Chattering Roots

Josephine Plummer

To all my friends and family who continue to encourage me to keep writing.

In the Meantime

Meanwhile, flowers still bloom.
The moon rises, and the sun.
Babies smile and somewhere,
Against all the odds,
Two people fall in love.

Strangers share cigarettes and jokes,
Light plays on the surface of water.
Grace occurs on unlikely streets
And we hold each other fast
Against entropy, the fires and the flood.

Life leans towards living
And while death claims all things at the end,
There were such precious times between,
In which everything was radiant
And we loved, again , this world.
— Tom Hirons —

Contents

1

Vernon

THIS IS NOT A usual night for me except for the sound of the lake on the dock outside my window. Somehow, I was able to convince Mr. Owens that the boathouse was livable. I know by the hooks along each wall of this building, it was constructed to hold the canoes and kayaks for summer fun, but as my PTSD grew increasingly more persistent, I felt the need to become one with the water. My mind wanders back to Bagram, attempting to take up sizeable proportions of my day. I knew the only thing that would calm me is the consistent sound of the water. Well, actually it is a noise that covers my mental chaos.

I am Vernon Fitzgerald Cannon, born in Miami, Florida, to Birdie Edwards. My father is unknown to me, at least. We lived in a war zone, just me and Birdie. Liberty City was a roof but an unpleasant environment for the first seventeen years of my life. That is, until Birdie went out one night to party or whatever else she did on her nights away from our dive of an apartment. Her silver briefcase was packed full of handmade beaded bracelets, postcards, crocheted key chains, or whatever else she concocted to sell to tourists. She always came home every morning smelling the same: sand, sea, and tequila, carrying her tube of English muffins and six oranges. One day a week, the grocery bag included eggs, pepperoni, and pizza sauce. Our menu never varied, but we didn't go hungry. Her hair would sparkle in the morning sun shining in through the white gauze curtain as she made my breakfast. Every morning, it was the same as if she had slept here and risen to make me breakfast, but that was not the case. I was here alone at night to hear the gunshots, police radios, and bull horns, people running around our building trying to escape the police and from each other. Turf wars, drug lords, prostitutes, wanna be gangsters are the worst since there is no one to guide them into the professional criminal life; they navigate on their own terms. I saw it all through the window of my bedroom, covered with a flat gray bed sheet, so holey it should not have been used as a window cover, splotches of sunlight moving across my wall as the day progressed. The palm tree that cast shadows on my window from the security lights installed by the housing authority was a lifesaver. No one could see me in the shadows that existed when the light was triggered, but of course, it wouldn't be long after each bulb change that someone would shoot the bulb out.

At sixteen, I seriously considered getting on a boat, any boat, any job for a way out of here, but Justin, who lives two buildings over, had left school for a deckhand position and returned a few months later. I don't know what happened to him out there. Maybe he wasn't cut out to leave this lifestyle, but I knew once I left, I was never coming back; escape was my final destination. After weighing my options, having decent grades, I saw the military was the only choice that could take me far from here, give me a paycheck, and a roof. I put in extensive hours to improve my GPA and was accepted into the army without telling Birdie, as long as I left on my eighteenth birthday, June 23, 2012, and didn't wish to enlist earlier. I would have needed her consent to enlist before then.

Birdie would have never approved of me leaving; she would have cooked English muffin meals for me forever if I let this go on, but I had to get out. The gunfire, police activity, and whatever else was a constant that was ingrained in my existence had to stop. I don't think I could have obtained a job or gone to college and stayed here. The mentality in the neighborhood was oppressive. I signed the forms, took the physical, and promised to appear on June 23, 2012, @ 0600 hours, 7715 NW 48th St., Miami, FL, 33166. Always knowing Birdie may have only had public housing, state medical, and food stamps because of me, I am sure she did her best by me and still maintained her free spirit. I am not sure where my decision will lead her, but I cannot be the anchor that holds us together any longer. After extensive testing, I was assigned MOS 12P, they say I am fit to be a Prime Power Production Specialist. This sounded fine to me as long as they relocated me, anywhere that doesn't have palm trees. I think the swish of the fronds blowing in the wind will forever blow in my mind.

On June 19, 2012, I was going through my insignificant amount of earthly goods, a couple Pokémon cards, some marbles from a game I had won at school years ago, a couple sets of clothing which I wash in the tub every other day and my prize possession a post card from our trip to Montana when I was four. I always hung onto that souvenir, remembering the cold nip traveling with the air, mountains, and open space, just the quietness of our time in the little motel next to the bison ranch was stuck in my mind. All of these items fit neatly into my backpack except the clothing I was wearing, my toothbrush, toothpaste, comb, deodorant, razor, shaving cream and the spoon I preferred to eat with. Birdie will be broken hearted, but I cannot bring myself to say goodbye face to face, a letter will have to work. It isn't as if I am her son, just someone she feeds and tells occasional stories to. I never discuss my meager life with her, no talk of school. I was sitting near my window, watching the grass corridor between the buildings. I saw a Miami-Dade Sheriff's car pull into the parking strip, which is unusual since Miami Police generally patrol here. Two officers get out, walk behind my building, and turn, I cannot see where they go from the angle of my room. Not that it ever matters to me, as I have not had any incidents, they aren't after me, and Birdie seems to keep herself out of trouble. I hear a ruckus on our stairs, boots, we live on the second story. I instinctively know from watching out the peephole at the neighbors across the hall, who always have police visits, that the tapping on our metal door is from a flashlight of the sheriff I saw earlier on the walkway. I am tempted to hide and act as if I am not home, but why? I haven't done anything except live here, and that makes me suspicious to start with. They knock again. I wish Birdie were home; she is supposed to deal with adult stuff, but she has already gone out for the night and won't return until daylight. The sun is just beginning to set, the sky casting a purple, orange glow off of our glass table we have eaten English muffins at for nearly eighteen years. I am suddenly hungry as I open the door and look into the deputy's eyes that are far off, like he doesn't wish to attend this meeting either. He asks for me by name, Vernon Cannon. I am surprised he knows it, but he explains I am the only next of kin listed on Birdie Edwards' ID card. I see Birdie's briefcase on the well-worn doormat. She was found on the beach, slumped over after slipping on a boulder and hitting her head. The EMTs were not able to revive her, and the other deputy stood behind the one talking, saying strings of words I didn't wish to hear but had no options. They had come to deliver the news, take me into custody since I was a minor, and place me in emergency foster care. I invited them in only because I needed to sit; my legs would not hold my body upright any longer. I was already packed but not going anywhere just yet, certainly not with these two men. I explained to them that tomorrow was school, I had to obtain my high school diploma for the military service I was scheduled for in four days.

They asked to review my military paperwork, looked in the cupboards, refrigerator, wanting to see my room, ran a warrant check on me, saw I didn't have any prior criminal record, apologized for my loss, shook my hand, and left. I heard the taller deputy say on the way out something about letting this issue go. I couldn't believe Birdie was gone, but I knew she would not have survived my departure, nor need to find another way to obtain a roof, so this worked out, although it was not as I wished. I still felt I needed to write a letter explaining my military service to her. I carefully constructed the letter, leaving it on the kitchen table. I dug into the washed-out Crisco can containing change and a few dollar bills. I went to the store miles from our home since there was no reason to stay there, using all the change, and got exactly what Birdie would buy: English muffins, cheese, ham, and jelly. Taking some oranges from a tree on the way home, I returned and ate just as if she were there until I left town. I don't know what I will do without her, but it is better than her being here without me. She may not have survived, I was her clock, the person to come home to at 7:00 am every day to cook the same thing. I always wondered where she got the oranges. Which store did she shop at? Birdie......... I know she loved me; otherwise, there would not have been consistency.

2

Vernon

APRIL 2025

I REPORTED TO DUTY on the morning of June 23rd, still reeling from grief, the depth of Birdie's death sinking in. I took a couple of her items, a ring with a green stone, and a necklace with beads that she had made. There were no pictures of us in all our years at Liberty City, it is as if we never existed. Birdie didn't talk about her past, never mentioned school, where she grew up, or who my father was. It was just me and her in the Miami Housing Projects, or at least I resided there, she was never home. I know she loved her nights out and had fun selling her wares.

They cut my hair, which their style wasn't much different than the one I had. I had the option of getting to Fort Leonard Wood, MO, on my own, or they would transport me. I boarded an olive-green bus with my backpack and rode for what felt like days. Birdie and I had never owned a vehicle, didn't ride the bus unless it was necessary, like a trip over five miles, or a school field trip that I went on if it didn't require money. If it did, I would remain in the school office for the day. We kept our circle small; no one knew us, I don't think, no relatives, friends, or money. Birdie told me daily, "Be invisible, keep your head down." The further the bus took me, the palm trees gradually disappeared from my rattling window. I had never been out of Florida, maybe not even out of Miami, so I was watching the signs as we passed through Georgia, Tennessee, Alabama, and Missouri.

I thought the humidity was bad in Florida, but when I got off the bus at Fort Leonard Wood, there was a wall of water in the air. It hit me so hard I wanted to get back on the bus and return to my crappy apartment in Liberty City. I knew I had signed up for three years, one year stationed here for training, then onto wherever they sent me. My first year went fast, I studied, made a couple of friends, but had been warned not to since we would all be stationed elsewhere once training was over. I kept hearing the term military life. The food was tolerable but being told what my every move was hard to get used to since Birdie had never even asked what I had been up to. We were up at 4:00 am for PT, mess hall at 5:30 am after our showers, then training all day, motor pool, guard duty, and CQ on rotation. I can't say I didn't enjoy this as I was out of Florida, gaining my Prime Power Production Specialist education and onto somewhere.

A year after the training started, I was allowed a week of leave to go home and visit family before my first deployment in Bagram, Afghanistan. Everyone I attended training with was going home, so I checked into Studio Z, a luxury hotel chosen because of its location about two miles from the base. I spent my week swimming, eating exotic food, and relaxing. I had never stayed in a hotel before, let alone a fancy one. I was used to being alone, and truthfully, it was beautiful, but once you are in the four walls, it isn't any different than Liberty City. I was still on my own.

One week later, I reported back to duty at Fort Leonard Wood and was flown out to erect tents and run power lines from generators to ensure shelter and meals for incoming troops. I stayed there two years, went back to Fort Leonard Wood and Studio Z for two weeks, and volunteered to go back. I didn't have anyone to see, I am not even sure what happened to Birdie's body, which I feel awful about. I remained in this loop for three tours: 2013 to 2015, 2015 to 2017, 2017 to 2019, then I was done. I was ready to be discharged mentally. They said I couldn't go back. I didn't want to be stationed stateside, so the Army and I parted ways. They say I am a disabled veteran. I have PTSD, I don't know why they think this, maybe from the discharge testing they did. I don't think the military is what has allowed me to have this mindset, but growing up in a war zone is where it started.

I had to decide where I wanted to go home to, since they were buying my airline ticket. I chose Duluth, MN, due to Lake Superior being there. I saw a real estate listing online for a nice house, one all my own, three bedrooms, two story on Jefferson Street. The house fit within the budget of Army guidelines, I stayed a year, of course, this wasn't home, I was still looking. Nowhere was but I could access medical care at the VA Hospital, and nights were pleasant down by the lake a couple of blocks from my house in the bars. The louder the better, I could come into the overcrowded bar, have dinner, a beer or two, and leave remaining anonymous no matter how many times I showed up.

After one year in Duluth, I was starting to unwind, the sound of palm trees long gone from my ears, and sand was still in my head from the three tours. Honestly, I may have stayed in the loop of Fort Leonard Wood to Afghanistan for years, as it was a system I understood, but they pulled the plug. Now I am here on US soil with nowhere to go. I don't think I am a threat to myself or anyone else, but the Army has not released me to work yet. I pack up my Jeep Rubicon and move to Moosehead Lake, Maine. I have decided to remain at each location for one year, then in the fifty-first week, choose a new location. The sound of the lake helps with whatever the Army says I have. I think I could go to work and come home every day, but they think otherwise. Since I am not allowed to leave the country, I had to travel a couple of hundred extra miles going south through Chicago, then driving east so I don't travel into Canada. This new location is a cabin right on the lake with almost no one living here year-round. Greenville, the neighboring town, I would estimate there are about 1500 people residing there. Going from Miami to an Army base, then onto Duluth, I have never lived anywhere where people were not milling about.

Six months into the year have been healing. I do all my VA-required visits online; they say I am making progress, I feel I am wasting time, but the noise in my head has become quieter. These people here are genuinely nice, want to get to know me, but I know I am moving on in exactly six months, so friends are not what I need. Plus, I can only see myself residing in a city with noise, motion, energy, something that is not found here. This is only a stop for peace to come.

I am not sure why I chose my next location, except for the cabin on the Glover River, the population is approximately 900, not many houses in this area, and I already regret committing to a year. I hope by the end of my stay here, which looks like a pleasant place to land, I will be released into the workforce and be able to use my military skills in the civilian world. About nine months here is all I could take, a serene, well-meshed community, but I am looking for more action. The lease is broken; I paid for the entire year, only used nine months.

My next location is Lake Las Vegas, a condo in Henderson, which I figure out is too tight of quarters for me. I need space all my own, not people coming and going right in front of my door. Every morning, I would go rowing, the solitude on the lake being my only solace in this journey leading to somewhere I cannot foresee. I did consider staying here for the rowing and people I was meeting, but I had made a vow to myself to move on each year until I could work.

Agency Lake, Oregon, was my next stop. The population is growing, but still not even a tenth of a major city. This lake is large and nestled in the trees, I am not sure why I keep picking places that don't have any action around. Duluth had a bar close to home I could show up and get lost in. Everywhere else I have chosen to be, I am watched, an outsider, people want to know me, I don't want to know them. I need to settle in a larger city.

3

Vernon

MY TIME HERE IN Oregon is almost up, I don't fish, swim at this time of year, or do many outdoor activities except hiking. The VA says there is a program to integrate my skills back into society, which is held at American Lake VA Medical Center. The success rate is high, it is on a lake which has been my nationwide following, and Washington is north of here. No better place to go except up. I still do not understand why they waited six years just over the amount of time I served to comfortably place me back in society as a civilian worker or have not hired me on as a civil service worker on base with the skills they provided me with, but I have gotten to see America like I never would have if I had just gone to work when I returned from the desert. I would have gotten a job as a journeyman electrician and stayed wherever that job was. I am thankful for being able to unwind not from my tours of duty but from my childhood war zone. Every year on June 19th, I set up a memorial of stones spelling out the name Birdie and place a few beads along with it. It has been six years, but it feels as if it were yesterday. I am certain she would be happy with my travels.

I load up my belongings and travel northbound I-5 through the tall pine and fir trees, seeing signs for the University of Oregon in Eugene, traveling to Portland, stopping at Powell's City of Books, a store I have always wanted to go to. Purchasing a jigsaw puzzle and a couple of books for my new life, one that may take root. I might be here over a year. The thought of me staying anywhere longer than a year seems overwhelming. I am always on the move or planning my next departure. The last time I was anywhere for a length of time I was stuck, there wasn't a way out of Liberty City or Afghanistan. Fear grips me as I merge back onto I-5 and across the Interstate Bridge and see the houseboats that appear as if they are small industrial buildings on the Columbia River.

Somehow, crossing that bridge has given me the freedom I need in my spirit. I know this is the right move and feel energized from the few minutes I spent in the city, looking for parking, fighting traffic, and walking a sidewalk with strangers. That is the life I need, a place to be but yet have enough people around to remain anonymous. That was how I grew up, I knew a few, everyone who lived around me recognized my face, but didn't know anything about me. I need that feeling again. I hope Lakewood has enough people in it to live under the radar, and I can just be me.

I drive through places that look the same, Centralia, Kelso, Castle Rock, wondering how people live there. It doesn't look as if there are enough jobs to support an entire town. I follow the directions emailed to me by the VA, getting off at exit 124, Gravelly Lake, on my way to a new life. A place has been set up for me, a cabin, they say, right on the lake. I met Mr. Ownes right on time, who has a contract to lease his rentals to military personnel, or should I say former soldiers who have not been released yet. There are seven compact cabins on the well-manicured property, a house down by the lake, which I believe is Mr. Owens' residence, and the boathouse. He shows me the third cabin down the hill, the one closest to the lake on the left side, carrying paperwork, consulting it as he gives his spiel about no drugs, asking if I do them, no alcohol, do I drink, no parties, will I have them. I assure him I will be the quietest guest he has ever had, no visitors, no family or friends to swim in the lake or party, it is just me. I ask to see the boathouse, which he explains is for residents only, except all the boats are long gone, too much liability these days. I explain I need to live there and not the cabin on the hill. He tells me it is not insulated or wired for occupancy. I tell him of my military service, inform him I do not need 220-volt wiring, and will keep to myself. I simply need the waves to be close, as near as possible. He explains the rent is the same, $925.00 per month, if I wish to sleep in a boathouse or under an actual roof. I signed the contract, crossing off cabin #6 and replacing it with #7. I know I will be here more than a year, adding insulation and a canoe, maybe even some furniture.

Monday morning, I walk the short distance and report to the VA hospital building #148 Vocational Rehab, wondering why I have been required to show up here. I have marketable skills and certifications, have never screwed anything up while overseas and now they want me to start schooling. I am increasingly agitated as I wait in the hard, government-issued chair for the speaker to arrive. I should not have left early, this lag time here is not helping, my mind is going a thousand miles an hour, picturing myself in school for what? Being a nurse, a cable installer, or a house builder? I don't want to do any of those things, I want to run wire. The instructor, or whatever you call him, walks in, introduces himself, and says we will be boarding the bus to Seattle VA Medical Center. I was not prepared to leave Lakewood; shouldn't they have told us we were leaving? I am not technically in the military and their property any longer.

Sixteen of us were loaded on a white military bus, all of us seated apart, none of us speaking. The instructor gets on the PA system, stating this was a test to see how flexible we were and if we are committed to the program. The jobs are all in Seattle, training could be in Pierce or King County, depending on which program we choose. I do not like their approach, but with the possibility of becoming employed in Seattle, I remain in my seat.

We pull into the circular driveway with mirrored buildings. I see the city and Space Needle for the first time, knowing I will be living here and mentally abandoning my boathouse by the lake with a year's lease. We enter as a unit, me having flashbacks to Fort Leonard Wood of basic training and operating as a group of strangers. Maybe this is why they wonder if I am fit for society, to be free of their program, I cooperate today. I had never operated as a group outside of school before basic training. Doesn't everyone have memories? Mine aren't that bad. We take the elevators, needing three to take us all to the third-floor conference hall. Presentations were set up for various schools and open positions at Seattle City Light, King County Metro, Seaport Steel, and other roofing, lumber suppliers, and a few white collar jobs. I knew I wanted to work outside, or at least in the field, never in an office; I have spent enough time indoors in Miami. Seattle City Light appeared to be the obvious choice for me, but something drew me to traveling the city on a bus, where I could see it all at street level. No matter what the neighborhood, I was used to sketchy areas, and I am positive the buses didn't operate in areas worse than I know. I signed on just like that, had a job as long as I could pass their drug test, which I knew I could since I didn't even drink soda or smoke anything. I had to wait for everyone to make their decisions for my ride to Lakewood to depart so I went outside and looked at the views of the Emerald City that I have been placed in to protect its citizens hoping I hadn't made too hasty of a decision but felt in my spirit this was the proper choice for me.

4

Vernon

THIS THOUGHT HASN'T EVER run through my head before, but I have never filled out an employment application until the one through the VA. There wasn't any negotiation for this position, I just became employed on the terms set by the US government and King County Metro due to my disability. There was an option to do the drug test onsite, but not many others did this or even signed up for employment or education, just milled about as if they were interested. I wanted out of the holding pattern I was stuck in because I had served our country and was ready to move on. I passed the drug screening as I knew I would and received an email a couple of days later with instructions to complete orientation and training.

I showed up on Airport Way South, reported to a class of seven, was issued a uniform, given testing that provided them with my mental state, and sent to the Van Pool Lot to process vehicles as they return and leave for two days. This is not the place for me, I quickly inform them I need to be on the road, in the city, not caged behind a fence with vans.

The next week, they bring me back in. I feel as if I should have chosen Seattle City Light since I am an electrician, but I also think that title is behind me; I left it in the desert. This is a new start, and I want to be out there seeing the city. They assign me to a temporary plain-clothed Metro Transit Police floater position to see how I will do. They say I will need to start my routes at various locations, always from a park and ride or bus garage.

On Saturday before my first shift, I board bus 594 to Seattle from the Lakewood Park and Ride, getting off at 4th Ave and Pike Street to connect with my assigned route but seeing the commute of an hour and a half will not work every day, being confined to the bus is one thing if I am working but just to arrive at a destination it is not for me. The buses I am assigned to and the bus I arrive on do not connect unless I work at 4:00 am. The Sounder Train schedule isn't any better.

Since I am up here already, I may as well explore, take a few buses to be current on the types of routes I will be placed on. Seattle is certainly not as warm as Miami, but I would like to find a beach and set up a memorial for Birdie. I walk to the Pike Place Market and find my way through to the back, where the stairs lead to the waterfront, and take a ferry to Bremerton, as I have not ridden one before. There are job listings advertised in the hallways, which I tuck away in my mind if this gig doesn't work out. Since I was without my vehicle, I ate at the closest location to the ferry, Anthony's, at Sinclair Inlet. I took the ferry back, walked up the hill to the market, purchased a map to study, and returned to 2nd Avenue to catch the bus back to my Jeep, realizing I know nothing about this city. Today I feel as if the decision to move here may be wrong, but willing to see what Monday brings.

On Monday, I have a swing shift on the Rapid Ride E line, between Downtown and Aurora Village. At check in, they let me know my shift will consist of four trips north and four trips south. I arrived early in Seattle at 2:30pm using the Diamond Parking lot at 4th Ave and Dilling Way, walk the short distance to Prefontaine Place and Yesler Way to start my first shift as an undercover bus attendant.

As we inch our way out of downtown and onto the Aurora Bridge going over Fremont, I see how beautiful this city is, while being disgusting in other areas. The day shift is leaving their allotted posts for home, students are on their way to and from various schools, and the vagrants are asleep on the bus for a warm place to be before nightfall. Not positive if I just let them ride for all of my shift or if the driver polices their actions. At the end of my second trip north, I get off and eat at Taco Del Mar, where I may have had the best spinach wrap since leaving Miami. I make two more trips today up and down Aurora Avenue, observing the clientele as night falls, the obvious trying to hide in the alleyways and behind bushes, drugs being sold in the open with drive-through customers. Motels used by the hour with businessmen pulling in, wishing to be invisible, and girls too young to be away from home. All with a story, one I hope to not hear but know if I keep being assigned to this route it will be just a matter of time before our worlds collide just as a slew of bullets pass before Rapid Line E. The driver slows not blowing my cover if he even knows I am here as an extra set of eyes, he waits patiently as they spew bullets at each other with their imaginary grid placing a turf war. The driver, having a front row seat but wishing he hadn't seen a thing, reacted as if this were a daily occurrence. Me sitting back here past the accordion seats on this red articulated bus, knowing the plastic sheeting would not stop a bullet nor the metal sheeting of the bus. I am sitting in a fishbowl and need to get back to my Jeep. The trip south back to Yesler Way was uneventful after the driver of the British Racing Green Toyota pulled the barrel of his handgun back in the window. As soon as that knowledge hit my brain, I questioned myself, why I would meet Ralph on my second tour in Afghanistan, who had returned from Camp Zama, Japan, and showed me the car he had purchased over there, a Toyota 86. Could my knowledge bring trouble down my road? As for now, I didn't see anything. That worked for me at Liberty City, and this isn't much different, at least I don't have to live in this. Now, after one shift, I know what I am up against.

Tuesday night is quiet, even though I am on edge from last night's actions. It is nearly 10:30 pm, and I have been safe thus far, but it is just me who is not right. This job and the gunfire have put me on edge, and I do not know if I can continue this. My mind is strong, but pieces inside of me are trying to return to Afghanistan and Liberty City. Just as I process my options, a man gets on the bus, sits in the first seat by the driver, seated sideways. He is wearing an old quilt as a cape, has a patched-up purple corduroy backpack with oversized safety pins holding it closed, as the zipper hangs below the bottle holder. It is my job to observe and read the intentions of people. He carefully opens the backpack and pulls out a naked doll, brings out the snap-up clothing, dresses it, and proceeds to comfort the imitation child. Then sits back to snuggle with it as we cross the Aurora Bridge back into downtown. As the driver announces the Galer Street stop, a tall lady enters the bus, walks down the aisle, and sits in the seat behind me. I know she is carrying; I am trying to give a description in my head as I can no longer see her. Hair decided red short, long legs, army jump boots, jeans that are six inches too short, boot cut, a jean jacket, OD green, fluorescent flowered shirt, chest flat, then it hits me she is wearing a bulletproof vest. Starting to panic but not wishing to appear agitated, I sit still, barely breathing, as she says, "Excuse me" and hands over her business card. I turn it over and see she is Detective Serene Allard with Seattle PD. She says she doesn't wish to blow my cover, and I am wondering if the guy up front would even notice, as he is still tending to his baby. I turned to look her in the eye for no other reason. She says she wants me to come to the station after work to ask some questions about last night, or we could Zoom if that works better. I write my email address for her to send a link. Immediately regretting my choice of paper and wishing I still had her card with a cell phone number on it in case of an emergency, such as last night, and knowing that if I continue to be employed here, I will need the police frequently. The driver told me his last few assistants, as he called me, have all quit. Some, before the shift is over, just got off the bus. This makes me want to stay. I am tougher than this; it isn't even as radical as Miami, just colder. I ask for another card as she rises to leave, she turns to look back at me but doesn't give me another card. Her partner picks her up at the open rear door of the bus facing the wrong way in traffic to retrieve her and speeds off. Having given my email to Selma, no, that's not her name,

I don't remember except it started with an S. I will wait and see if she is who she has told me she is, or from the side of the shooter wanting to know what I have seen. Nothing is certain in a world of crime, and I have been dumped into an area as a floater to protect what or who? Maybe tomorrow I will be on a different route, but I think not.

I return to my Jeep walking tall and sure, this area is not the best at 11:00 pm either. I drive down I-5 to Lakewood, knowing the lake and solitude will calm all the pieces of me that have been in overdrive since last night, but wishing at the same time I didn't live this far from work. The drive seems long tonight, and this is only two of how many nights. I wonder why the VA didn't team up with local companies. What has happened to the other fifteen people I went to Seattle with? My required weekly meeting is tomorrow at 11:00 am, I bet I am the only one employed. Certainly, one of the only ones who has been involved with gunfire and the police.

My phone alerts me at 1:26 am. I have a new email. I know it is from the lady on the bus, no one else sends emails except the VA, and advertisements. I signed in and clicked the link, having Zoom already installed for my VA meetings when I lived too far away for a facility. I see her name is Detective Serene Allard, the email looks legit, she joins me almost immediately, and everything in the background tells me she is at a police station. She wants to know how long I have worked there; I answered that it has been two days. So that was your first night? Do you recognize any of the shooters? What can you tell me about them? I feel at this point she thinks I am involved. That is the last thing I expected, I thought she would think I would be of assistance, not a suspect, or maybe I am taking this line of questioning wrong. I answer all her questions, remaining calm, then she asks what I do remember. I tell her of the British Racing Green Toyota 86 and about Ralph in Fort Leonard Wood. She responds with "Ah, military, that is why you weren't afraid to come back." I always knew from growing up that you never talk to the police more than needed, so I let her have her thoughts without any elaboration on my part. Then she asks where I live and where I am from. I tell her both ends of my story, even though they don't pertain to this interview, Miami, or Pierce County. She says she grew up in Liberty City, Florida, and got out in 2008 on a scholarship. Seattle is about as far away from there as you can get. I knew we would be able to work together as long as she didn't want too much from me. I was just hired and barely made money paying for gas and parking each night. I wasn't sticking my neck out too far for anyone. She appeared satisfied with my observation of the rare Toyota as she introduced her partner, Detective Metevior, who took her away to another piece of Seattle that needed tending.

At 3:07 am, my phone alerts me to another email. I check my phone to make sure it is not an emergency, but I know I do not have friends or family, so it could only be Detective Allard. Maybe she has an update from the information I provided earlier. I sit up, suddenly mad, who does she think she is, waking me up in the middle of the night to do her work? She sent me three full sheets of photos with names attached to watch out for on the bus. These are people she is looking for; she hasn't even provided their charges. I don't know if this will jeopardize my life. Where I come from, you don't meddle in business that is not yours to stick your nose in, and if you are in it up to your nose, don't open your mouth.

I sit and study these individuals, Raven Wells, Melvin Scriptnor, and Don Montgomery. They all blend into the faces I see daily; nothing stands out as unusual. I will look for them, but my job description states I will keep order on the bus, not do police work. I did not respond to the email but lay down annoyed and tried to sleep.

5

Vernon

I HAVE BEEN ASSIGNED this route for thirty days now as a floater. I am used to the repetition, have arranged parking at the bus garage as if I am a driver, and have gotten into the routine of my schedule. I am even enjoying having dinner at Aurora Village, but I have not gotten accustomed to this new way of life. Having to watch my back for hours on end out in public.

Two days after the email came through, I spotted Raven Wells on the northbound route leaving downtown at 3:23 pm. I consulted my cell phone for a photo, and I know without doubt it is her. Her hair may be lighter now, but it is Raven. She is alone and takes a ride almost to the end of the route, exiting the bus at N 145th Street, walking east. I gain my composure, feel my company badge that is tucked under my shirt, and peel it from my skin on this scorching day, and hope Detective Allard has no idea of my knowledge. Raven was only on the bus, not committing a crime.

On July 2nd, the same actions were taken at the exact same time and locations with Raven, who I hope does not realize I am watching her. I don't even know what she is wanted for, or if I did turn her in, where that would leave either of us.

On July 4th, I showed up for work as usual and was instructed to board bus #40. They tell me I am a floater, and this is my route tonight. After this, I will be permanently assigned to the Rapid Ride E route. This new route covers the fireworks show at Gas Works Park, a route that doesn't normally run with such frequency. This information throws me off as it was not scheduled, but at least I get to see the fireworks. I grab a few items from the vending machine in the driver's breakroom since I will not be having dinner at my usual stop tonight and am on my way to another part of the city.

At Mercer Street, a redheaded lady between forty-five- and fifty-years old boards the bus with a toddler in a stroller, talking to the child about the fireworks show. A couple stops later, Raven enters the bus from the back door since it is a ride-free zone. Immediately recognizing the lady with the toddler, she walks towards them, calling out the child's name, Enzo. The red-headed lady moves the stroller over to Raven and says, "Bring him back on Sunday morning so no one will know I don't have him." Then she rings the bell, gets off at the next stop, and walks back the way the bus had just come from. I see the compartment in the rear of the stroller is loaded with two backpacks, a small ice chest, and a duffle bag of toys hanging from the handle. Enzo is clutching his blue bear as if his life depended on it. His little arms extended to the older lady, but Raven is holding him tight as if she knows he could get away from her. Raven's story has just gotten more interesting, and I need to find out if I can work this route next Friday or call in sick because I will be on this bus.

Raven gets off at the stop closest to Gas Works Park just like everyone else on this monster limo, leaving every seat vacant except mine. Enzo looks at me with excitement as if he understands fireworks, or maybe he knows the word park. This route runs late tonight due to the fireworks show starting at 10:15 pm. I have been instructed to stay on the bus until the final route of the evening is completed. My mind is working out a route from Gas Works Park to 145th and Aurora. I am already worried about Raven and now Enzo getting home at that hour, but I know the E line runs late enough to deliver them. A lady and baby on their own in the city at night, a baby Raven possibly doesn't belong with. I hope this is not why she is wanted; she acted overly protective of the child and treated him with care during my observations. I will see if there is a way to check criminal records.

At 11:30 pm, I see Raven about 20th in line to board the bus, along with what appears to be a few thousand others, many will be waiting for other coaches to board. She patiently waits, looking tired, holding Enzo. I should not know the baby's name. She boards without help, carrying the stroller with the weekend gear in it and everything else that goes along with a baby. I want to help her, but I know she saw me on the trip here since I was close enough to hear the conversation between her and the lady to whom she will be returning the baby on Sunday. I wonder how the switch of custody goes and where it happens.

I remain in the back of the bus, so she doesn't see me. I am happy to see a family takes the stroller from her and loads it on the bus as their small girl holds Enzo's hand as if it were her brother. I think she has met friends or family there, but they quickly find seating away from her, the little girl kissing Enzo's fingers before parting ways. Raven sits in the handicapped area holding the stroller with one foot, and Enzo is asleep on her lap as if he is at home in bed. I hope they had a good time tonight enjoying the fireworks. At North 105th and Aurora, Raven gathers her gear, most people have already gotten off at their stop, and with the bus nearly empty, I do not wish for her to see me, especially if she is wanted or even has suspicions of that. I pull my hoodie over part of my face and act as if I am sleeping but keep my eye open a bit to be certain she gets off the bus safely. A lady seated by the door offers to hold Enzo, and Raven is skeptical but hands him over as she needs to safely get the stroller down the stairs and to the sidewalk. It is nearly midnight as she retrieves the baby and places him in the stroller.

As Raven passes the bus with me on the passenger side, she looks around, then up at me. I see recognition on her face, but I do not move and continue to act as if I am asleep, but I think we both know I am not, and she is onto me. I am suddenly worried about her being alone and wish I could follow her only to be assured she got on the Rapid Ride E line arriving for departure shortly after 12:03 am and delivering her and baby Enzo home to North 145th at 12:15 am. My mind wanders. Will someone meet her at the bus stop on Aurora? How far does she have to go in the wee hours of the morning with the baby and gear? Where does she live? Who does she live with? All questions that are not my business, but I make them mine since Detective Allard has brought Raven to my attention.

6

Vernon

I AM BACK ON Rapid Line E Monday the 7th; the day seems un-eventful, just as the rest have been, except day one. For the most part, people get on, people get off. There has not been a commotion I have had to call in until today.

An elderly lady boards, happy as a clam, smiling at everyone, wearing mismatched pink clothing from head to toe, sits down in the side facing handicap zone with her aluminum utility cart full of groceries. She talks to the man next to her about the price of groceries and how she saves a dollar here and there to purchase enough food for the month with her supplements, whatever those are.

Approximately three more stops, it is hard to remember when you ride for a living, a gentleman gets on, smelling up the entire front of the bus. It is packed being rush hour, people are opening windows, but that only lets in the sweltering air emanating from the pavement, making this commute the worst one since becoming employed. I am not sure what my responsibility is in this situation since it is simply odor; everything about this man stinks. Then he pulls out a vape pipe, says, "This will cover my smell". The lady wearing pink says, "That is a stimulant, and it will kill me with my heart issues." He proceeds to take the biggest hit I have ever seen and exhales right in the pink-clad lady's face. She clutches her chest, holding her breath, but starts to turn a tepid shade of gray, which deepens as I reach for my phone, dialing 911 for medics and police assistance.

The lady falls to the floor. Someone checks her pulse and shakes their head. The foul man doesn't believe she is dead or that he has anything to do with her death. He sits next to her on the floor, rubbing her hand as if she were a child he knows, asking for her to wake up. He sees the Seattle FD with EMTs, and Seattle Police enter for statements. They ask if they can do that outside. The foul man gets up from the dead woman, tries to make a run for it, leaving his bag of filth in the aisleway for all to smell. Detective Muncer winces as he takes the man by the arm and escorts him to a patrol car, not being sure of the charges that will be given, but knowing he needs a shower, and the clothing burned. He returns to his car, gets a bottle of water out to pour over his hands, wipes them on a towel, then uses sanitizer to finalize the deal, throwing the towel in the mesh garbage can attached to the bus shelter.

This is my initial police encounter out of necessity; I couldn't have asked for a more punctual response time or professionalism from everyone involved. I can't help but feel remorse for not being able to save the unfortunate lady who was so happy with her cart of groceries just moments prior.

This is just the start of my shift; we wait for another coach to load the passengers into so the medical examiner can do his job, the scene can be investigated, and everyone can get on their way. I carefully stand with my back to Ruby Sanders body and ensure each passenger's departure through the rear exit just past the accordion portion. Some people push to get off, others are in shock. I am just hoping this delay does not affect Raven and her commute now that I am watching.

7

Detective Muncer

JULY 2025

Even though the sun is just beginning to rise on this summer morning, my mind remains on that bus entering downtown with the unfortunate death of Ruby Sanders. I do not respond to many murders where someone intentionally administers something that another person was allergic to or would have a reaction. I am sure Jacob Mullins didn't understand that he wasn't helping his smelly situation but was committing murder. While taking witness statements, I was told by each person that Ruby Sanders had repeatedly asked him not to use the vape and recited issues with her heart. It happened so quickly, I am not positive there was time for anyone to take the vape away from him, or else they didn't wish to get near his emanating aroma.

I am not a fan of summer as it brings light in the morning earlier. I prefer to arrive home after my shift, and it will still be dark. It also affects the crime rate; people are out later and in groups partying or just escaping the heat of the city. The domestic violence rate is almost as high in the summer as over the holidays.

This morning, I am meeting Agent Ford at Three Girls Bakery in Pike Place Market to get any updates he may have on my family that was abducted in Mexico. I wonder when he sets a location to meet, what his agenda is. Will he meet someone after me, and am I just being fit into his schedule? He never makes me feel that way; he appears to act professional and be genuinely interested, and he even acts as a friend would. I order the Raspberry Cream Cheese Danish and am tempted to order Jill a Chocolate Croissant but know it would go bad before I see her since she has been staying with Hector most of the time lately. Agent Ford orders the Lemon Bar and tea, always being healthy.

He sits for a few minutes that feel like hours enjoying his breakfast, then looks up and says he has no information and needs to talk to Jill about specifics. So far, Jill has remained behind the scenes on this case as she wished but dead ends are all he is running into. With the abduction being nearly twenty years ago, there are not witnesses only Jill. I know he is doing his best to investigate, but nothing has been found. My family could still remain out there being held hostage as Jill was. Where are mom, dad and Joshua? This question ate at me nearly every minute when they first disappeared then after a few years it wasn't at the forefront of my mind but now with Jill returning there is a new hope of reuniting with my family.

I will call Jill tonight when I wake up and stress the importance of a meeting with Agent Ford. She can't not care about the rest of our family. I think she got through the past twenty years using denial to make it through each day.

I return home to write lyrics and unwind; my dinner being taken care of. I enter and Jill is at the kitchen table, she is supposed to be at work, but she is here cooking. She doesn't even live here, the perfect opportunity to talk with her about a meeting with Agent Ford. I worry about Jill in the city without a car, but she commutes with Hector. I couldn't have handpicked a more streetwise and loyal person. He is aware of his environment, knows the streets since he travels them by bus, and appears to adore my sister.

I ask Jill why she is here cooking, she says, "You are late." She appears irritated, which rubs me the wrong way. She stayed here, some of her stuff is here, she still has a key but doesn't live here, and now she is lippy with me for being late due to attempting to find answers to her mess. I know from the streets that reacting to another person's attitude doesn't help getting information, so I tell Jill I was with Agent Fred Ford, now wishing I had the Chocolate Croissant. She purses her lips so hard they are almost nonexistent, if it weren't for her lip gloss that has made a row of shine, I don't think I could see them at all. She turns her back, fills a plate with rice, beans, and a taco, puts it in front of me without asking if I am hungry, and turns to do the dishes, not eating herself.

I ask her to dish herself up a plate and eat with me. We eat, talk about the weather, and any other nonsense, then I tell her we need to meet with Fred Ford, purposely not using the word agent so as not to frighten her. She agrees to meet with him as long as I and Hector can attend. I will need to set this up, she also requested it be when she gets off work at 4:00 pm. That is a time I am generally sleeping or just starting my day, but I will cooperate with her wishes to help this investigation.

Jill never told me why she was cooking at my house or waiting for me, but it is nice to know she has the option of being here whenever she wishes.

I think back on the past few weeks and months; I am amazed that Jill has made a way for herself and transitioned into life here. Then ask myself why I can't get it together with Naomi. We both work different shifts, are off sometimes one day and not a weekend like normal folks, but we should be able to make time for each other. I took a vacation in February we had a date the first and last day of my time off but with me heading out to Neah Bay and getting stuck in the snowstorm that didn't help, and we both know we are used to being on our own time and five straight days together would be too much. Maybe we should take an overnight trip to Ocean Shores. I will stop by some night soon and ask what she thinks of that idea.

8

Vernon

JULY 2025

My shift is not ideal except for the commute, going in the opposite direction than most workers. I have met a few people on my route, always repeating the identical story of living in Snohomish County and transferring buses at Aurora Village. So far, no one has asked what I do for a living, my answer would be security. If anyone has ever watched, I generally get off at the last stop, Aurora Village Bay 3, and walk over to the restaurants for dinner. Four trips north, four trips south. There is one gentleman who gets on downtown frequently who seeks me out for conversation. I do not prefer this as my eyes need to keep assessing the scene, and I need to be mobile at a moment's notice, so I have taken to sitting on the aisle seat for flexibility. His usual stop is 3rd and Seneca, except he is early today. He says, "hi" and slides past me to the window seat, then goes into whatever spiel is on his mind. He appears to be with it mentally, says he lives in the homeless community by the Duwamish River, the one that is threatening the Roxhill Bog with the runoff of pollution coming from the encampment. I am not sure how it all works; he informs me of the dealings there, dealings of merch as he calls it, transpo, which I assume are stolen bicycles, and underground products, he says. I wonder if the encampment has such an enormous impact on the environment, why does the city deliver dumpsters to the site when they go unused? He says his name is Joe Connely from Portland, Oregon. His occupation used to be selling candy on the street down there, to tourists, and recycling to buy things like underwear. Now I didn't ever need to think about this man's underwear or how he acquired them. Why has he sought me out? Every few days, he approaches me. I may appear safe, but I prefer not to make any acquaintances here or anywhere else.

I know this is the time of day Raven gets on at Bell Street around 4:00 pm. I don't want him yacking my ear off when there is a chance, I could overhear something Raven says, even though I have only seen her speak to one other person, the lady who handed her Enzo. Joe continues to talk, Raven boards through the back door with her earphones in, closes her eyes after she is seated, but while watching her, I see an occasional hint of a smile, thinking she must be listening to a podcast or audiobook. I then wonder how the weekend went with Enzo, even though that is not my business. While in thought, Joe says in a loud baritone voice, "Gotta go, my methadone is waiting at the clinic." His voice bypassing Raven's earphones, she looks up at me in recognition as if she now knows something about me, but I am positive there is nothing to know. I shake my head and hope no one thinks I am friends with Joe, am connected to him, or was with him in any way.

Just as we approach 145th and Aurora, Raven gathers her gray backpack, pulls up her socks, zips the ankle-length biker boot, makes sure her earphones are secure, walks by me and gently kicks my boot, smirks, and leaves through the front door. As she gets off the bus, I see an older man, short, skinny, with ill-fitting clothing, behind the bus stop. They immediately start arguing as the bus pulls away from the curb, Raven glancing back, me acting as if I didn't see anything. Then it hits me that man was Melvin Scriptnor lurking behind the bus shelter with all the windows broken out. Now I have questions. How do they know each other? Are they related? Does he know the red-headed lady and Enzo? The pieces of this story are all facts I shouldn't know about these strangers' lives, but they have been placed on me by Allard.

Just as I am absorbing the new piece to this puzzle, I must have been lost in thought for a while because the bus stops at North 65th Street, and Detective Allard boards. She walks down the aisle with an overconfident look on her face. I wonder if she knows about my omission to her puzzle, but I actually don't care. She saunters over to me, stopping next to me, saying scoot. I move to the window seat, wondering if she travels through her days with this bossy attitude. She looks at me and says, "Well, what do you know?" I look at her again and realize why I can't stop staring at her. She has the same mannerisms as Birdie, maybe it is the confidence and surety of her movements. This immediately makes me sad. The detective in her picks up this shift in my attitude and asks what I am hiding. I explain the best I can that it is personal, but she can't or won't let it go. I finally told her a lady I knew had a shirt like hers, I hadn't thought of her in a while, and it just brought up memories. She may actually be human and not all detective by the look I saw flash across her face for a brief second. She probably thought I was harboring a memory of a past girlfriend. Then she returns to, "What do you know?" I respond with, "About what?" She looks at me as if she knows I have been watching Raven and now Melvin Scriptnor, but then says, "Joe spill any important info to you?" At this point, I am comforted by the fact that they are considering enclosing the drivers, and my job may come to a halt. I do not wish to play this game; I was not involved in the repetition of the hood when I grew up, and feel she is trying to force me into a role I do not play.

I am relieved that Joe is her mission today and tell her about the dumpsters being delivered and his quest to get methadone that he announced to everyone on the bus. She says, "Good, he is staying clean. He's from Portland, you know. Let me know if he gives you any other information. He is one to watch." To appear cooperative, I tell her about his mention of merch, transpo, and underground products. "Those are the ones I am looking for, not the stolen bicycles," she says, then gets up to leave through the front door, crosses the street holding up traffic with her badge, and jumps into an SUV with her partner. My whole body relaxes when she is out of sight. I wonder what trouble Joe is into, and I can only imagine what goes on in an encampment where everyone says they are your friend but are only out for themselves. Joe will be another story to build and something else to watch for. Thankfully, she didn't board the bus while Raven was here.

I breathe normally again, scoot back to my aisle seat, and know the most exciting part of my shift is over, or so I think. Today I simply wish to be at home by the lake, hearing my calming noise, visiting Gus the mallard, and not the continuous hum and vibration of the bus.

9

Detective Muncer

I DON'T FEEL IT could be any hotter over 100°and my day has not officially begun. Agent Ford, Jill, Hector, and I will meet at Ford's office at 4:00 pm to try and get more information out of Jill. It is as if she graduated, left Seattle, went to Mexico for a week, and returned like any normal vacation, but that is not what happened. She has spent twenty years of her life missing, and either she cannot or will not disclose the information. To me, it appears she thinks the twenty years had not been lived anywhere. Personally, I do not think having Hector there would help at all, but I am not Jill and have not been through whatever it was that happened to her. Maybe she will talk with the support of Hector.

We meet in front of the FBI Headquarters on 3rd Avenue, all the windows look as if they are staring back at us. I think of the cases that are handed to me and can only imagine the complexity of the ones investigated here. Jill walks up holding Hector's hand; they are nearing forty but appear as teenagers. Riding the bus, having their first relationships, living at Hector's inherited condo. I am thankful

Jill has returned, but I hope she can help us find the rest of the family; she may not know anything. We enter through the lobby, the front desk agent recognizes me and says, "He is expecting you." I know the way to Agent Ford's office and start down the long hallway, I turn and see Jill walking in slow motion, contemplating her next actions, and feel she may run or freeze. With the fluorescent lighting and reflection of the marble walls, it appears Jill has turned green and may become ill. I return to her side, not being sure what will help. All I can be sure of is I am up early in this heat, not my normal time. Agent Ford is working hard on this case and has made time to meet with us, and Jill knows whatever she remembers, so she needs to talk.

We proceed down the hallway, enter a conference room, and I just automatically sit by the head of the table where Agent Ford is. Jill hesitates in the doorway, and Hector leads her into the chairs on the opposite side of the table from me, but at the other end. It occurs to me that Jill may have told Hector this story already. I count six gray padded captains' chairs between the man asking questions and the girl with the answers. I wonder what Ford thinks of my family now, with her strange behavior. Her actions don't seem to faze him. He flips open his leather file holder, introduces himself, and tells us he will be taking notes on the meeting. He asks us all to state our names, then proceeds with questioning Jill. I am sure he gets all kinds in his line of work.

AF: Do you know how long you have been gone?

JM: Twenty-one years.

AF: Do you know where in Mexico you were held?

JM: It was many miles from Mexico City where we were abducted, and where I caught a train back to. I don't know the names of the cities.

AF: Where did they take you after abduction?

JM: It felt like hours, but it was probably about an hour of pavement, then an hour driving slowly on an unpaved road.

AF: What did it look like where you were taken?

JM: We entered a garage, and when the van doors were opened, it was a two-story enclosure like a warehouse.

AF: What type of vehicle, color, and size?

JM: White Toyota HiAce. When we were loaded, we always did a high five. The name of that van helped me decide to have a good day. Oh ya, the hugs and kisses on the license plate made me happy, but the X made me sad knowing my family was gone.

AF: Hugs and kisses?

JM: Yes, Oaxaca. I had to grab onto whatever would make my mind stable. I worked hard, never gave them trouble, learned some Spanish, and did my work perfectly. Some people would purposely do a job wrong and be demoted. Like left in a 3' x 3' steel box at the sleeping quarters. They would show it to us with someone in it periodically, just to keep us in line. Not enough room to stretch out, and only one meal of rice a day. Your length of stay in the enclosure depended on your violation. If you intentionally messed something up at work, the punishment was longer.

AF: What did you do at work?

JM: At the first plant without windows, I never thought I would see outside again. We made circuit boards, inserting resistors, diodes, and capacitors. Only one time did I put a diode in backwards, and that didn't go well. I saw it starting to smoke and cut it out before it could explode, marking the board as defective. Better to have a mis-aligned board and burned fingers than be sent to the box. Anything to stay out of that box. Then in the second place I escaped from we made technical fabric. There was always someone who could speak English to give instructions on the equipment we used, but they would never speak of anything else. Not even a hello.

AF: Did you feel trapped?

JM: Yes, I knew this was a carefully planned operation and there were no glitches in the system, like doors only opening and closing when triggered, or time alone. I lived in a small room with a bed, a blanket, no books, pencils, nothing, not even playing cards. Everyone would get off work from a twelve-hour or more shift, stop at the dining room, eat the same meal every evening, then go sit on our stoop. They didn't encourage mingling, everyone seemed like they were from different countries. Not many of us spoke the same language.

AF: Do you remember anything else that would help us?

JM: That it was hot, it never cooled down, especially at night with our enclosed living area, but at work, there was A/C. The boxes said Xavier Manufacturing at both plants.

My phone buzzes in my pocket, repeatedly. Knowing it is something I need to attend to; I pull it out of my pocket and read the message while holding the phone under the table so as not to break Agent Ford and Jill's trains of thought. It is Metevior, he has Joe Connely in custody, and us off the books our CI Steven Watkins is dead. The tent went up like a dried Christmas tree. All evidence points to the fire starting outside, and they allowed the tent to burn with Steven inside, but Connely swears the fire started inside the tent. I wonder how Metevior can add this much information to a text, or why. We all know Connely and Watkins have been sworn enemies since the incident under the bridge a few years back with the baby.

I rise feeling like I am abandoning Jill, who swore she would never be able to go through this interrogation but is now acting as if she is visiting with long-lost friends. Maybe it is reassuring for her to get her story out in the open. Hector patiently sits at her side, occasionally rubbing her arm or shoulder. It feels odd for me to observe his moral support to this woman who, in my mind, is still my little sister, but is now an adult without normal daily experience in life. There is no way out of this meeting without interruption. I explain that I am needed by the Duwamish and leave, knowing Jill is in good hands with Agent Ford and Hector. I look Jill in the eye before leaving so she knows I am here to support her. I will text her tonight and thank her for her bravery.

My first thought on my way back to my cruiser was to call Rubio. He works in South Seattle and may have some insight into the population of the encampment. He answers, groggy from sleep, and asks what I am doing up this early. I explain about Steven Watkins death and our issue with Joe Connely. He says he has heard the names on the street but stays away from that area if possible.

I arrive on scene, change my shoes into ones I know will be deposited into the dumpster on the way out, and retrieved by a resident of this establishment. These are last year's shoes. I wish I had older ones, but it seems I am frequently throwing a pair away. I start to walk in and assess the area. People are everywhere, and movement is in every direction. A bicycle is carried down the path between two tents, the BBQ is fired up, and a line has formed, others bringing plates, even the dogs are in line for a meal. The community clothesline is loaded, and baskets full wait to be hung. I would guess there are about seventy-five tents or more in the area I can see, and I know the encampment runs to the river at least another football field in length through the trees and towards the river. Prime real estate is to be had by the leaders of this establishment. It is hard to tell how many residents there are as no one wishes to live close to the other, so they pitch a tent here and there, one in the trees, another down by the bog. My mind automatically thinks of mosquitoes, as I live next to the water and need my screen door.

Forensics and the medical examiner are on site, but I don't want anything moved, so whoever called in the medical examiner was premature, inexperienced. The tent is melted, a scene at many encampments in the winter with people trying to stay warm but not so much this time of year, unless intentional or drug manufacturing was a factor. I suspect if the fire was started inside it would be from a candle.

Joe Connely is cuffed and sitting in a yellow and white webbed lawn chair a few yards from the burned tent. He won't shut up, just keeps yapping, "I am not guilty." He chants this over and over again, his long hair waving as he rocks back and forth while spouting his words.

I round the corner by the ash tree with burn marks extending up the trunk and see the Nike Air Force print of six rings burned into the soil that was mud a couple of hours ago. I asked Joe Connely, who was visiting Steven Watkins, to bring me all of his shoes. I knew I wouldn't find the shoe with the sole I was looking for. I am wondering if this is our man for Meade's murder, the death of Stephanie Thomas runs through my mind, and I think of Little Mel wondering if he got off to somewhere better or into a more precarious situation.

Joe takes me to his tent, pops inside, and comes out with a pair of hiking boots, sandals, and an off-brand pair of shoes. He is wearing Nikes, but not ones anything like what I am looking for. He asks why I needed to see his shoes. I don't answer but ask him if he knows who wears the Nike Air Force tennis shoes. He says, "Don, the one who lives just south of here, or used to. He was a supplier but left town, then came back for a spell. Those shoes are all worn through now, not sure why he doesn't get more. That is who set the tent on fire, I tried to tell them before I was cuffed. They didn't believe me. Said I was a junkie just making things up and if there was a Don I would be able to provide his last name. I didn't run with that crowd, so I don't know his name. Don and Steven were smoking something in the tent. I kept hearing Don say, "No, keep your own. I have some", but Steven must have kept offering because Don repeatedly told him no, then it was quiet for what seemed like an eternity to me, lying in my tent across the way, listening. Next thing I know, it is bright as daylight, which doesn't happen in these dense trees. Then I heard a few fast footsteps and splashing. I suspect Don or Steven took off through the water. I don't know who is truly in the burned tent, but

I would like to know so I am aware of who to watch out for since they killed that person." If I find the enemy, then I will know the victim.

I ask patrol to uncuff him, tell them I have his statement, and he has agreed not to leave town. I know he will not be going anywhere since he is an undercover officer of the Portland Police Bureau, traded to the Seattle Police Department with the worst assignment in history. Just thinking about the commitment, he has to his job is honorable. I would never take on a role like this. While leaving here, disposing of my shoes and writing the report, I text Rubio and ask where we can meet. We need to get Don off the streets this time. Last time he disappeared, this time they have all gone MIA. Raven, Melvin Scriptnor, and Don, which may not even be his actual name.

Rubio wants to meet at Huckleberry Square on Ambaum. I pulled in in a matter of minutes and suspected he was already here or on his way to this location when I called. I have driven by here a thousand times but have never stopped. I see him impatiently waiting in the side parking lot. We enter through the red front door; he is in another of his silent moods. I don't push him, wait until we order him a Mountain Man Scramble and me a Huckleberry Mountain Burger, then tell him of Don being back on scene. I do not blow the cover of SPD's CI being as Rubio works for the King County Sheriff. Our waitress Tina delivers our food, Rubio says mid bite, "Aleene, my ex, who has the baby, doesn't want to keep him anymore. She wants me to take him full-time. How am I supposed to do this job and raise a baby? Does she know what she is asking? Do you think Raven could raise her child?" I interrupt at this statement and ask if he knows Raven's whereabouts. He shakes his head no, saying, he suspects she has left town, is on her own mission to find Don to deliver justice for her sister, or is just lying low somewhere. Maybe Little Mel has set up shop elsewhere. There have been no sightings of any of them for a few months now. People don't just disappear, especially not a group of them. We don't even know of Meade's existence prior to us finding her body, let alone where she lived, as she didn't have any identification on her. Or anything else. I ran her name, Meade Wells, through the database but came up with nothing. We need to find Raven, to find Don, if that is even who he is, so I can figure out the baby. Aleene says she can't keep him forever. I don't want Albatar leaving the military to come home and raise his child. What would he do, work a minimum wage job, put the baby in a state-run day care for the entire day? This baby needs his mom. Raven has to surface."

I tell him I understand his point and am seeking the same individuals, but for a different reason. Meade, Stephanie, and now Steven Watkins and all the others did not deserve to die from a bad batch of drugs, even though they chose to do them.

10

Vernon

AUGUST 2025

IT IS A HOT Friday afternoon, August 22nd. I have not seen Raven on a regular schedule for the past three weeks. For a couple of weeks, she was riding daily, then after Melvin met her at the bus stop, there wasn't a pattern to her appearance. Also, since I am a floater without a permanent route, they pull me off this route whenever I am needed elsewhere. I was on the Rapid Ride F Line for a couple of days. That is the most zig-zag route I have ever seen. The second day, I saw Joe Connely at the Burien Transit Center just behind bay 6 in a heated discussion with an undercover King County Deputy. I could spot his badge when the hot gusts of wind picked up. His vehicle was parked in a designated police only spot, he appeared to be making a point about something the deputy was not agreeing with. I felt it was a good thing he missed this bus if it was the one he had been waiting for and was occupied in his discussion, so he didn't see me, but I could have gained information if he had hopped on. The last thing I need is for someone to argue with the police, then be seen talking to me. I am positive the deputy would not know I work for Metro Transit

Police, and it would make things awkward to explain to him and not blow my cover to other passengers and Joe. I was glad to get off that route. I never did get back to the #40 route the following Friday to see if Raven was there to retrieve Enzo.

Everyone who boards the bus today looks weary, the summer has been a long, hot one, and everyone living on the pavement that is not able to hold the heat. I am thankful for the reprieve of my lake house. It is hot when I arrive for work, but the rest of the evening, the heat wears off with the A/C of the bus going if people would leave the windows closed.

On my second trip north at the stop on Seneca Street, a male boards the bus, he either has a hair dye job gone wrong or is wearing part of a woman's wig, a portion of the blonde curls are covering the right side of his face. The left side is towards me, he doesn't move his head, probably for fear of his newfound hair failing him. His eyes shift about at a high rate of speed, he is wearing clean clothing except for the black mark on the left sleeve of his mustard - colored hoodie. The hoodie puts him in a class to be watched, in my opinion. It is almost 90°and he is wearing long sleeves. He moves from the front of the bus to a forward-facing seat three rows up from me. It was easier to watch him when I could see where he was looking. I am almost always towards the rear of the bus for the best possible viewpoint. We inch through traffic at a slow rate of speed. I think I see Raven walking not far from one of our last stops downtown. She boards the bus through the rear door, turns to sit up front, then thinks better of that and proceeds my way, looks me in the eye, taps my boot with her white Converse high top, and moves on to sit a couple of rows behind me.

I don't turn to make contact with her since she would be one that I shouldn't get to know, even though I want to know everything about her. A few minutes later, the man with the blonde unruly hair gets up, looks around me, and starts walking my way. He passes me and sits somewhere behind me, but I am not sure where. I wish I had a mirror. I took out my cell phone and reverse the camera, hearing whispers at high volumes back there. He is sitting with Raven, his hair at a different angle as if it had fallen off and he repositioned it. She is not happy to see him, whoever he is. I notice she is trapped in the seat with the man not moving as if frozen in place. I get up and ask Raven if everything is ok. She looks at me with tears in her eyes, but then screams, "he killed my sister." I grab the man who smells of burned plastic, call 911 for assistance, hoping I can hold him until they are on scene, but at the same time, feeling ill from touching him. As we are on 107th and Aurora Avenue North, the police presence is high, so their ETA should be short being as any call from Metro gets high priority since there is always the possibility of multiple victims. The driver has stopped the bus, and passengers are not sure if the lady, who states there is a murderer among us, is crazy and debates whether to get off the bus into a large group of prostitutes parading in the street. A man outside the bus was yelling for us to get out of his territory or to remain on there with the possible murderer. Raven suddenly realizes that the police are on their way and must know she is wanted and hops over the seat in front of her, streaming towards the rear exit as the driver yells, "You didn't pay your fare." I watch Raven slink behind the buildings as if she knows the area and its routes. The blonde wigged man is squirming and attempting to get away. If it wasn't for his intentions to follow Raven, I would probably let him go since I am tired of holding him. He smells like sweat and heavily of cigarettes, and I'm not sure what my responsibility is in this situation; so far, all he has done is harass a passenger. Since I started this job, I have not had to detain anyone before today. I am just glad he is not fighting and is much smaller in stature than me. SPD officers board the bus with Detective Allard trailing them. They apologized for the time it took to arrive on the scene, saying they had instructions to wait for the detective. He grabs his hairpiece and throws it to the back of the bus, defiantly faces the officers, and repeatedly moves his arms so as not to be cuffed. Allard says, "Don Montgomery, you are under arrest for the murder of Meade Wells, Stephanie Thomas, and...." The charges went on listing other names I didn't recognize. He doesn't stop wiggling around like a rag doll, but that only makes the cuffs more uncomfortable for him; it doesn't prevent Allard from making the arrest and escorting him to the patrol car. I hear Don is already trying to get out of this and making deals, talking about Raven being right here and fleeing into the neighborhood. He says he knows PD is looking for her, but he hasn't done anything except throw trash. His wig, we can call that trash. He asks if he can do this over again and get his hair, so he is not charged with littering.

Detective Allard looks at me accusingly and says, "I will pull the bus cameras and see who was on here. Why didn't you alert me about Raven?" Then she has the patrol take Don Montgomery and deposit him in the back of a patrol car. I look out the window, knowing this may be my last shift, but don't see how the two issues, my work performance and being a forced rat, could be connected. Now I am torn between getting off the bus and taking a cab to 145th, where Raven gets off the bus and warn her, possibly get the rest of the story, or to simply stay out of their mess. If Raven's sister was killed, why would she be wanted? I will search articles online when I get home for Meade Wells' murder. Another name in this story has been revealed.

11

Vernon

AUGUST 2025

Monday, I showed up as usual for work with no emails from Allard over the weekend. I have not been able to fully relax after seeing that accusing look in her eye. Having lived honestly my entire life, I never had anything to watch my back for. I don't lie, so the story always stays the same, and now it is a detective I am uneasy about. This time it is a sin of omission, but is it actually that, do I have the responsibility of doing anything above my occupational duties? I have extensive military training about personalities and their disorders. I feel Allard is using her power to overachieve and get others to perform. At this point, I feel I have done the right thing and will continue to act as if I do not recognize Raven. She isn't even aware I know her name or that I know about Melvin Scriptnor or Enzo. I do worry about her having run off into the chaos of the streets in that area last week. Today's shift went quickly, the heat has either made people irate or distraught. No one wishes to commute in this weather.

Tuesday is humid, and the temperature has dropped to 86°with the rain falling and evaporating as soon as it hits the pavement. Clouds of steam are rising off the sidewalk, smelling of motor oil, dried grass, and whatever people have been walking through. Nausea hits me each time the door opens to let a passenger off or on.

There is a commotion on my second trip northbound. One teenager, a male, chases another onto the bus. One gets on the other is impeded by the bus door that the experienced driver closes so as not to have a fight onboard. The one that was fortunate enough to escape his pursuer is short, has dark wavy hair, large brown eyes, and has a single tattoo of an ear of corn on his left forearm. He can't contain his energy, leaves his original seat, and quickly makes his way back to my area while the bus is in motion. He sits across from me and starts in conversation like we know each other and have been talking all along. He says," You know that jerk that chased me. He can't run, not like I can." I am watching his corn tattoo as he turns his arms at odd angles like they are stiff, or he thinks the odd tattoo makes him tuff. I see his fingernails are covered in various colors of paint. His story keeps going; one of his biggest mistakes in life will someday be not having kept his mouth shut. He turns to me, putting out his paint-encrusted hand as if he wants to shake my hand, not noticing I am not reciprocating, and says, "My name is Kernal, as in Korn with a K, not Sanders." Then he gets off the bus at the next stop and walks east down North 115th Street.

On my last trip southbound, leaving Aurora Village at 9:51 pm, I see Raven walking across the transit center from another bus bay, but am not sure where she has come from, and she is in such a large crowd for this time of night, I can't be sure she is alone. I slouch in the seat as if I am sleeping and see her board through the front door. She is carrying five large shopping bags from Fred Meyer. I don't know this area well enough to know how far she has walked with her bags, but she looks exhausted. It has been four days since she hopped off the bus and disappeared. I am relieved to see she is safe and will be onboard with me shortly, even if it is a short ride to 145th. She gets on, sets her bags down looking for her transfer, finds it in the top of one of the bags, shows it to the driver, and proceeds down the aisle, bumping the over-packed bags on empty seats as she comes towards me. She smiles as she goes by and sits in the rear-facing seat so there will be enough room for her groceries or whatever else is in there. I expect her to get off at her usual stop on North 145th Street, but she gives no sign of exiting. She stays on past the Aurora Bridge and into downtown and gets partway off the bus at Denny Way, trying to hand the bags to the red-headed lady whom she met on the 4th of July, but the lady refuses the bags since they are so heavy.

I jump up and ask Raven if I can help. Her demeanor is not the usual neutral person I have observed prior to this; she is frazzled, as if scared, like she could possibly be in some sort of dilemma. The red-headed lady remains on the sidewalk unsure of what just occurred, the driver needs to go to keep on schedule and makes her aware of this, hoping I am not overstepping my bounds by telling the red-headed lady the bags will be delivered shortly to wherever they need to go and carry the bags to the rear of the bus, glancing inside the one closest to me I suspect this is food for Enzo with the children's fruit snacks on top. I place the bags on the seat in front of where I had been sitting. Raven walks back and asks, "What are you doing? This food belongs to my son." I know this will blow my cover but tell her my Jeep is a couple stops away at the bus garage, and I will deliver the bags and her wherever she needs to go. She looks at me like I am crazy and whispers at such a low volume I almost couldn't hear her words over the roar of the bus. "Do you know what page of this story you are jumping into, and is that where you want to go?" I quickly nodded yes, at least I am in the story tonight, with regrets or not, I am pleased to help.

I know I cannot let Raven into Metro property, due to liability, all passengers have to exit the coach before we enter the gates for maintenance to inspect the bus after each of our shifts and ensure everyone is off. As I ask the driver to let her out by the gate, he gives me a look I am unsure of, but I am in this mess now and will be delivering groceries somewhere along with taking Raven to her destination. I carry the groceries across the bus yard to my Jeep, start it, and don't wait for it to warm up, not wanting Raven to be on the street any longer than necessary at this time of night and in a sketchy neighborhood. Using my badge to open the gate, I see Raven just on the other side; she appears still leery about this setup, but I intend to get her home safely. With her reluctance to get into my vehicle, I show her my badge and tell her of my position with Metro.

She asks if I am still on board with all this and informs me that the groceries need to be delivered further south. I tell her to direct me where she needs to go. She says since I was seen by Aleene, now I know the red-headed lady's name, I could pull up in the alley, so she won't have to carry the groceries far. Raven sends Aleene a text, or I assume that is who she is texting, her phone buzzes a couple of minutes later, and Raven says, "It is ok if you wish to carry the bags to the back door." I am again relieved to be able to help even further.

We drive over the West Seattle Bridge and get off on Admiral Way, make our way over to Alki Avenue SW, and turn into the alley right after 59th Avenue. I may be in danger, but I don't think so. I am paying careful attention to where I am going, just in case there is trouble, or I need to return. The house is a one-story stucco like they have in Miami. This is the first one I have seen here. Alki Beach was my destination the first weekend I spent in Seattle but never made it. The salt air is refreshing after being corralled on the bus all night.

Aleene opens the door as soon as the security light turns on; she must have been watching for us. She inspects me like a cop would, says, "Thanks," and to Raven, "I will catch up with you Friday."

Raven thanks me, then tells me in a muffled voice to drop her downtown on the E Line route, and she can make her own way home. I don't feel this is a good idea and am perturbed with her feeling she will be safe everywhere at any time. She explains that Aleene insisted at a late hour that she needed groceries for Enzo. I think of my original plan to build my yearly memorial to Birdie and ask Raven if she would mind, since we are here, if I took a short walk on the beach. I pulled into the empty parking strip waiting for her answer. She says, "I don't suppose you would harm me and leave your Jeep here, Aleene knows who was with me." I look at her with astonishment, but glad she has some sense of her well-being, and tell her that would be the last thing I would do.

We stepped into the sand; I told Raven of Birdie and my delay in spelling her name out in rocks, something I do every year. Raven walks away, returns with her jacket folded up, small rocks falling out of the sides, then asks, "Who is Birdie?" I tell her the story of my mother as we spell her name in the sand. She listens carefully, not saying a word until she says, " I would like a ride home when you are ready. Thank you for helping me tonight. I will never tell anyone you are bus police." Even though the beach closed a couple of hours ago, we sit on a picnic table in silence with our own thoughts. Me having no idea what to say. I am just thankful I could be of assistance tonight, even though she doesn't know me at all. I am still, for the first time all day, thankful to be able to help and learn more of this unraveling story. I am grateful Raven is safe, and the heat has been taken away with the night sky and breeze off the water. I find this place calming, but I need to take Raven back over the bridge to the other side of the Puget Sound as I see the lights and Space Needle across the way. I asked Raven which building is her favorite, and she points to the one where green lights hang in the window about thirty stories up but says she would never live off the ground.

We agree it is late and time to go. I have her program my number into her phone for future reference. That way, any contact will come from her, and I will not be tempted to check on her. She looks as if she is relieved, and then my phone dings, which never happens unless it is work. I check it, hoping it is not Detective Allard since I am having a relaxing time and don't need her in my private life. It is Raven saying hello and giving me her number.

I let Raven direct me to her house, I-5 north. She has a way that doesn't seem direct and keeps looking behind us, but I don't let on that I have noticed. We drove down N 145th Street, then she asked me to make a U-turn and pull over. She thanks me again, says she can't get out in front of her house, and exits my vehicle. It dawns on me that her and Melvin could be a couple or even married. I tell her I will stay here until I see her enter a yard and then leave. She smiles, and I see relief on her face that she knows I understand she may have some complications. I know this lady may be more than I signed up for, but this is where I enter her story, and I am committed to it now.

My radio turns off suddenly as I reach the Federal Way exit, my halfway point from the bus barn, certainly more than halfway home from the drop off for Raven. The radio starts ringing, and I realize it is my phone hooked up to Bluetooth. It has never rung while driving since I have owned this vehicle. The screen scrolls across with Raven's name. I don't know which button to push, so I get out my phone and answer. Raven is out of breath and whispering. I look at the clock on my dash, it is 3:17 am, Wednesday, August 27, 2025.

Raven is frantic but not telling me what she needs. I get off the exit that points to The Commons, knowing I am not going there, but lack a place to pull over and listen. Raven says he didn't care for her coming in so late, breaking curfew, waking him, and he has now kicked her out, taken her key, and she is a few blocks away from where I dropped her off. I ask what her plans are, does she have a place to go? She replies with, "Never mind, I shouldn't have called, you have already helped me enough tonight." What she doesn't know is I am already turned around and on I-5 traveling north. I don't know where Raven will go tonight or any other night, but she won't stay on the street. I am thankful the weather is not treacherous, and she called to ask for help. I ask her to get somewhere she is safe and tell her, "I will be there as soon as I can." She will wait at the bus stop right in front of the Goodwill.

I pass the exits with a mile between them, except it feels as if there are ten. My mind is racing about what happened to Raven tonight. Will she need medical care? I already know or suspect who the "he" is, Melvin Scriptnor, but I am not a hundred percent sure. What if he is chasing her or out looking? All speculation at this point, I glance over in the left-handed exit only lane for Stewart Street and see an undercover SUV cruising at high speeds, ready to pass me. I can tell by the reflection of the streetlights in the grill onto their blue emergency lights. The SUV passes me, ready to exit, when I see Detective Allard in the passenger seat. She waves, but I wonder what is in her head. My driver's license and vehicle plates still have my Oregon address on them, so she doesn't know if I am returning home after a night out or a shift at work. Certainly, I live closer than Oregon, but she doesn't know which direction. To my relief, they got off the exit, and I sped up over the speed limit, and suddenly there is an urgency to get to Raven, knowing Allard would not be in that vicinity.

I get off the 145th Ave N exit quickly, find the Goodwill, and am thankful I know this area at least a little, and spot Raven sitting at the bus stop. I am not sure why she called me, and then I had to tell her twice to get in. She climbs in, clutching her phone as if it is her last possession, and it very well may be. I ask where she wishes to go, but she doesn't have anywhere. States Aleene can't know about this since she lets Raven take Enzo from Friday until Sunday. I tell her I can drop her off at a motel, a friend's house, but she shakes her head no. I tell her I will pay for wherever she wishes to be. She opens her pocket and shows me a twenty-dollar bill that has been ripped in two. I offer to take her to my house, which I know is not something that should have ever come out of my mouth, but there is no turning back now. I tell her I don't live around here; she looks at me and smiles the biggest grin I have seen on her face. I know this may be the right decision for her, but not for me, I suspect.

During the next fifty miles, she doesn't say much. I am careful not to scare her, but I need to know who may be after her. The first thing she tells me is of her twin sister Meade dying, Don spotting her on the bus, then about Little Mel and his mom who just passed away, the move from south Seattle to north Seattle, leaving the other people in their ring behind, and getting clean. Little Mel was really mad when she got home because she woke him up; he wasn't too happy about Enzo staying the weekends either. Since he has been on his new medication, he needs everything to be absolutely quiet.

She tells me about Albatar leaving, having the baby, Detective Rubio and Aleene, his ex-wife, filing for custody, and not having a place to keep the baby besides at Little Mel's, which was being watched by the police, Seattle PD, and King County Sheriff. They won custody, and Enzo has lived with Aleene ever since. Recently, Aleene has been demanding groceries and overnight visits. "I love to be with him and will always feed him, but her demands at unusual times when I don't even have transportation make this hard. I am fortunate to see my son, but it is all on her terms, and Rubio doesn't know about any of my involvement. He visits Enzo on Monday mornings. I would like to keep him with me, and I suspect Aleene is tired of being a full-time parent." She explains.

After getting to the 512 interchange, Raven says, "You weren't kidding, you do live a long way away. I wasn't expecting this." I inquire if she is still ok. She says, "the farther the better except on Friday. I will get back there." I pull into my driveway, making our way clear down next to the boathouse with my lights off. Since I have lived here, there has never been a thought about cameras on the property, but I am hoping Mr. Owens does not have them installed, but it wouldn't surprise me. Raven waits, looking out at the lake as I juggle my coat, lunch box, and keys. We enter, she sits at the two-seat kitchen table and looks relieved to be somewhere no one can find her. I have to blow that moment of comfort by asking why the police are looking for her. She whips her head around and says, "What?" I am not positive this is my best decision, but I pulled up the sheet sent to me by Detective Allard, omitting the other ones, Don Montgomery and Melvin Scriptnor. She stares at it for a couple of minutes, is silent, and then shakes her head no. She then says, "I have no idea why they want me, they know who killed my sister, Don Montgomery. I haven't done anything wrong. I just moved from Little Mel's to his mother's house when he sold it. I wouldn't even know who to ask about this, but I don't want to find out I have a warrant by showing up there. You aren't turning me in, are you?" I shake my head no and am already thinking of a way to find out why I have this poster.

I am wracking my brain trying to think of a way to ask about what the warrant is for, if there is actually one.

I ask if she is ok and assure her, we can somehow get to the bottom of this. It is past 5:30 am, I need to be up and ready in just over eight hours to travel north again so I change my sheets, being glad I purchased the second set, offer Raven my bed even though this is a studio apartment, and we will be in the same room, but I hope she is comfortable since this is all I have to offer. I think Raven was asleep before she hit the bed because the second, she laid down, I turned to give her a blanket and she was out. Possibly recovering and feeling safe for the first time in many years, the load has lifted at least for this moment. I covered her and went across the room to the couch, laid down, and knew there would be no sleep for me tonight. I know no one knows we are here, but I need to get to the bottom of this story.

I wake at 7:28 am, and the screen on the front window, next to the door, is being moved. I know it is Gus wanting his daily supply of worms that I feed him, having forgotten when I returned home earlier this morning. I'm unsure if ducks eat worms, but I saw a bait sign at the corner store and have been feeding Gus worms since then. I quietly open the fridge, retrieve the worms, and go out to visit with Gus. He is not being quiet at all, quacking away as I exit, trying to enter my residence, not considering any boundaries at all. A few minutes later, Raven joins me, not being scared of the worms, and feeds Gus. I am sitting here with the most complicated lady I didn't even know, who may be wanted by the police and others, who was chased out of her residence by someone named Little Mel, found by Don on the bus, possibly involved in the murder of her sister, has a child she doesn't have custody of with the son of a cop and now she is feeding Gus with me. This is not a story to share but one to keep under my hat until Friday at least. I tell Raven I have to leave for work by 1:30 pm and don't think my landlord would appreciate anyone staying here. If he asks to say she is my cousin and don't use your real name. She says, "It will be nice to just sit and watch the water from inside, of course, until Friday, then I need to get to Seattle." I don't ask where she will take Enzo but suppose we can figure that out tomorrow. This is only Wednesday morning, the longest twenty-four hours I have ever lived. Raven asks, "Where are we?" I laugh and reply with Washington. I know this may not appear as if it's the right thing to do, but if I can help her get on her feet, untangle her legal troubles, regain custody of Enzo, and find her own place, I know I have done the right thing. Someone needed to help Raven, and she was put in my path for a reason.

12

Detective Muncer & Detective Rubio

AUGUST 2025

AT ABOUT NOON ON Thursday, my phone rings and a text come in simultaneously. Both are from Rubio wanting me to meet him at his hangout in White Center, the one he used to frequent. I know if he is there, life has been throwing him unusual twists. He hasn't been the same since Little Mel and his crew disappeared. I am not even positive he knows of Don's recent arrest. I suppose that is reason enough to get up from my last bit of precious sleep, see what my friend needs, and deliver that news.

It takes me a bit to get dressed like a person and not my required cotton shirt, slacks, tie, and jacket. I feel off leaving home in this attire and not going to work. I am attending a social event, but it is still business.

The transition from outside to the interior of the dive bar with mostly green Tiffany lamp shades with beer logos, I am taken back to a few other times rescuing Rubio when he drank himself under the table and knew who to call. With those thoughts, I immediately regret my decision to answer the phone and wish I were still in bed.

Rubio sits at a table in the back corner in a worn vinyl booth, one of his boots is off, his coat lies next to him, and a beer that appears to have grown warm by the perfectly round puddle growing at the base of the glass. When I first entered, he didn't see me watching him, then turned with recognition and waved me over. I hope I do not regret this meeting.

Rubio automatically motions toward the beer on the table but says he hasn't touched it. The ritual of being here involves a beer, so he bought one hours ago. A friend is what he claims he genuinely needs.

Rubio starts in without any small talk. I guess that he has been here for some time, mulling over his tale. This story may be new to me, but he has been examining it for days. "Aleene doesn't want to be a full-time parent anymore; I am not capable of that role either, with my job, and truthfully, I love Enzo but am only his grandparent. Don't grandparents pick up the child, then the child makes its way back to the actual parent? Brobowski wants to move in together and raise the two like brothers. I am not ready for a relationship, either, not now, probably not ever. I am not skilled in that department. Let alone one with two toddlers, at our age." I interrupt at this point as he starts laughing like he told the funniest joke, since I have not heard about Brobowski before. Rubio answers while holding his head, looking into the beer glass, "I met her on a case. She is a dispatcher for 911 Communications. Her daughter was struck by a stray bullet on I-5 and passed away, but her child in the back seat was luckily fine. Tiffany Brobowski now has full custody of her grandson. We have been seeing each other for a while, and with our common interest, I guess I let the relationship become deeper than I am probably ready to live up to." My only thought is, why is he asking me? I can't seem to keep any personal relationships together. Not because I don't wish to, it just doesn't line up. Naomi is the only person I have dated in a long time, and that is mostly done in fifteen-minute increments at Harborview around 3:00 am in the closed cafeteria. With these thoughts, I start laughing and ask Rubio why he called me and relayed the thoughts on my love life. He replies, "That is why I called you; you are my friend. You will tell me the truth." I ask about the mother of Enzo, about Albatar, can they not be involved? Rubio says he saw a flyer with Little Mel, Don Montgomery, and Raven's pictures on them put out by SPD, but could only find a warrant for Don. He was hoping for me to look into the reason Raven is being sought for questioning. She still hasn't surfaced, but when she is found, Rubio wishes to speak with her about filing for custody or inquire if she even wishes to.

I tell him of Don Montgomery's arrest on Rapid Ride Line E he was supposedly harassing a female who screamed, "he killed my sister," then jumped off the bus before being questioned. The description didn't fit Raven, so maybe it was someone else he had killed the sister. At least Don is in custody for the murder of Meade Wells, Stephanie Thomas, and at least eleven more that we know of. What we don't know is where the lethal batch of methamphetamines is. Don is not budging on that information; he keeps saying he has a bigger case to talk about, but then shuts up, deciding not to spill his story without the promise of a stay at The Maple Lane Campus for his entire sentence. He states he is insane, always has been, and will do anything to make a buck, including murder now, he guesses, to support his habit, which started at fourteen. He didn't know anyone had passed away from the addition to the manufactured drug; he is not a chemist or a smart man, just someone trying to make a buck, and it wasn't even him who added it. Then yells for the guard that he is ready for his return to his cell and book; he needs to find out how the story ends. Don always turns and states, "See you next time when you are ready to negotiate."

I don't know what Rubio will do, but I know he still remains sober and has some life-changing decisions to make, but I will be here for him. We leave the bar with the smell of beer lingering on our clothing and hair, step out onto 16th Ave SW, the sun almost too bright for me since I am not generally up at this hour. We shake hands, I look him in the eye, and he knows he will call me when he makes up his mind about life, since he has shared the first part of this difficult story with me. I say, "Raven is the priority." He knows I will look into the flyer. We part ways, him going south to his house by the airport, and I travel north to Fremont, back to my trusted hideout on Euturia Street to lay down some lyrics since I am up and there is no chance of going back to sleep. I pull in thinking of Jill, picturing her at work. It is interesting that she can miss two decades of life and pick back up appearing normal. Then there is me, who missed her for two decades, and I cannot form a typical relationship. I do know many people and have lots of friends, but no one close. Everett Sunshine is my responsibility, and I enjoy his company. Agent Ford is on that list of friends, too. I picked up the phone to call Naomi but decided against making the contact at this time of day since she is probably just starting her day, and I don't want to be a speedbump in her routine. Then set my phone to remind me at 1:00 am to text her.

I walked up the exterior staircase, deciding on plans to bring it inside this year. I grab my guitar, turn on the amp, and since it is fully daytime, I do not wear my headphones but listen at a respectable volume as the words flow out of me. I sit with my laptop and write the lyrics pertaining to my summer and life on the streets. I laugh, but not against Rubio, but the laughter is for my freedom that I create and cherish.

Seattle Hot

(Verse 1)
Seattle overnight, the rain's a flushin,
Hot wind blowing, ain't no love for another tears gushin.
Trees flappin leaves, dreams rare, it's a ruthless scene,
Morgue's got a line, little peeps caught in between.
Random shooting, cars rolling through, everyone smokin blunts
Innocent victims caught in the bad drug fronts.
Cold hearts, they chill, the streets don't feel,
Crimes gone wrong, but they're out for the thrill.
(Chorus)
Bare summer, hot winds blow,
Squad moving silent, but we run the show.
Big dreams in the alleys, beats on the streets,
Territory life, no retreat, no defeat.
(Verse 2)

Summer is here, but the past won't die,
Seattle's got a pulse, we keep our heads high.
Passengers on the coach, sweet dreams turn sour,
We're plotting for greatness while the darkness devours.
Crimes gone wrong, the clock's ticking slow,
Detective in the shadows, looking for that glow.
Everyone's a suspect, trust is a ghost,
Ruthless ambition, we do what we love most.
(Chorus)
(Bridge)
Wind Swirling through buildings, echoes of sin,
We're chasing the shadows, where the battles begin.
Seattle's a concrete jungle, but we're born to survive,
Committing unthinkable, just to feel alive.
(Verse 3)
Squad on the corner, plotting our next hit,
Life's a hot summer, but we're never gonna quit.
Cars rolling through, chaos in the night,
Every crime tells a story, man, you gotta get it right.
Leaved trees, drunk dreams, we're hungry for more,
In this ruthless city, watch the legends soar.
So we hustle hard while the clock ticks away,
With the beats on the street, we're carving our way.
(Chorus)
(Outro)
So here's to the crime, here's to the fight,
Seattle's our canvas, and we paint it right.

Cold hearts, ruthless souls, we stay in our zone,

In this heated summer, we won't die alone.

#Seattle Strong

#DJ Muncer

#mun det J

Every 24

(Verse 1)

Seattle overnight, last of a cold heart cry,

Trees thirsty, summer's end, wilting and reach for the sky,

Wind blowing in alleys, ruthless grind,

Random shooting, no warning they ain't blind,

Cars rolling through SOAP zones, no peace to find,

Big dreams splattered, crimes gone wrong,

PD lurking, but they don't belong.

(Chorus)

Every 24, we hustle on the low,

Squad rolling deep, man, we steal the show,

Innocent victims, while the body gone cold,

Deals sweet, but life's bitter and bold.

(Verse 2)

Pioneer Square, shadows in the night,

Freemont lights, but the vibe ain't right,

End of Season blues, just trying to survive,

Thug life living, tryin to stay alive,

Files in the closet, secrets in sight,

New in town, but I'm ready for the fight,
(Chorus)
(Bridge)
Beats on the streets, where the pain is raw,
Greatness in the struggle, can't ignore the flaw,
Cold hearts thumping, we push and we strive,
In the emerald city, just trying to thrive,
(Verse 3)
This season almost done, but the past won't quit,
Crimes gone wrong, not solved, yeah, we're living it,
Ash falling down, gotta keep it moving,
When the world's so dark, stay ruthless, keep grooving,
Seattle's my playground, chaos in bloom,
But in every 24, we carve out the room.
(Chorus)
(Outro)
So here's to the night, where the shadows creep,
In the heart of my city, we rise or we weep,
Every 24, with the weight of the world,
Seattle's alive, watch our stories unfurl.
#Seattle Strong
#DJ Muncer
#mun det J

13

Vernon

AUGUST 2025

THE PAST TWENTY-FOUR HOURS have been brutal. I have driven over 150 miles, am seriously deprived of sleep, and feel more fulfilled than at any other point in my life. After taking Raven to my home and asking her about the warrant, I am unsettled being as I don't know her at all. Either she is an excellent actress or truly doesn't know she is wanted. I didn't want to make this call in front of her or let on I have any connection with the police other than my job; my intention is to help and not put her in a place of panic making her run. On the night of Ruby Sanders' murder, Detective Muncer was on scene and handed me his card. I stuffed it in my pocket, thinking of Allard and her pushy ways, never intending to use Muncer's number at all but taking the card anyway to appear cooperative and not rude, although I am becoming testy and on edge, not knowing when Allard will appear and what her actions towards me will be. I didn't know when or if I would run into Muncer again. During this encounter, he has acted professionally.

I reluctantly dial his number after pulling over to figure out my Bluetooth radio. He answers with music in the background, heavy metal or rap, something I hear just a slice of, since he silences the volume almost immediately. It takes him a minute to bring the scene to mind I am describing, but he remembers, giving my description, about 6' 4", brown hair, green eyes, Metro. "Can I call you that?" he asks. Telling me about how the incident and word association help him. I bring up the topic of my call and let him know I am aware he may not be able to release this information to the public, but I am wondering if I am looking for Melvin Scriptnor, Don Montgomery who I found, and Raven Wells why can't I know what they are wanted for? It sounds as if Muncer is humming, but I think he is digesting the fine line of police work and what help I can give. He has been silent for so long. I think maybe it was a mistake to have made this call. Then he says, "Sorry, you are the second person to ask me about these individuals in the past six hours."

It sounds as if he is typing but is silent. This phone call is awkward to say the least. He tells me he has only had a couple of hours of sleep due to helping a friend. I laugh, only imagining what messes he may get into. He asks how I heard about these three individuals; I tell him of Allard, being on the bus and asking for my assistance the night of the shooting on Aurora. He says Don Montgomery was wanted and charged for a series of murders relating to methamphetamine distribution. At this point, Melvin Scriptnor is just someone we need to question, and there are no active warrants out; we can't prove any of his crimes if there are any to attach him to, it is too late in the investigation for that. Raven Wells is in the same situation as Melvin, although she didn't appear to be involved only lived on the property. "I am sensing you feel uncomfortable with this situation." I let him know I just don't want to put myself in danger when I am not police. I don't want to let on about the emails and repeated bus visits from Allard.

"Maybe you can help me," Muncer says, "I am investigating something else in the Aurora area and may join you undercover if you are working tonight. When I am on board, of course, you don't know me." I am suddenly relieved that Raven is at my house and will not be on the bus, also hope Muncer is telling me the whole story, and Raven won't be arrested with me as an accomplice. I am not sure who to trust at this moment as I merge back onto northbound I-5.

I get to the bus garage and park, more unsure of my actions than I was two days ago. Life was definitely less complicated then. Just as my shift starts, my phone rings. Mr. Owens is not screaming but being authoritative, "I know you have left for work as normal, but someone is in your residence, I can tell from the exhaust of the shower." I calm him down, explaining my cousin came into town late last night for a couple of days. This story will at least get me to Friday when Raven will need to leave for her weekend with Enzo.

I get on my bus as the first passenger and start my shift, ride up to Aurora Village without incident. On our trip southbound at 3:45 pm, we travel through the congested streets with rush hour and commuters picking up. Downtown, around Pike Street, Kernal comes running onto the bus, not paying, and sits behind me, crouching in the seat so as not to be seen. I do not need any trouble, especially behind me. I watch as another person about his age chases the bus.

I have never seen someone run this fast, but with rush hour traffic, he catches up easily and board at the next stop. He gets on, looks around, and starts down the aisle towards me. He gives me a look as if he thinks I am involved. I glare back, he passes me, turns around, and I wonder why he didn't stop to visit Kernal, if that was why he chased the bus. He walks back up the aisle towards the driver. Just as he is ready to exit, Kernal jumps out from under my seat and laughs. I knew this kid was trouble, just then the other kid comes barreling back and I have to get between the two, which isn't easy with Kernal spewing words and basically playing chicken with my body as the barrier between them. Once the fight had started, the bus stopped, 911 was called, and punches were thrown around my body. I recognize Muncer as he boards in Fremont wearing jeans, a baseball hat, and a rock and roll novelty shirt that says *Green Pyramids*. He walks down the aisle, through the scene, going to the back seat, and sits like someone not involved.

Patrol officers take these two into custody and criminally trespass them off any bus in the system. Stellan Lind and Ludolf Korn are both under arrest, I am not sure what for, but I hope not to see them again. We headed into downtown, late as the incident got us off schedule, inching south as rush hour picked up. We get to our turnaround point and head back north. Just as we cross the Aurora Bridge, there is a lady at the stop whom I recognize with dread as Detective Allard. She boards the bus, sits in the seat behind me, which is also between me and Detective Muncer. She is furious, I can see from her actions, the air pulsates from her anger. I am nervous about Raven, but know she is in a safe place no one knows. I don't even have any utilities in my name, there is no way to trace her there. Allard asks if I have seen anyone interesting lately. I know she is looking for people from the stack of flyers she emailed. I tell her, "Yes, I saw Don Montgomery and called." I know that is not the answer she is looking for since it is information she already has; her demeanor becomes more intense. I just look at her as I know Muncer is, too. She turns and yells at Muncer, not recognizing him, treating him like he is a passenger but irritated he has gotten into her business, "What are you looking at? Mind your own business."

She tells me a green Toyota 86 is registered to Stellan Lind; what do I know about that? I tell her of Ralph again at Fort Leonard Wood. She doesn't appear to believe me and announces that I am always in this neighborhood and am in on something or know something but not coming clean. Then she gets up and leaves, crossing the street in her style with her badge in front of her. Hopping into the passenger seat of the dark SUV. I see her white ankle above the top of her expensive boots and wide-leg pants.

I am relieved she is gone, that Detective Muncer has seen her actions and did not react. I continue on with this game as if it is real and turn to Muncer and apologize for my visitors' actions. He acts as if he is scratching his head, but is signaling, he will call me.

14

Detective Muncer

AUGUST 2025

I BELIEVE AUGUST HAS been the longest month of my life; that incident on the Rapid Line with Allard was uncalled for. I have suspected she is up to something, but harassing another officer, well, basically another piece of law enforcement, is not how this should have gone down. I don't think her escape and way of crossing the street is too special either. She flashed her badge to stop traffic and ran to the SUV. I need to talk to Metevior about her and see what she or they are up to.

Agent Ford left a message asking if we could meet to analyze the meeting with Jill a few days ago.

We meet at 6:00 am at Seattle Sunshine Coffee again, holding our meeting upstairs, as I think of Everett Sunshine and will arrange a meeting here with him soon. I really need to work on my personal relationships with everyone. It feels as if I am being pulled in so many directions for work that I am just exhausted and don't want to see anyone after my shift, but the people I am avoiding are the only ones I need to see. Maybe we should have a BBQ at Everett's place soon.

This brings a smile to my face as Ford says to be careful on the stairs since I am not here mentally.

I apologize and tell him I am thinking about Everett Sunshine again. Then invite him to the BBQ that Everett has no idea about yet.

Agent Ford says he will not be using names since we are in a public place but wants to give me the information about the meeting with Jill. He goes on to say that "she is emotionally 17 or 18 years old, she did give a lot of information, at least the area is narrowed down to a few hundred square mile area that can be searched. Her memories are vivid, but if she was there and safe for over twenty years with her actions now, she blocked out many days, weeks, and years. She probably has memories of other things that would help us investigate this case, but she will either need counseling from someone who specializes in these types of cases or a hypnotist. The latter being faster, but ultimately it is up to her if she does this. I would encourage it since more people remain missing, even those not related to you. If it were just her, I would say she is happy and let her be. It isn't likely in her case, since she is no longer there, that we could make an arrest unless we find others." I agree to speak with her about her options and we part ways. He then yells across the parking lot, "don't forget to send me the specifics on the BBQ." Oh boy, I had better talk with Everett soon.

This meeting and anticipation of summer's end is the best reason to trigger my mind of the tasks needed to hold a BBQ at Everett's house. Once back in my cruiser, I text Naomi to invite her, make a grocery list, and set my alarm to call Micky, Everett's caregiver to see if next weekend is a good time for them. I quickly add Agent Ford to the list, so I don't forget his invitation.

I decided to go north on Aurora up by where the shootout was a few months ago. As I near N 100th Street, the outside lane is closed due to a downed power wire with Seattle City Light in their bucket truck and SPD rerouting traffic. I turn left, unable to scout out Aurora as I wished. On N 97th St there is a traffic jam with people not being able to navigate an uncontrolled intersection, I turn north taking the alley between N Evanston and Dayton Avenues, a reflective windchime catches my eye a few houses down the alley on the west side and I see a green Toyota backed into a garage with its hood poking out of the dilapidated partially opened doors. I park off to one side of the alley, put my police placard on the dash out of habit. It isn't like anyone would question my choice of parking here. I know I should call for backup on this car as it appears to be the vehicle involved in the shooting a few weeks prior. I can positively ID it from the oversized wheel well, flat spot on the front of the hood, and odd shape of the headlight I can see from this angle. I set foot on the property which no warrant is required, nor is one for the garage, since it is hanging wide open. I place my hand on my service revolver and round the corner just as a male about forty years of age rounds the corner on the opposite side of the garage. I tell him to halt; he places his hands in the air and stops, not fully making his way to the vehicle in question. A female announces out the back door, "Billy, breakfast is ready." He yells, "Hold on." I ask him to place his hands on the hood and search him while asking if he has any weapons. He replies quickly, "No, sir, what is this about?" I tell him the car is wanted as evidence in a recent case. He says, "Stellan, that little slime ball. I knew I should not have given him permission to park his car here. He asked if he could bring it here to work on about a month or two ago and hasn't been back. "I would like my garage closed, I suspect the homeless have been sleeping in there." I ask if he will remain at home if I uncuff him, and if he knows Stellan's whereabouts. I feel it is safe for him to wait inside, as Stellan is in custody and Billy is not wanted; I do not fear he could alert Stellan of my visit. He responds with, "Yes and no, sir, I do not." I uncuff him, return to my cruiser to check the report for Stellan's last name, run the plate to verify they match, check property records on the residence, and see that William Lind is the owner, then call for a tow truck to take the car into custody.

I am not sure why, but while waiting for the impound, I called Vernon Cannon, even though it is only 7:30 am. I let him know the Toyota 86 and its owner are in custody. I hear a female laughing in the background, and I am happy that at least someone has a normal life and some laughter.

I knock at the back door when the tow truck arrives to give Billy a chance to come out and lock up his garage. We talked a bit, and I told him Stellan is in custody already from an incident last night. He seems pleased with this tidbit of information, smiles, pulls a padlock out of his well-worn jean jacket, and before turning to the back door, he adds, "Thank you for not shooting and coming to get me to lock up."

Micky texts back, loving the idea of a BBQ, agreeing on next weekend, saying it has been a long summer without much activity for Everett. He hasn't wanted to go out in the sun. She texts back a list of what she has to contribute, though I wasn't expecting anything, This get-together was my idea. I let her know I will take care of the rest and pick up something from Seattle Sunshine Coffee. Micky sends a laughing emoji's as we as we end the conversation. I know the source of her laughter is the name of the coffee company. Everett will be pleased, sharing the name.

15

Vernon

AUGUST 2025

ABOUT 11:00 PM, I text Raven to let her know of my arrival. The reality of inviting a stranger into my house and then letting her stay is so unlike me since I have never had anyone to trust before, but somehow, I am not bothered by this situation. What feels off is the fact that I would return home and tell anyone about my time away. During my childhood, no one would ask about my endless hours alone, my day at school, anything about what I had done, or ask if I had eaten or was safe. I could have robbed banks, and no one would have been on to me. All Birdie ever asked was if I liked her cooking, English muffin this or that. It is a staple at my house now, a comfort almost, like Birdie is always with me.

I pull in, the night just starting to cool, feeling the breeze off the lake, and Gus waddles around my ankles. He is used to his worms that I purchase at the corner store. I suppose this is the calmest part of my day, thinking of the duck I am friends with makes me laugh. I am positive Raven has seen the container being one of a small number of things in my dorm-sized half fridge. She probably imagines I fish living on the lake. I enter from the front, leaving the door open while Gus waddle dances in the doorway and Raven laughs. She rises from the couch, runs to the fridge, and retrieves the worms, handing them to me. Raven is almost giddy. I have only seen her sullen, in a withdrawn state on the bus, and now I have heard her laugh. We stay up all night again and laugh about past, present, and future tales. She grew up on a farm with her grandparents in Sedro Woolley, her parents left her there for a month every summer, and the year she was twelve, they did not return. She says, "There are worse places I could have been abandoned. Grandma and grandpa were good people. The chores were hard, and not being in the city made making friends tough, so I had horse, cow, and chicken friends. One of their geese didn't let anyone on the property until we went to the gate and assured him it was ok. Gus reminds me of home, or at least where I was raised, through the end of school. I think they kept the farm since I was still a child, but once I graduated, they posted a *for sale by owner* sign on the dirt road out front and bought a three-bedroom house in town. I lived there for a short while but then applied for jobs in Seattle and worked at a warehouse by the airport, packing meals for the airplanes. That is where I met Albatar, we were not a couple. I am not sure where it all went wrong, but I did have it together. Albatar left for the military before Enzo was born, and it seemed like he didn't want to be involved. He stopped talking to me, quit coming to work then I heard he had joined the military. Aleene watched Enzo while I worked. Then I was probably bored and overwhelmed. I partied with people at work who were friends with my sister. I started using for like a week, Aleene and her ex, Rubio, saw the difference in me and took

Enzo, filed for custody, and I felt so defeated. I failed him before I had even really settled into parenthood. They are very by-the-book kind of people. I quit working and moved in with my new friends, where my sister Meade lived. Aleene would only let me have supervised court-ordered visitation. I have always shown up for that, so now I want to apply for custody again, but without a job or place to stay, I feel I would be denied. You let me stay one night and get my whole story, I shouldn't have unloaded this on you."

I shake my head, which causes Raven to put her hand over her face. I pull it away, thank her for her honesty, and assure her I need to know what direction she chooses if I am going to help in any way. First, I ask, "What is your plan for your weekend visit with Enzo?" Her expression withdraws, she appears to sink into the couch and disappear. I don't even know her well, but I still see anguish and regret coming to the surface. I see this is a topic she does not have an answer to. She reminds me of her previous arrangement at Little Mel's and Aleene calling all the shots, her requirement to be present on the #40 route after 9:00 pm in the summer, so no one will see Aleene hand Enzo off to her before dark. "Rubio cannot know of our colluded agreement, Aleene says he would not approve."

I am still not sure of my suggestion before it leaves my mouth, but I turn to Raven, whom I just noticed is wearing one of my old T-shirts, which takes me by surprise, and I stop mid-sentence. This action makes it appear that I am not sure of my offer, which is only partially out of my mouth. Raven looks at me and says, "You have done enough, this is my mess. Look, you are all set up and have your life together. You don't need these troubles." I know that at that moment, I had never hindered or helped anyone, but this is my moment to decide to help. I offer a place to stay, knowing it can't be here, but somewhere. A hotel, which doesn't feel right to leave a little guy confined to a room all weekend without access to run. An Airbnb of her choosing, I will pay for this weekend anyway, ensure she can get to Seattle to be on route 40, make sure she has adequate food for the weekend, and drop her off. Then I realize Raven has no clothing or personal belongings. We will go to Target and shop in the morning for a few outfits and something for Enzo, along with food. I have never spent any money on much through the years. Getting Raven through this weekend and on her feet is manageable as long as she gets a job. I do not tell Raven of my plan other than to find a roof for the weekend. I am positive by the quizzical look on her face, she is wondering about food and other needs with all her belongings at Little Mel's. I don't know if she has plans to try and retrieve her stuff, but that can come later. This weekend is a pressing issue, so she doesn't appear unreliable in her undetected care of Enzo.

Thursday morning at 11:00 am, we are at Target in the Lakewood Towne Center. Raven says she will wait out here while I go in. This is where I tell her of my plan to help her with more than just the roof. Raven looks away from the store, not being used to receiving help from anyone, and asks," Would it be better if I went to a food bank?" I was shocked since I had never used one or even thought of that option in this situation. I get out of the driver's seat, open the passenger door, and motion for Raven to get out without touching her. This will have to be her choice; my thoughts are that a few hundred dollars should cover today and the weekend. I tell her, "I have never done anything like this before, and it should be an adventure." Once inside, I escort her to the lady's department, leaving her there for privacy, and go to the men's department for some warmer clothing for the season ahead. I see children's clothing across the way and locate the food and toy department before returning to Raven, who had picked out three outfits. I ask her to get a set of dress clothes for interviews. She says, "I will get it together." I nod in agreement as she places her clothing in my red Target cart, and we proceed with her more at ease and hopeful to the children's clothing for Enzo, toys, and groceries to cover the weekend. I am unsure what will happen after this weekend, but I know Raven and Enzo will at least be provided for over the next few days. Raven gets in my Rubicon and is silent except for an almost whispered thank you. We ride back to my house with only the radio on quietly and thoughts in our heads. Raven probably wonders what I want from her. My answer is for Enzo and her to be happy and safe.

16

Detective Muncer

SINCE I WAS THE one to locate the Toyota, I felt it was on me to complete the case file. At 10:00 pm, I showed up, found the guard, and requested Stellan Lind be brought to questioning room four. When I arrived, the chairs were in place, but the table had been exchanged for another one. The thought of touching anything in this room is eerie, which had been the safest bet before this scene is now my only option.

Higgens, a newly hired guard, saunters down the cinder-blocked hallway with Lind as if in slow motion, closing the auto-locking doors behind them, escorting a beaming-faced Lind. He glares at me, enters the room, and sits, never removing the evil smile from his young face. I glance at his file while keeping one eye on him. I see his birth date is August 22, 2007. Acquiring his recent age, he has landed at this establishment and not juvie like Korn. I am not even aware of their separate charges or why they were involved on the Metro, but the shooting and green Toyota are what brought Lind to this room.

He looks like that smile is tattooed on; it must be his defense mechanism, but it is not working for me. He hasn't said a word since being seated. I see notes on the file from Allard, who has left the suggestion of trading time served for information. I do not let on that I have read that note and now understand why the amount of happiness is radiating from him. He either has spotted that portion of the file or has talked to Allard and been assured he will be leaving, but neither of those options are correct. He thinks he is leaving after our conversation and doesn't understand how the system works, like this is an exit strategy. This will have to be seen in court, with new charges filed. Allard does not have the last say in this or any at all. After she yelled at me on the bus, I saw her true colors and need to track down Metevior when he is off shift, since he has been partnered up with her to find out what cases they have been following.

Being as Allard has recommended his release, I am quite happy with my decision to have stopped in for a visit with this young man, given that the grin will be on my face once I leave this room. I am in no way happy he is here or that he committed the crime, just happy he has been caught since he chose these options.

He tried to own city blocks, own people, tell them when to sell, walk, steal, or whatever wishes he imagined, then drove the car, shot into businesses, and at innocent people, even some that allowed him control. He didn't care who he hit, just used his weapon like he was having a temper tantrum and now sits here smiling as if the situation is over. It has only just begun. Luckily, no one was hit, but he thought he was king of a few blocks that belong to the city and people of Seattle, and he is not returning to his parents' house to play video games, steal cars, sell drugs and go out in the evening for a shootout when he pleases. He will remain in custody until trial.

I ask what his involvement was during the shooting on Aurora back in June. Me knowing full well he was the only shooter and had fired off approximately one hundred rounds into businesses. The footage retrieved from a local business shows bystanders from the sidewalk all running for cover, hiding behind whatever they can locate to be safe. Meanwhile, Lind keeps shooting with someone controlling the wheel from the passenger side. He must not be a very good shot; I see one frame shows him slowing down to a female on the sidewalk, shooting at her and missing.

Lind asks for something to drink, the first words he has spoken since his arrival. I leave, making certain he doesn't have anything to harm himself, and retrieve an orange soda from the vending machine to match his jumpsuit. I return, he sees the can, asks for coffee, a man's drink. I tell him my theory; I purchased the drink with him in mind.

The smile has faded since he understands I will not cooperate like Allard, and she is not the only one with a say so in this case. In truth, we just investigate, arrest, and interrogate. The outcome of the story remains with the judicial system.

Lind suddenly looks like a young child, a pout has replaced his smile, and he shared with me, "Detective Allard and I rehearsed my version of the story for over an hour; I am sticking to it and ready to go back to my cell. Mom always made me go to bed by midnight, and I still need to brush my teeth." I know now that there is no point in being here; call the guard so Lind can get to sleep. At least his mom would be proud of him for it, and he will have good teeth.

After leaving, I check the schedule and see Metevior is off tonight, immediately I text asking if he is busy needing his time but not wanting to interfere with his off-duty plans. He texts back in about ten minutes, saying he has been meaning to see me. I feel the hesitation in the words I read on the screen. The next text comes in almost simultaneously. Meet me at the corner of N 62nd Street and Phinney Avenue in fifteen minutes.

I check my phone, know that at this time of night, I can arrive in ten minutes. I travel up 99 to assist my friend in sharing the story he has held onto for a long time. I pull over on the southwest corner in front of a closed business, get out, imagining the animals at the zoo a couple blocks away, and am listening for them when Metevior shows up in a battered white Honda Civic, parking on the north side of the street. I am not sure he has seen me, or maybe just needs a few more minutes alone to hold onto his story and rearrange his thoughts. He cuts the motor by releasing the clutch, leaves the keys in the ignition, walks around to the passenger side, and leans on the car. This is not a vehicle I have seen him drive before, and I have known him for over twenty years.

He sees me crossing the street, nods, but I can tell he is carrying a heavy load as he tilts his head from side to side, releasing the tension in his neck and shoulders. I ask how life is treating him. He gives me a look like I should know things are not easy. Then says, "It is against my better judgment to share this with you, but since we have worked together for two decades or more, I will divulge the information that I have been holding onto for what feels like an eternity."

He was approached by intelligence not long after Allard was brought into the department and promoted to detective. "They gave this case to me, saying they could trust me. I never wanted to be part of her scheme, just wanted to work my last years and retire, but here I am being forced into her mess. I police the streets, not the department. They gave a brief rundown on her actions and their suspicions, but nothing concrete. I have been watching her every day, but she gets out here and there, talks to people, chases down buses, especially the Rapid Ride E line. I know she has her fingers in something, but I can't figure it out. How does she have all these connections if she just moved here from Portland? I am not sure if I did know what she is up to, I would want to let on that I knew, no one needs enemies in the department. She has been obsessed with finding Melvin Scriptnor, and I have no idea why. Isn't that a guy from down south that Rubio and you were working a case on?" I tell him he is the third person who has asked about him in the past couple of days, just as an animal sound comes from the zoo, possibly a lion claiming his territory on this hot night as summer begins to close.

Metevior and I part ways, me not knowing any more than I suspected, but now understand why he drove the battered Civic, the purpose of the grin on Linds' face, and the reason for the harassment of Vernon. It all stems from the plot of Allard and the fate of this investigation. Me being involved prior to hearing it from Metevior and now Allard's enemy due to my discovery of the British Racing Green Toyota and not her, who may have made the vehicle disappear.

17

Vernon

AUGUST 2025

It felt strange to drop Raven off at a rented duplex for the
weekend. She assured me she would be safe from Mel and was capable
of getting on the #40 to meet Aleene for the transfer of Enzo. I know
she is capable and has kept herself out of trouble for many years
before the almost three days we spent together, well, at least the parts
of the days with me working. Mr. Owens didn't give me any more
trouble, but I am certain he is watching my movements. I was true
to my word that Raven would be gone by Friday. The one thing I
will miss the most is hearing her laugh when feeding Gus worms. She
didn't appear bothered when handling them or if Gus nipped her
fingers.

I hope since it is Friday night and a four-day weekend for most,
that it is quiet, but do the types of people who cause the chaos like I
see leave town for Labor Day weekend? After leaving the bus garage,
we follow our normal route. I see an unusual teenager not too far
north of downtown. She boards the bus, looks me directly in the eye
like she has found her target, and sits in a seat near the front with her

back towards me. After we cross the Aurora Bridge and get to the first stop where three people board, I am thinking of Ruby Sanders and her family, wondering how they are doing, when the unusual girl gets up and sits across from me. I am fortunate to have remembered to sit in the aisle seat, so no one joins me. The girl hands me a note and says, "Ringer, is my name." I look at her and can only wonder what words are on the piece of paper in my hand and imagine how crazy this girl is. Now I know she boarded this bus specifically to see me, or so I think, without reading the note.

I carefully open the well-worn note, making sure there are no powdered substances falling out. I feel like my life will change if I read the written words and wish to return it to the girl. I pass it back across the aisle, calling out her name to get her attention as she looks out the opposite window. Ringer turns as I say, "No thanks," and hand the note back to her. She demonstrates her teenage eye roll, rises, starts to leave, dropping the note in my lap and walks up the aisle, ringing the bell across an empty seat as she proceeds. She exits the coach, places her hood on her head, this hot afternoon, stands on her tip toes to see in the bus window, and points to herself, then to me. I can only imagine what business this wacko girl named Ringer would think she has with me.

After a few blocks, I have to read the note, my curiosity not resting. It is a message from Kernal in such small writing I almost need glasses, but I do not own any. I take out my phone and magnify the pencil-written words. He can be released from juvie under the conditions of an adult going with him to sign up for a community service program called Ethan's Edge. His mom is not around, and his dad works all the time, so he is on his own, and since I am bus police I could help. I stop here, wondering when I told him that, and know I did not. I continue reading the blue paper asking me to help in a program about graffiti. I carefully fold the note and place it in my side zipper pocket, knowing for some reason I will help this child named Kernal and his messenger Ringer, but am still mentally in denial, shaking my head, smiling as I bring to mind his crazy corn tattoo.

18

Detective Muncer

AFTER MY TALK WITH Metevior, I have been trying to think of how to help but not be involved. He has been put into a no-win situation. I thoroughly look at every case Allard has open and try to make a connection to the end result of her motive but see none. Before being transferred to downtown, she mostly worked south of here, and our paths rarely crossed. She was with the Portland Police Bureau before that.

I locate Joe Connely's number just in case but prefer this meeting to be off the books and remember he travels daily for his methadone on Aurora, taking Metro from south Seattle and making a day of his excursion so he can be present during the night when most of the activity happens.

I locate the clinic, almost missing Joe, who sits at the bus stop across the street. If it weren't for the neon orange stripe on his shirt, I may not have seen him. Turning around and hoping I can cross five lanes of rush hour traffic before he boards the bus, I get to the center lane, and Joe stands, seeing me. He has always been an off-the-books cooperative CI, even though it is not me he reports to, and seems to enjoy the fact-finding missions he is sent on. He has been in Seattle for a few months and has always been cordial to me. I wave, and he dodges two lanes of traffic, standing at my passenger door holding the handle. Then he thinks better of getting in there with my hesitancy, which wasn't due to him getting in but the shock that he avoided getting hit while running across the lanes of traffic. He looks through my passenger window and points to the rear door. I hit the unlock button as he slides in and belts himself. I generally do not transport anyone but call for a patrol unit to make the transfer from the crime scene to lock up, so having a passenger is not common for me.

I am wondering what to do with Joe now that he is in my cruiser. Up ahead on the south side of Aurora, I see the golden arches and ask Joe if he is up for a meal. He smiles, saying, "Always." I pull in and decide not to go through the drive-thru with what appears to be a man in custody. I let him out by the dumpster, giving him the rest of the pack of smokes, always located in my console for others. He gets out, knowing my plan to come back with food and lights a cigarette and something else behind the dumpster as I continue behind the building to the order sign. Getting us each a meal in separate bags, I pull over and place Joe's identical Quarter Pounder meal in the back seat and drive cautiously so his soda doesn't spill before retrieving him.

Once I back in next to the dumpster, he hops in the backseat with the smell of tobacco permeating the entire vehicle. He knows I am looking for information but is not talking since he sees many crimes but is not sure about which one I will be inquiring about, nor does he know I am aware he is a paid CI. I ask how life is going at the encampment. He knows I am aware of the case involving the burned tent, so he starts to talk, "At least it has been warm and dry, but since Steven Watkins passed in the tent fire last month, things have been different. It wasn't even like Steven had been there long or knew many people. He had met Don somewhere and was brought to us. We were a tight-knit group, but since Don recommended him to stay, even though Don wasn't a resident, we allowed him in our area. He was always in his tent. Sometimes we would hear him crying, but just like the others who showed up to stay one by one, they had to adjust to our way of life. There was word through the police that Steven had gotten custody of his baby after the mama ran away, then he lost his roof and was living under a bridge away from others, but with the baby. It was taken by CPS, and that is when he came to us. Don tried to get him to come out and participate in meals when he showed up to drop off product, BBQs, and food bank runs, but Steven was flying solo. We never would have let Don hang around there if we had known he was the supplier of the crap that killed so many. I am still not positive it was Don who set the tent on fire after Steven was found dead, but I do know Don supplied him with a tad bit of drugs for the $26.00 left on Steven's food stamp card. You know, the funny thing about that day was that there were other detectives there before the tent went up in flames. The lady, Allard, came to talk to Watkins, and her partner stayed in the vehicle. Whew, this street life and encampment living sure hangs on me when I wish it didn't. It is a hard system to shake. You know I have an upstanding wife who works as a nurse and three children living in Portland. Maybe I shouldn't have told you that, but I work for the Portland Police Bureau and am up here on a case we have been following for about a year. The only thing that is getting me through this assignment is the picture of the house up the road from mine, since it would be too dangerous to have photos of my children, wife, or own residence on my person. I take this long trip daily to stay sane, but am at the encampment nightly, and while I am out daily, I can call my children when they return from school, and my wife, Rachel, too. She works nights, and her mom stays with the children. This assignment has been hard on all of us, but since Allard pulled out on this assignment after signing up and being hired on to SPD, I was approached and basically forced into this role." Joe sits in the back seat with his head hanging, I know he is one of us and not them. I also know more about Allard and her connection to Portland and tent city, but not what that tie is yet, but I bet it has to do with the neighborhood we are sitting in, Stellan Lind, and wherever else she leads me. I will not tell Metevior of my findings yet until I have some solid evidence. Nothing worse than hanging around someone and not being able to blurt out what you know about them. Just as I am thinking about this Joe blurts out, "Allard was transferred out of Portland for misconduct, my thoughts are she was using or making money off the dealers in connection to overlooking their actions but there wasn't sufficient evidence, and the upper ranked panel decided to let her move on, but she knows I am here from Portland and also is aware I knew about her previous actions. She has warned me not to talk, of course, she finds me away from my temporary home. The reason I am telling you this is that if anything happens to me, she should be your first suspect. She is an underhanded, double-faced arm of the department. I would watch yourself around her." Now I know a meeting with Metevior is in order.

The BBQ came together easily, celebrating the end of summer. A great excuse to get together with everyone that matters to me. Everett is happy in his tank top, shorts, and tourist hat to shade his eyes. He always asks to see my badge; this time, I introduce him to Fred Ford as FBI. Everett says he will be watching for him on TV. I am glad to see Micky and Daniel are still together. I sit back and realize everyone here is an important piece of this city and introduce them as they interact. Jill declined the invitation. I thought that was strange, but I know she may feel odd in the presence of Agent Ford. There is more going on with her, and I will find the underlying cause of that. Naomi leans over to tell me she didn't know I knew people to have fun with. I have told her about this duplex and the occupants but have never had a reason to bring her here.

Micky and Daniel cook, Naomi and I get out the picnic table and chairs, just as August and Willow walk in carrying a chocolate angel food cake for dessert. Everett is drinking his soda out of a Seattle Sunshine Coffee cup, pointing at the word sunshine and then pulling out his ID, showing us that the two words are the same. I wonder what I have started with him and am glad he does not know it is just a few blocks from his house. Otherwise, he would bother Micky to go all the time. We sit and eat. Everett says he gets one shot of beer a day and runs in the house for his shot glass. Overall, it is a relaxing day and great to catch up with Daniel. He says Simone has had the tire company up and running for about three years now. We play lawn darts, corn hole, and disc golf. The two duplexes may be identical, but my backyard is small compared to this one. We decide to do this every year and have a dinner together at the start of each season. I am fortunate to have this close group of friends.

19

Vernon

SEPTEMBER 2025

THE WEEKEND HAS BEEN peaceful, except for the excessive number of boats on the lake. Gus has been staying in the wooden crate I have placed inside the bushes by the lake. I have noticed him allowing a female to stay in his crate, too.

This is the first time in my life, except when I was in kindergarten, that I have felt alone, the most difficult year of my life so far. Birdie would drop me off for a few hours at school; prior to that, it was just the two of us playing all day, mostly on the beach. Then, when I started school, I would sit there for those hours, having separation anxiety, convincing myself she was not going to be standing outside when the final bell rang. Making all sorts of scenarios up, she would get hurt on the beach, hit by a bus, struck by lightning, which was common in Florida, or maybe she just liked her life better without me. I got through that year somehow, in the summer, not yet being old enough to stay alone, Birdie would take me with her, and it would be just like before again. By the time first grade started, I knew I could go to school, and she would always be outside waiting for me when the final bell rang. Kindergarten was the last and only time in my life I missed anyone. During all my other years, I knew, even though I was alone, that Birdie would return with the English muffins and oranges.

This weekend, after having Raven here for a couple of days, I discovered I miss her. I have not texted so she can spend time with Enzo but have no idea what her plans are tonight after returning him to Aleene's. This would be easier on her if I helped, but I am not positive she wants that after all I have done, and I leave the next steps for her to ask if she chooses.

There are so many questions. Can she stay at Aleene's? Will the cop ex-husband, Enzo's grandpa, try to take her in? Is she actually wanted? Where will she go once she drops Enzo off? I hope not back to Little Mel's. There has been much thought this weekend about whether Raven wants to work. I don't know what skills she has or what her plans are. Just as I complete this thought, she texts asking if she can stay one more night; she needs somewhere to gather her thoughts and make a plan. Her last sentence is "Can you meet me at the 512 park and ride at 7:04 pm?"

I find relief in text and know she will also be helping herself. I am not positive if the feeling is more from Raven returning to my house or whether she has shown the initiative of being assertive and not taking my generosity for granted. At 6:30, I prepare to leave and spot Mr. Owens in his garage; I stop to inform him about Raven coming into town for another week or two. That should be long enough to give me some leeway with him and for her to decide. Mr. Owens looks at me and states with authority, "This is my property, and last time she was here, there wasn't any trouble, so I trust it will be that way when she comes back again. I did enjoy hearing the laughter floating through the open window." I thank him, smile, and drive up the hill to Veterans Drive on my way to pick up Raven.

I am suddenly hungry. On Sunday, I usually BBQ by the water, but didn't go to the grocery store or prepare for that with my mind being preoccupied. I take I-5 for a couple of exits and make my way to the park and ride just as the southbound 594 bus arrives, not even needing to park, just as Raven spots me. I imagine her and her twin; she is someone who has always had someone her entire life, and now that person is gone.

She gets in and asks if I would like to go to dinner. We go north on South Tacoma Way and stop at Dairy Queen. Raven offers to pay, but I tell her to hang onto her money, wondering how she obtained it. Once seated, she tells me about Aleene, who gives her $100.00 for her time with Enzo, just in case. Sometimes they go to the zoo or a carnival, but his favorite is the pet store or beach to throw rocks into the water, always putting a few in his pocket, saying, "next time". After eating, she pulls out a list with the columns marked needs, wants, now, and later. At the top, under needs, are names of temporary agencies, shelters, housing options, and avenues for legal help to gain custody of Enzo. She says Aleene is aware she will be filing soon and is still willing to watch him in the daytime until he starts preschool, probably later this year.

I am relieved I do not need to ask any of this and only say, " I am impressed with your plan." Then I wonder where she will work, if I will see her, and if we should have a Blizzard. I inform her that she is welcome to stay at my house for the next couple of weeks, and we will try to find a place for her to be with Enzo on the weekends. I do not want to pay for the Airbnb every weekend, but I will if it is needed. I tell Raven about Kernal and his dilemma. She says she saw information about Ethan's Edge on the shelter website over the weekend, and it is located at the women's shelter downtown. She asks if I have the phone number to call on Tuesday, since Monday is a holiday, like I have already made up my mind and probably have to help Korn.

We spend the evening watching corny movies on the DVD player since I don't have cable and have not gotten the Wi-Fi password from Mr. Owens. I am glad to have the holiday off and relax. I may have been off work for a few years except this bus gig, but I am not sure I have fully relaxed. I look over at Raven, who is wearing my shirt and sleeping on the sofa, her backpack being used as a footstool.

She wakes about 11:00 pm, with a start, asking for Enzo, then remembering she has returned him to his grandma. She tells me that is the hardest part of being a parent, not being one full time. That is her child, and she let them convince her he would be better off with them when they weren't ready for that, neither was she, but she would not have jeopardized her life with him and gotten back on the right path. If she had fought the case, she might have lost him forever. Then Aleene started contacting her without Rubio's knowledge, she says, "I don't know what he would say about me taking Enzo, but I am positive Aleene proposed the idea to him of keeping Enzo full time. Like a night shift policeman would have time for a small child full time."

Tuesday, I sleep in since work is on my schedule in a few hours. When I go into the living room, Raven is not there, I panic thinking she has left but see her backpack still by the sofa. I locate her in the wooden chair outside the front door. She holds her finger up to signify one minute, hangs up, and says she has an interview tomorrow at 1:00 pm in Seattle with Tempo, a temporary agency. I am exceedingly happy for her, but just as I am getting used to her being here, she will be back in Seattle again. At this moment, I can see my current house behind me and wonder about Gus when I move to Seattle.

Raven's interview went well, she has a drug test to schedule and two placements to choose from. Both off of 6th Ave, one at Amazon and the other at August Island Rike Paper Company. Both daytime warehouse positions. Daytime was a requirement for her since she is trying to get Enzo back and attempting to find housing. The bus ride from here to there is long, it could work, but I know Raven will be making other accommodations soon. I bring myself back to this moment and congratulate her on the interviews.

I report to work distracted. Ringer boards the bus, and I feel as if I am in a capsule that anyone who wishes to meet with me can just enter. I think I should put in for a transfer to another route. Ringer walks up and says, "Well?" I am not exactly sure my business is with her, but I know I will call Ethan's Edge in the morning to find out about their services. Then I ask Ringer how to reach Kernal if I choose to. She wants my phone to enter his digits. Says somehow, he got out of juvie on house arrest, he is waiting, and the number belongs to his dad for messages only. Kernal's phone was lost in the shuffle from the bus to juvie and never returned.

On the last run into town, I was ready to go home. The only thoughts I had were stopping to buy worms for Gus on the way home and seeing Raven laugh. At the last stop before I am done, Allard is at the gate and walks over to me. Now I am stuck with her on the street and not entering the bus yard with her, not even positive she is supposed to cross the gate path. She is interrogating me. Where are Raven and Melvin? Why did I turn in Don and not them? What are they paying me? I just stand and look at her, then ask, "What are they wanted for?" She whips her head around and gives me the evilest glare, knowing her partner in the dark SUV is watching us from somewhere nearby. She doesn't travel alone, just then he appears, parks in the road with his lights on, and exits the vehicle. Now there are two of them, like she had called for backup, and I hadn't done anything. The partner asks us both if there is a problem. I quietly say, "No, I am just trying to go home since I just got off work, showing him my badge and pointing to the buses." He looks at Allard, and she shakes her head, mumbling something derogatory about noncooperation under her breath as she turns her back to me and slides into the SUV parked a short distance up the road. The partner gives me his card and asks me to call, but not tonight. Now I wonder what I have gotten myself into and if I should ask Muncer before contacting Metevior.

I call the number I found online listed for Ethan's Edge the following morning, not positive what I am getting myself into, and leave a message. I receive a return call almost before hanging up, both lines showing up at the same time on my screen. I tell my story about not knowing Ludolf Korn, aka Kernal, at all, but have been asked to help. Tell this man named Carl how I met Kernal and Ringer, who delivered the note to me on the bus, and about my occupation. Carl invites me to their Belltown location, asks if I am familiar with the city. Giving me brief directions and scheduling a meeting for any day this week that works for me, he says as he informs me, he is looking over Ludolf Korn's file as we speak. He laughs, giving me a chance to back out, feeling reluctant, and then says, "Sounds like this guy is a bit like Ethan." That statement makes me know I am going to this appointment tomorrow before work, if only to hear the story about Ethan. Time will tell if I am going to help Kernal get out of his self-chosen dilemma.

I work without any more intrusions from Allard, and I am torn between contacting Muncer or not. I feel I can trust him with the information of this harassment but have no idea if being involved any further is recommended, especially since there is a third member of the force wanting contact, Metevior.

After finding parking several blocks down from the women's shelter that Carl said they only use for programs now, I walk the few blocks south to meet him at the front door. The sign in the window says by appointment only and points to the bell and lists a phone number other than the one I called to reach Carl. This is a rough part of town, and I watch my back while waiting, but don't feel threatened since I have been in places more sinister than this.

I ring the bell and can hear someone approaching, a man in his forties or so, looks out the floor-to-ceiling window, and smiles. He doesn't know me at all but remembers our appointment about Korn and the process of getting him back on the right track if he wishes.

I am led through the building down a long-carpeted hallway, past many doors and some open spaces with various items such as toys. This is my first visit inside of a shelter. Carl thanks me for being punctual, saying some people don't show at all, and others show up hours late. He says they need volunteers and was intrigued by my call to help someone get in line, whom I didn't actually know.

We enter his office by the back door, which, by my calculations, is half a block deep into the building. Carl says, "I keep this office since it was my grandmother's before she retired, and it is the closest to the parking spots in the alley. Some days the place is full, others, like today, I am the only one here in this monstrosity of a building. It used to house many, but now the housing has been transferred to our other facility called Charlene's Place. This is probably more than you needed to know, and we haven't even touched the subject you called about." I see framed photos of children with certificates, one without a certificate, and is just smiling. I ask why he doesn't have a certificate. Carl bends his head and pinches the bridge of his nose so hard it is extremely red when he pulls his hand away and speaks a couple of minutes later with an ear-to-ear grin, saying, "That is my Ethan. The one who started this program with his tags. He didn't take the course or get in trouble, even though he should have from all his tagging. He suffered, or at least I did, more than if he had been caught. Ethan was murdered, and this program is a dedication to him." I am not sure how to respond to that statement. I have great empathy and can feel anything in a room, but this cuts deep in Carl and now me. My mission will be to help Kernal turn a corner and prepare himself for the future.

There are a few stacks of business cards on a table under the photos, a few are from Seattle PD. I see Detective Muncer's card towards the back. Taking a gamble, I ask Carl about Muncer and tell him about my current occupation, past military experience, and meeting Muncer while on duty. Carl laughs again and says, "This city brings a smallness to the vast area. As life unfolds each day, it brings what and who you need into the scene. Detective Muncer was who showed up the night Ethan was murdered at the train depot and was there every step of the way until the case was solved. He even attended the funeral, not knowing our family personally, but stood right by us. We are still in contact now and then, especially when a case is turned over to us or he is investigating someone in our care. People come to us escaping various situations." I can sense he is not in this room mentally but remembering specific cases that have been through this building. He is a man who has probably seen more heartache and success than most. I think of the people who started working for a company and stayed there until retirement. They see one avenue of life all the way through, but Carl has seen many variations at this facility. The roads people did not plan on taking, and they need help getting back if they can.

Carl hands me the brochure, I assure him I will read it and get back to him by Thursday if that works for him. He nods yes as if he thinks he will never see me again with my sudden departure. I had looked at my phone, realizing it was time to leave so I wouldn't be late for my shift. I assure him I will call one way or another but still do not know much about the program since we talked more like old friends catching up on the city.

I lose no time getting back to my Jeep, that I am thankful is still parked where I left it, the stock luggage rack making my vehicle look out of place on the street with economy cars being the majority. I wonder if Raven ever owned a vehicle, then I picture her at my house. This will be a long Wednesday night, but at least the week will be more than half over when this shift is complete. I can almost feel the vibrations of the bus from the motor and the well-traveled road before I enter the bus garage parking. I park in my usual spot, not being sure how it is open every day when I arrive being as MTP shifts are staggered throughout the day and many do not park in here, mostly drivers. I am not even through one eighth of my segmented shift and am full of dread, not knowing if Allard will show up again being as we were interrupted by her partner last night, and she possibly didn't finish. I don't think she is aware of Metevior asking me to call since her back was turned at that moment.

The first segment ended up taking fifty-seven minutes precisely on schedule, a layover of exactly twelve minutes and exchange of passengers, none of which I know, and only recognize a few. Then on the first southbound route, we were stopped on Aurora, not at a light but to let a fire truck proceed, and I see a person in the window of a three-story apartment building that looks like a warehouse converted to apartments. I count sixteen black mailboxes mounted by the side door; they must be studios by the size of the building. Then I notice a person is in the window watching me make observations of the house. There is an eerie feeling emanating from the guy in the window, a young man who is wearing a t shirt so old it is not only holey but is almost tan which I can see through the perfectly clear window onto a table that holds a spray bottle of window cleaner and a roll of paper towels. The person also had a pair of large scissors, a handheld mirror that he repeatedly picks up to look at himself, aims at the parking area, and cleans the mirror and window consistently. The bus takes off with a jolt, the driver most likely feels irritation from the pressure to stay on schedule in an unpredictable world. With my curiosity piqued, I check on our northbound trip when we pass the man in the window, but I cannot see due to traffic backed up from the intersection. At Aurora Village, I exit, get dinner, and wait forty-two minutes for my layover, catching the second bus southbound. I am aware of the location of the man in the window and make sure I don't miss what is happening, even if it is nothing. On this trip, my final one of the night, I see the man with his paper towel in one hand as if ready to clean the window, but his face is pressed against the window with his mouth open like he is screaming. Now I know why he continually has a need to wash the glass; he is the cause of the dirty window. I wonder if he does that to his mirror also. There is no reason that I can think of why I saw this man I have passed possibly over one hundred times before and didn't notice, but as Carl said a few hours ago, "this city brings a smallness to the vast area. As life unfolds each day, it brings what and who you need."

My thoughts and wishes are to get home to Raven, but I feel I need to call Detective Muncer and ask about Metevior. Muncer answers on the first ring, stating his name. I tell him mine, and he hesitates, being as probably half the city has his number, so I remind him of the name he placed on me last week, Metro. He comes to life then, bringing himself from the rolodex of faces in the sea of people down to one. He would be happy to meet, even tonight, if it isn't short of notice. I ask where and when. He wants to meet in the parking area of Lumen Field right at the front gates, will ten minutes work? I text Raven letting her know I will be a few minutes late.

I cut across town and arrive in five minutes, thanks to the absence of commuter traffic. Only semi-trucks with the micro cabs used for transporting containers from the port to rail, dodge around each intersection. The street traffic is connected to the multicolored tents, people jumping out here and there, bonfires on the sidewalks like street parties but this is their kitchen.

I turn onto 2nd Avenue and follow it into the paid parking, seeing a car behind me, knowing it is not an SUV but wondering if Allard could be on her own tonight. I am relieved to be in the enclosed area of the parking lot with the attendant's booth, feeling the safety of the open area. I get close to the dome, never realizing how sizable it is, and turn with the vehicle pulling in next to me as police do, sitting cop style. It is Detective Muncer I see, releasing my breath. Even if it had been Allard, I would have simply said I took a wrong turn and left.

Muncer asks, "What's up?" I tell him of last night's incident, and he asks if I could handle a bit more of this, meaning Allard's behavior. I thought this was a strange response from someone who I thought might help, but I had not asked for help officially. I was primarily making a complaint off the books. I ask about Metevior if he is to be trusted, and I am not sure those were the proper words, but I don't know who to trust in this mess I didn't ask to get into. Muncer asks if I will meet with him and Metevior sometime soon. He will set it up, I agree, tell him of my schedule, thank him for his help in this, and leave feeling I have not made any headway yet, but who knows what the next meeting will hold.

I drive home unsure if I have gotten in too far or not far enough, but I am in it now. Laughing about Gus and smiling as I travel home with the road noise from my oversized tires and my empty Jeep, wondering how hard it is to install a car seat in this vehicle, or if it is too soon for me to meet Enzo. I will leave that up to Raven.

20

Vernon

SEPTEMBER 2025

FRIDAY. IT'S FINALLY HERE after a long week; it rolls in bittersweet. Raven gathers the rest of her possessions. The air is thick with uncertainty; communication does not appear to be either of our best traits. I do not wish to pry and she not wanting to burden me with her mess. I do know that Raven will be traveling north with me and staying at her aunt Evelyn's house for the weekend with Enzo. I am certain I do not know Raven at all and realize she could be lying to me, just using me for a place to stay, for the last two or three weeks. I can't seem to keep track of time with the other elements added to my solo life: Raven, Little Mel, Allard, Enzo, and Muncer, plus my job, the possibility of Ethan's Edge, and VA classes. Based on the bits and pieces I have gathered from her story, she was living with Little Mel and had been for at least a couple of years before that. I would like to know how that was put together and why she was there. Without communication, I will be on edge all day, but I am certain I will not learn anything new on our ride north.

I break the wall of silence, asking Raven what her plans are beyond today. She looks at me, uncertain, because maybe she only knows life as far as this minute. I am dropping her off downtown, but she could stay at my house until it is time to get Enzo and catch a bus, since she will not meet Aleene for the keys until 7:45 pm. She is not comfortable on the E line anymore due to Little Mel and Allard looking for her. She says she doesn't know what she will do except get dinner and walk around downtown. Sometimes, communication can be challenging when we lack the answers or skills we need.

We plan today with only the facts laid out in place. Raven is leaving, will pick up Enzo, and I will go to work. She does not have the address of where she will be staying. I wonder if this may be the last time I will see her and ask. Raven turns to look at me with a pained look on her face. She blurts out, "I don't know where my life is going, but I would prefer for you to be part of it." Well, we have established that. She asks me if I would like to see where she will be staying tomorrow or Sunday. "I do know I won't be back here on Sunday night since I start work on Monday morning and have no idea how our schedules will come together, but I do want to see you. I don't even know how I will work in Seattle, where I have to live to get Enzo, but I don't have a place to start with."

It is time to go, the moment I have been dreading since I got used to Raven being here. She runs to the window before we leave to check on Gus, who is absent from the porch, maybe from her life forever, and the only source of happiness in the past few days. Raven grabs her backpack, disappointed that Gus was not present. I take it from her, and we load into my Jeep. Mr. Owens waves as we proceed up the hill. I am thinking my story may be true, of just in town for a short while, and Mr. Owens may be thinking Raven is a permanent fixture here.

There is not much conversation on our way, and I think about not hearing back from Detective Muncer about Metevior. These days, I am edgy whenever I am working, knowing Allard is up to something. She is trying to involve me, and I have to watch my back since I am not involved in anything up north or where I live, my ties are minimal anywhere. The last thing I need is trouble, especially to be involved in the drug ring on Aurora.

I drop Raven off at The Shake Shack on Westlake Ave N. She assures me that she will be fine, and deep down, I know this because of the way she fled into the neighborhood the night Don was harassing her. I somehow do not like for her to be alone on the streets for endless hours. Just as I have that thought, she says, " I brought a book, will check out a couple parks, catch the 40 and see Enzo in just a few hours."

I know I am acting uncertain about her story, but that is not it; I just worry about Allard and how she would treat Raven if she located her. All these thoughts are suddenly in my head and not my problem, but I am involving myself, something new to me. Would Raven miss picking up Enzo due to being brought in? Right before filing for custody, it wouldn't look good to have been detained by SPD even if you were not guilty of a crime. I decide there is a better chance of her remaining free here than with me on the E Line and drop her at the corner of 8th Avenue and Westlake, kissing her as she turns to retrieve her backpack from the rear seat and ask if she thinks I should purchase a car seat before my visit on Saturday. This is our first kiss; a driver behind us is not patient and is blaring his horn. Somehow, I don't care; he can go around. This moment could change the entire course of my life, and I am not giving that driver the option of changing anything for me. Raven is clearly in shock as we have never touched before, a kiss being the first contact. I hope I have not blown this just now, amid all of my worries, I wanted her to know I care. She smiles and gets out, says. "I will send a picture of the car seat that will work, thank you, and the address for your visit over the weekend." Then leans across the passenger seat, having to get up on the running board, but kisses me, steps down, turns, and walks away, waving, not looking back, which makes me wonder if I will hear from her again.

I pull out onto Westlake and continue south to the bus garage, not paying attention to my routing, just as I receive a text from Muncer asking if I can meet him at 10:45 tonight, a second text comes in at N 62nd and Phinney. I am antsy but hope this meeting will relieve the stress of Allard, even if I simply gain knowledge of her motive. I pull into my parking spot and pin the target location on the map so when my shift is over, I will be on time for this meeting. Shifting from missing Raven, I am suddenly glad she is not at my place waiting, and I am free tonight for whatever happens.

The shift is long up and down Aurora, the usual suspects appear. I see Korn and Ringer along with the usual Friday night crowd at an intersection waiting for the walk sign to appear; some have already started in the crosswalk with horns blaring. This is not where he should be spending his time after dark, but who am I to actually control his actions? I am still on the fence about spending my time to help a total stranger, but from what I have read in the brochure, there is an 87% success rate with Ethan's Edge. To distract myself, I calculate my daily mileage, and between the eight bus trips and the drive to and from home, about two hundred miles are covered. Then it hits me that if Ethan's Edge helps clean up graffiti, I could find the locations, my mind bringing me closer to helping Korn, whether I wish to or not.

On my second northbound trip, a passenger was talking to me as they so often do when a car pulls out of one of the motels at a high rate of speed and nearly hits the bus. From my angle, I can only see the top of the driver's head, and only because the tall ringlets of blonde hair are stacked up. I am not positive if it is a high ponytail or man bun, but there is a lot of hair. We are on our return southbound trip, and the same car drives north along the side of the bus into oncoming traffic, so close as if the two are connected by magnets. The blonde hair is weaseling its way out of the top of the partially opened window. Our driver stops briefly and slows down to look in the motel parking lot, but the car is no longer there. I look at the lady next to me, who is still in motion from the northbound trip, and wonder why she didn't get off at Aurora Village or somewhere in between. With her story not missing a beat in the delivery. She is here for the commute, entertainment, or companionship, unaware of her surroundings, only staying in her story, and has not caught on that I am Metro Transit Police. She only sees me as someone to talk to. She is probably one of those who has a bus pass and rides for fun.

The rest of the shift is calm except for the ones who overextend their boundaries by having their music too loud or being so sprawled out that they are in someone else's lap. We missed the street racers going through downtown this evening, but there is still the evidence of car parts and rubber laid on the road from their circular tire marks.

I pull out of the bus garage at 10:20 pm. Leave my lights off as I get to the gate, knowing full well that I can be seen with the security and streetlights. I am also aware that Metevior must not be with Allard tonight since he is going to meet with me. My first instinct is not to show up and be any further involved, but I know if I don't dig deeper in this mess, I never asked to be in, I could be in danger and further entangled. I feel fortunate that Muncer trusted me enough to involve me in this meeting. I leave, turning left like normal, heading home even though I need to go right to attend the secret street-side meeting. No one is tailing me, that I can see. This entire mess with the pushy cop leaves me on edge most of my day, and I am glad I live far from this scene where I can unwind. I inch my way over to Aurora and feel as if I am on the clock again. My Jeep is the only variance. Nearly there, but not much time to spare as I wasted any extra minutes circling on my way here, the reflection of the streetlight catches my eye, funneling through the blonde hair of someone walking eastbound on N 47th Street. I don't have time to circle the block, but file that information for a later date, knowing it was the driver of that car who nearly collided with the bus tonight. This information may not mean anything other than they are an extremely reckless driver. Still not being positive if it is a male or female but will circle the block upon my return if I can figure out a way that allows me to cross the concrete center wall.

I pull in on N 62nd Street with no street parking available, I picture all the people sleeping in a horizontal position as I find parking and walk down the road towards Phinney, not being familiar with this neighborhood. I hope it is safe to walk here without trouble, but then remember I am meeting two detectives who should be nearby. I hear laughter up ahead and see two men leaning on a rusty Honda Civic. As soon as I get within half a block of them, they both turn as if their radar is on and see me approaching. Muncer greeting me with, " Metro, you remember Metevior."

Metevior looks me up and down as if to place a description into memory from a crime scene. I am positive he already has me on his list of people to watch, either from Allard's talk of me or repeated stops to visit while I am at work. The only scheduled time she could find me being as I hide; suddenly glad I live in Lakewood and there isn't a trail to my door.

Metevior opens the conversation with, "So you are our CI on the Metro?" I am shocked by his accusation and immediately deny any association with that title, imploring where he received that information. He informs me, "That is why Allard shows up as she does, since you are the CI and we, or at least she, need to meet in a private location. She says you are uncooperative about meeting where she would like, so she surprises you with her visits. I had never heard of you until Allard got to town and figured you came with her, like the others." I relay the short version of my story to him, omitting the pieces of where I live and Raven, and make certain he knows my visits with Allard are not my idea and I am not a CI, just employed by Metro. Then add, "The only reason I called about Don on the bus was because he was giving a passenger trouble." Then I wonder if I had said too much since Raven was that passenger, and she is who I want to keep out of this conversation.

Muncer gives us a brief rundown of what Joe Connely warned, with him knowing Allard from Portland. Metevior says they stop at Tent City now and then, meet Joe around town, and he is a CI. I tell them of his rides on the bus and acting like an addict going to the methadone clinic daily in north Seattle but hold back on my sighting of Melvin Scriptnor at the bus stop on 145th and Aurora. I figure if he doesn't have a warrant and no one has asked me about him except Allard, I should be quiet. If found, he may give information on Raven, and I should keep my knowledge of her whereabouts out of this for her safety.

I mostly listen to the banter between them. Muncer is on duty, and Metevior appears to be off, dressed casually and not in a suit. Metevior says he will try to get more on Allard and appreciates my time, then turns to leave. Muncer stays a bit longer and talks about this being hard on Metevior, his longtime friend, being pinned into a corner on this case. His phone rings, he answers and says, "Rubio, can I call you back? I am just finishing up here." He turns and says, "What do you think she is up to?" My response is not helpful, I shrug my shoulders, turning my head to clear it, and say, "I have no idea, but she is hiding something underground." Muncer asks if she has me looking for any other perpetrators. I shake my head, wondering why I was invited to this meeting and whom I can trust now. I have become informed of who at least one CI is, that I had been passed on as a CI and seen in that position, that Allard is being watched, and Metevior is in a spot. I think Muncer will be my point of contact if I need one, but I will try to stay out of their business altogether unless I see something that can get Allard out of my picture.

I walk back to my car on this nearly silent Friday night, the only sounds are tires on the pavement and a ship horn in the distance, probably on the Puget Sound. I watch the block as I get close to my Jeep, making certain Allard has not joined us or anyone else she may have sent. When I get to Phinney Way and turn south, I notice Metevior is long gone and imagine him living in this neighborhood. Muncer turns left and heads north. I can see his taillights in my rearview mirror for a few blocks. Being on edge after attending that meeting like cops and CI's have on the sly, I don't know who could be watching.

I do not know this neighborhood so I carefully follow the signs back to Aurora and instantly know where I am almost wishing I had not come to Seattle now that I am in this mess but then smile thinking of Raven, our surprise kiss earlier today and Enzo who will possibly be riding in my back seat. I hope Raven knows how to install one of those seats. Just then, she texts saying she hopes it is not too late, but wanted to wait until I was home, so the text didn't come through while driving. I am glad the Bluetooth system is installed, and I can talk to text, so she won't know about my meeting tonight. The last thing I want her to do is feel on edge with me. I see there is a link for a car seat attached to the text and I will order once I arrive home and pick it up in the morning.

In passing, I take notice of the three-story, yellow building that has the window-washing man in the apartment closest to the road and action in the neighborhood. Just as I am paying attention to my text, thinking about the car seat and seeing the man in the window again, a car pulls out, tires squealing. The driver has her head turned, hair flapping around like it isn't attached. Then she turns when she has straightened her vehicle in the outside lane. It is Allard wearing a long black wig and makeup like the street walkers. She looks me in the eye, and I regret being here at this moment. I imagine myself on another route, leaving two minutes before or later, but not now. Hoping she doesn't think I am following her. This has brought me deeper into the story without my consent.

Once I cross the bridge, I exit and drive through downtown. I see a clock on a bank and realize a new day has starting, it is 12:17 am. It was a day I was looking forward to, but now there is a burden at the top. I call Muncer, who I am positive was not expecting my call or story. He doesn't appear surprised by the information, of course, maybe nothing surprises him, but he knew where she had been due to the tracker that had been placed on her vehicle, just not why. I hesitate to ask, but I have to know what his response would be, "Who is Rubio?" He laughs and says, "King County, met him on a case years ago. He is a good guy; too bad he is not SPD." That wasn't much information, but now I know the most important part of my meeting tonight was to find out the connection between Muncer and Rubio, Enzo's grandpa.

I continue my journey home, checking my neighborhood for anyone suspicious and order the car seat. Gus comes to visit since he heard me arrive, and I wonder what the days will be like out here in the winter and alone, cold, and with just Gus and me. Will the lake, Gus, and my meetings keep me on track? Should I move? What about Gus? I think I need another occupation or to be rid of Allard. I can't even calm down now. I should let Raven know I ordered the car seat. It wasn't available in Lakewood, so I will pick it up in Federal Way, possibly on the way to see her, or if not, when she is ready. It is after 1:00 am, and I do not expect her to answer until morning.

21

Vernon

SEPTEMBER 2025

THE WEEKEND PASSED QUICKLY, starting with picking up the car seat at the Commons in Federal Way, where I turned around just days ago at the start of this adventure. Today begins another chapter with my trip to see Raven in Seward Park, which could be awkward being as I had not spent any time with small children ever in my life. Enzo doesn't appear to have a problem with me, though. As soon as he saw the box with a picture of the car seat, he climbed right in and started prying at the tape, asking for tools and the keys. Raven seemed unsure if his ways were ok with me and was watching for my reaction. I asked if he was going to help, just as Raven laughed and broke the tension.

The three of us installed the seat and drove across 520 to Grass Lawn Park in Redmond. We walked the trails, watched Enzo play on the toys, and had lunch. Then it was time for her to go back to Evelyn's house so Enzo could nap. She asked me to come in, then told me Evelyn would be back by 6:00 pm on Sunday when Enzo goes back home. Raven was hesitant in her next request. She starts work on Monday without a place to stay. She wonders if she can stay at my place for a couple of weeks until she gets a paycheck. She knows our hours will be different, and she would have to leave early on the 214 bus to get to Seattle but would be quiet.

I am hesitant to let her stay only because she may be leaving so soon, and I don't want to get used to her presence, and then she is gone. Of course, I agree as I am here to help her get back on her feet. Raven noticed my hesitation and asked if I was positive, it was ok. I tell her the reason for my hesitancy but know the facts going in and want the best for her and Enzo.

I spend Sunday looking at bus and train routes from my house to Seattle, not knowing where she will be working. Sunday night, Raven arrives at the 512 Park and Ride at 7:15 pm. We go back to my house after dinner at Dairy Queen again. Somehow, something has changed; maybe it was the kiss, or this has become real life, but something is different. It could be that she feels guilty staying after my admission of missing her in the future. Raven has to leave by 5:30 am, so we turn in early, neither of us saying much.

Monday, I go to work as usual. On my second trip north, I see Little Mel at the bus stop on N 145th Street, he is pacing back and forth the length of the stop, which is about four steps in each direction. Then he turns like a soldier and marches the other way. We continue on not needing to stop at that stop. On the trip south, he is still there, and I see the backpack that Raven used to carry; it is on the seat inside the bus shelter. Now I know Little Mel is expecting Raven to get off the bus and come back to his house. There is still a hole in the story that I haven't thought of. Where did Little Mel and Raven live before

North Seattle? Were they a couple, and where was she coming from daily when I met her on the bus?

On my next trip south, which is on the opposite side of the road, I see the backpack is somehow miraculously still there, with Little Mel walking about two houses down in the opposite direction from Aurora. I ask the driver to radio in that the backpack belongs to a passenger, and I am willing to retrieve it from lost and found if the next bus north can grab it.

I get off work without any major incidents, sightings of Allard or the blonde person with curls. I am torn between telling Raven about the backpack and Little Mel, but I wake her up to ask the questions that have been rattling around in my head all evening. I know her answers will not change the offer to her of staying here, but I feel she thinks it will. I just need to know and assure her that she cannot tell me anything that will make me force her out of here.

Raven groggily, after her first day at work, asks, "Why now? have you changed your mind?" I nod to indicate that is not the reason I asked and tell her I had seen her old bus stop and started wondering. She tells me of their place, all twelve of them in south Seattle, almost Burien, she can take me there if I wish. She adds parts about Stephanie Little Mel's girlfriend, who recently passed away right before Meade, all due to Don and his drugs. Then I ask, "Why were you on the bus every day when I met you?" She says she went to get little Mel's new medication that helps him stay clean, he doesn't like downtown, it is too close to the morgue, the last place he saw Stephanie. It gave me time to spend downtown at the parks and library, just to get out of the house. To me these all seemed like reasonable answers, and I didn't want to lie to Raven but didn't think it would help to tell her I had seen Little Mel tonight twice and the state of agitation he was demonstrating, nor about the backpack and get her hopes up for maybe some of her old clothes. I don't know what she had at Mel's place, but she hasn't seemed to be worried about it. I am hoping the backpack will be turned in and can be retrieved from the lost and found. I could pick it up before work on Jackson Street. I wonder what Mel has deemed important enough to return to her.

Tuesday and Wednesday are the same, with Raven being tired from her eight-hour workday at the paper company and five-hour bus ride. Me coming home after a late shift on edge, no encounters from Allard or contact with Muncer after my call to him last week. Thursday is a bit different. Little Mel is still pacing at the bus stop about the time Raven would get off the bus, same as Monday through Wednesday, but this time, someone is in his face. It is not a person I have seen before, maybe someone who is an old enemy or a newly created one. The man flings his arms, indicating as if he wishes to sit down, and Mel will not let him get across to the seat, drawing an imaginary line between the sidewalk and the metal bench with his pacing, arms flailing. Personally, I don't see why anyone would want to sit on the bench anyway, with the windows broken out so often, Metro has quit replacing them. Mel is insistent on taking possession of the stop, and so is the other man, then they stop and have a conversation as if they know each other. Mel backs up, the man pulls out a gun, Mel ducks behind the windowless stop, and the man shoots. Mel falls, and the shooter throws his pistol on top of Mel, walks around front, and sits on the bench.

The bus has stopped due to our being witnesses, and the incident took place at a Metro location. I call this into Muncer as the driver calls 911. Allard shows up first on the scene like she had been nearby, next is Officer Stanley. Both boarding the bus, wanting statements as patrol retrieves the weapon, cuffs the shooter, and SFD arrives to perform CPR on Mel. I can't tell from this angle if he is responding, but I feel the need to know to accurately tell the story to Raven. It is a good sign that the ambulance has loaded him and takes off with the lights and siren reflecting off the buildings. The eerie echo of the siren is heard for miles.

Allard keeps looking at the patrol car that holds the shooter, then looks at me, saying, "You are with me." I don't question this as I can catch another bus every fifteen minutes south and get back to my Jeep or onto another route, plus I may learn something useful. The only questions I do have are is this in my job description and who is the man in the patrol car. Maybe Raven knows him, so I file away his description mentally. All I know for sure is that I am not getting into a vehicle with her. My loyalties lie no further than this intersection. If she thinks and tells others I am uncooperative then I will be. I believe me abandoning my coach in midshift and agreeing to be questioned is more than cooperative. I even called about Little Mel, just not to her, but she has no knowledge of my call.

Steven Watkins was the shooter, so I learn. I had heard that name before just couldn't place where or how he is connected. I could see Allard is shocked when she gets to the patrol car and steps back, almost falling, but there is anger under her accusations towards me and with him. With his unwillingness to talk, she becomes more aggressive, slams his door, and turns to me. Yelling, "What did you have to do with this? How come you didn't tell me he was alive? Why didn't you call this in like you were supposed to about your sighting of Melvin? Where is Raven?" I respond by actually not answering any of her questions, only telling her, "The driver let them know of the incident over the radio." Allard gets angrier and asks quietly, "Did you call me? Do you know who the perpetrator is?" I shake my head no as I see the steam rising off her and she comes towards me as Detective Muncer pulls in behind the scene and witnesses this just as Allard grabs me by the shirt and I let her drag me over to her car but refuse to get in as she pushes me towards the open door of her patrol car, I am only a witness and am glad Muncer has seen her actions wondering where Metevior is and hoping she doesn't try to charge me with anything.

Muncer gets out and approaches us, in my line of vision, but behind Allard. He has not said a word, only observes and goes to the patrol car, opens the door, and steps back in shock also. I wish I could place the shooter somewhere on my timeline, but not being from here, I am fortunate or possibly unfortunate to know some of the people I recognize. All are recent bus passengers, police detectives, and Mr. Owens.

Muncer walks over to us. Allard has calmed down since there is another detective on the scene. He says, "Hi Metro." I was hoping he would get me out of this, then he asks for a timeline and why I am no longer on the bus.

I tell him what I had witnessed, with Little Mel at the bus stop arguing with the gentleman in the back of the patrol car, then a couple shots were fired, Mel was on the ground behind the bus stop looking like he was already gone but then they performed CPR, and I don't know his fate. Muncer asks if Little Mel had boarded the bus or the shooter, "it makes a difference in the investigation," he mumbles as if in thought, then asks if I have any knowledge of the shooter or Little Mel ever riding the bus. "I don't believe Mel has ever been on the bus and have not seen the gentleman in the back of the patrol car before a few minutes ago." "Do you know how they got here?" I respond with, "They were just at the stop." I don't tell him of my knowledge about Mel being at that location for the past few days or that I know he resides nearby. I don't think that is necessary since he was just there pacing.

Forensics arrives and tapes the scene off. I cross Aurora and take the next Rapid Ride E southbound coach that arrives. My thoughts are not here but with Raven, who I would believe by this time of night would be at my house, safely tucked in. I am thinking about how to tell her this story, and know I should, it needs to be in person, not through a text. I would like to see her reaction anyway.

When I arrive home about 11:00 pm, Raven is in the living room, pacing, and says, "Something is off, it's not right." I wonder how she could know about Mel, and if she knows the shooter. What are the chances of my being a witness to this crime? I don't know how to handle this exactly since I was picturing coming home and waking her up to tell of the scene I had witnessed. Now the story has changed before it has started. I don't exactly have good people skills since I grew up on my own, and I observe her for a moment, contemplating what actions to take.

I approach her in one of her passes, thinking of Mel and his pacing, then hold her; she is tense but doesn't seem to object. We stand embraced for a minute, maybe ten, I don't know, as she calms. Then I lead her to the couch, and we sit on either end facing each other. She says again, "something is off," and I know this is the moment the story needs to be delivered. As soon as I tell her about Mel, it is as if her face melts and then she relaxes, saying, "I knew it was something big." I do not detect any emotion on her; she just sits there and says, "I don't believe so many are gone, and now Little Mel could die and so violently, he helped me so much, but then I helped him too."

Raven stands, runs to her backpack and pulls out a set of keys, and asks if I will take her up north to get her stuff. I don't know if that is advisable, but after thinking it through, it is not where the crime scene is located, and this early in the investigation, most likely no one knows Mel lives on that street. We gather a few bags, Raven saying, "There isn't much." We get in my Jeep and take the fifty-mile trip north to get her stuff. I ask how she likes her job after being there nearly a week, and if she will be able to work later today with our late-night outing. She responds with a smile, telling me, "I won't mess this up, the job is a piece of cake, and a lady named Jill Muncer is showing me how the mail room is run tomorrow. I will be cross trained to float around the warehouse so when extra help is needed, I can jump in anywhere. August, the owner who is my contact, asked when my birthday was, like that is important for this position. They all seem like a nice group."

I am still stuck on Jill Muncer and probably tuned Raven out after that, but in a city this size, there could be a thousand people with every last name. We turn onto N 145th Street, and surprisingly, our drive was fast without commuter traffic. Raven did know Steven Watkins after I told her his name and the description. She says, "He started coming around Mel's before we moved, but I don't know him well, just that he had a baby when he showed up." I see Raven staring at the taped off bus stop, left that way until the investigation is complete or someone from the street swipes the tape, thinking it is treasure. Raven looks away, then back again, and I say, "Yes." She Understands what that means. I am just glad Mel went away in an ambulance and not the morgue. There are no police on the corner or at Mel's as we drive by. We pass by Mel's house again, making certain there aren't any people watching the place or us. Raven points out that there is only an older pickup truck in the driveway, and all the windows on the house are dark with the shades open. Raven says, "Little Mel would have closed the shades as soon as the sun set; he was a stickler for order. Rules, rules, rules."

We park and carefully watch the house for activity. My main thoughts are to make sure Raven is not seen, especially by Allard or any other police, since I have no idea what Allard has convinced them after hearing her concocted story about me.

With my vehicle parked a few houses up on the street, I ask if I should follow for her safety. She nods, yes, and is silent, taking steps, retrieving Mel's extra key carefully hidden in the rotted window frame next to the front room, and enters after knocking with no response. We have been placed into a house right out of another decade, but there is no time to explore it. I let Raven take the lead on what needs to be done as I check the rooms for anyone and the back door and windows to make sure they are locked. She uses her cell phone flashlight after closing the floor-to-ceiling linen drapes, which are like the ones we had in Miami, old. I ask if she is ok, and she nods. I don't know why, but tell her I am from Miami, with my memory being triggered by the drapes. She laughs, and that takes a bit of tension off this task. Then says, "Tell me later, please." We enter a room that looks as if she had been the one living there with only girl stuff and a couple of baby toys. She throws select items in a bag and starts to leave with a bit of hesitation, she runs to what I think is Mel's room and grabs his wallet, taking out a credit card, showing me, it is hers, and then goes to the kitchen for a spoon saying, "Enzo loves this spoon I have no idea why." We grab the collected bags off the 1970s console TV next to the door and leave. Raven locks the bottom lock and runs to put her key in the kitchen drawer on a ring of others before closing the front door. We get into the Jeep, looking around to ensure no one is watching. Since the street is quiet this time of night, it is easy to see we are undetected and alone. I take directions from Raven on how to get around the barrier on Aurora and travel south. Raven says, "I didn't see my backpack there. I wonder what Little Mel did with it?" With the mess that happened tonight, I had forgotten about checking lost and found and decide not to say anything until I know for sure it is there. The rest of the trip is silent, me wishing there was somewhere close to hang out for the next few hours, so Raven doesn't have to take the bus in four hours, but that is what is in store for this Friday morning. Then it hits me, where will Raven and Enzo stay this weekend? As soon as that thought crosses my mind, Raven says, "Aunt Evelyn is still planning on being out of town again for the weekend, so you know where I will be if you wish to visit. Enzo seemed to have liked you." I look over a mile or so down I-5, and Raven is asleep. We get back to the house on the lake, safe, and stay in the Jeep since her alarm will be going off soon. I think back on my last few hours and see how fortunate I am. I may have no idea where my life is going, but I am happy and realize I need to get out and feed Gus when he waddles up the walkway between my house and Mr. Owens' garage, making a ruckus. Raven wakes with a start when I open the door and the dome light turns on, a feature I need to turn off with all the secret trips I have been taking. We grab her bags, go in, sit out front, and feed Gus the rest of his worms and sleep for a couple of hours before she leaves for the weekend.

22

Detective Muncer

IN ONE OF THE first hours of Friday morning I have left the scene on Aurora shortly after Little Mel had been shot multiple times and transferred to Harborview ICU in critical condition, a few floors above the morgue, the place we met him not long ago, a few floors below the cafeteria where we spent a portion of an early morning silently drinking a cup of coffee nine months ago when Stephanie Thomas was found deceased. I need to call Rubio and tell him that another person from the case he has been working on for over two years has been shot, and it doesn't look good. I know Melvin Script-nor was operating on the other side of the law from me, but I suspect he had a fondness for the dozen or so people he was helping, who were all probably out for themselves, but Little Mel still provided a roof and security for them. Maybe he considered managing his crew a job, or he may have made a mint off of them, and that money is hidden somewhere with no access to a bank for him. No one is watching his old property any longer in South Seattle as far as I know. Everyone from Mel's house is accounted for except Raven, and we weren't sure of the identities of the two males after running them through records with no facial recognition. With everyone gone, dead or alive, I am not sure there is a case anymore.

I wait for them to fingerprint and process Steven Watkins and request to interview him first, before other detectives get a chance to talk with him, since I had made the report. Allard may have been on the scene first, but she was spending her time walking around and harassing Metro. I don't know what she has against him. Steven is brought into room four, my favorite, along with his booking records and data on any previous arrests. What I want to know is who occupied the tent when it caught on fire at the Duwamish Encampment, if it wasn't Steven? Steven was not talking at the scene, but is that due to an issue with Allard or police in general? He has to have information; he wouldn't have escaped from the tent and shot Mel without cause.

I wait for the guard to bring Steven into the room, sitting away from the door, my back to the wall. I don't know this guy; most of my suspects I have had at least a couple of minutes with before our interview, but this one has only been silent. He enters in a gray jumpsuit, which only differs from the orange ones when intake is high and there is not enough clothing for the population; the only other color jumpsuit is rust, and that is worn infrequently, only for mental holds. At a meeting last week, the Captain was addressing an increase in homicides in the past month, I am hoping the jail population has grown because there have been some arrests and not just petty crimes.

He sits and stares at me with vacant brown eyes. I can't decide what nationality he is, which doesn't matter, but he is making me uncomfortable with his deep stare. I look at his arrest record for any previous violent crimes committed. Surprisingly, he doesn't have a record at all, I flip through the pages again, making certain I have not missed anything. Attempted murder is not usually the first crime someone commits.

Steven Watkins looks at me and says, "I didn't shoot Mel because of anything he did. I just wanted him to come home and was tired of jeopardizing my freedom with him out there in the open. Mel told me Raven used to get his medication for him, he was scared to go out for fear of the police seeing him, so he went to the bus stop three days in a row to find her. Even took her backpack full of money as an apology. He wanted her to come home. He was letting me sleep on the couch there when I escaped from the tent right before I saw her set it on fire." I interrupt Steven to ask who set it on fire. He looks at me and says, "One of your own, Allard. She was always after me to purchase large quantities of opioids, heroin, fentanyl, meth whatever I can get my hands on. Her customer is one person, but I have no idea who that is. I only drop to her at the location of her choice, then get out of there. She always watches me make the purchase, won't release the cash without my exact pickup location, and then meets me a block or so away for the transfer. This made it simple and less risky for me since I only had the product for a short while, but I was always fearful that the police were onto her, and she was being tailed. I texted Allard the night of the fire and stated I wanted out and was done now, not later, I wouldn't be making any more transactions for her. She was furious that I had quit and that I used plain English in the text. Later that evening, I was in my tent when she visited, saying her partner was there, pointing to the road. She was in a hurry and was going to change my mind on this visit; she didn't have time to come back, and I needed to cooperate and stop wasting her time. I didn't get out of the tent until she said so. She also informed me there is only one other way out, but didn't specify, just said I knew too much. I knew that was death by the look of fire in her burning eyes. I told her ok, tomorrow expect a text with the time to meet for the money and drop. She nodded, I pretended to get in the tent but lay along the side for a moment as I saw her pull her lighter out of her jean jacket and light the corner closest to her on fire. The tent melted almost immediately, like a bubble popping, except someone was inside, as I could see from my vantage point closer in the bog. I pictured all my clothing, pictures of my baby, and other belongings going up in flames. I know we are not supposed to enter that area of protected wetlands, but this was an emergency. I had to get out of her sight, and I was only there a couple of minutes. As soon as I saw Allard trek across the mud-encrusted field, we called home and got in the black SUV that had been hidden out of sight. I walked to the road, ducking to the side if any vehicles passed, and called Mel. I may not have any other possessions, but my phone, wallet, cigarettes, and lighter were on my person. I had no idea someone had entered my tent while I was out talking to Allard, but they had to have heard everything we said."

DJM: Where did you meet Melvin Scriptnor?

SW: At the compound south of here

DJM: On 119th Street?

SW: Yes, I was at a low point when I left there. Mel was going to sell the place to developers. Inez, my baby mama, had relapsed after rehab, and I took custody of our baby. Mel let me and my baby stay at the compound, then he sold the whole place a few months later, and I ended up living under the bridge with the baby, having no income since my time was used taking care of the baby. I figured a roof was better than the woods, but people called it in. I relapsed, too, when I went to see Inez, and we lost custody.

I look up and see Steven has a racetrack of tears running down both cheeks, but he is telling me the story like emotion and fact are separated.

DJM: How did you end up at Melvin Scriptnor's other residence, and where is it located?

SW: I took the bus, hoping Allard didn't have people looking for me or her herself but then reasoned if I burned up in the tent, how could I be on the bus, and why would she have anyone looking for me if I was dead due to her? She is a murderer. The only reason I started selling the drugs for her and living like I did was to raise enough money quickly for an attorney to gain custody. Living at the encampment meant there wasn't any overhead on rent, eating from the food bank, and trying not to spend anything.

DJM: Steven, you still didn't answer my question about where Melvin's residence is located.

SW: Sorry, it is on North 145th right by the bus stop, about three houses down the block on the same side of the road. I have a key in my confiscated possessions. No one should be there unless Raven came home, or Mel has been released, but I don't think she would return after the story Mel told me of chasing her out of there one night a month or so ago. He wanted me to get his medicine that keeps him clean, then decided Raven would get it, but Raven is not there. She's been gone a while. Mel didn't know I was supposed to be dead; I didn't tell him about my encounter. A couple of days before I shot him, I checked my P.O. Box, and there was a letter there about custody being finalized by the state, and I didn't have any more time to petition for custody myself. I don't know why I thought this way, but I figured I could never live a normal life again with my baby out there, whom I let down. Allard would always be after me, I was getting messed up in my mind with all the pressure and shame. Since I was dead, Mel was acting like a fool, wouldn't listen to reason, or shut up. I wanted to limit my options, so I shot him and stayed at the crime scene. I wanted to be locked up forever and not have to make my own way, plus let Allard know she hadn't won because she is going down too. I had no reason to work for her any longer with my baby living at someone else's house. I sure messed that one up.

DJM: Can you write a statement of everything you just told me?

Steven Watkins slumps his shoulders and grabs the pencil, placing the eraser on the page and staring at the painted cinderblock wall, knowing he had made the wrong choice. He could have traveled many avenues but chose this one. One being to disappear and start over, but this one may be the hardest since Allard or someone she knows always has access to his whereabouts. I can't even imagine what is going through his head at this moment, but this is the part of my job that defines the boundary where my responsibility lies with the person who may be guilty, and where the judicial system takes over. Steven Watkins has a lot of information to give in exchange for his future, but does he care? So far, he has only told me, Detective Jeffery Muncer.

23

Detective Muncer

IT IS NOW JUST after 3:00 am and I know I have no other option than to wake up Chief Stewart. I have never in my twenty plus years with the department had the need to call him or any other supervisors, captains or chiefs in the middle of the night. I wonder if he answers directly, or if it goes to an answering service.

I take a couple of flights of stairs down to the lobby and locate the only person I know on duty, and they find the captain's number. He answers before the first ring has completed, "Stewart here." I know the voice and can picture him from our meetings, and his words remain with me. A rash of homicides floods the streets, patrol every sector thoroughly, and send undercover deep into the neighborhoods. As I am thinking about his orders, he clears his throat, and I know he has most likely been asleep at this time of the morning, but I am wide awake and am sure it is time to give an account of the recent confession I just received, leading up to this moment.

I start to tell him of the chain of events, he says, "You have never directly called me and have taken care of all your cases on your own.

I see your name and reports cross my desk frequently. I can meet you now somewhere other than the precinct."

We chose to meet at the Fremont Troll on N 36th Street due to the rain that had started. There is at least some cover there. I pull in as some teens scatter from smoking weed up on the hill, they run in all directions, likely have snuck out of their homes, one almost being plowed over by the chief. He gets out laughing, "What did you do, Muncer scare off the troublemakers?" Then looks at me, knowing that will be the only humorous moment of this meeting.

I start with what I have witnessed Allard doing, referring to the moment on the bus when she reprimanded me for looking at her. He asks why she didn't recognize me. I am sure it had to do with her anger, almost like a blackout drunk, but I was in plain clothes. I finish my end by telling him about her repeated trips to N Aurora, the wig, her grabbing Metro's shirt, leaving out the pieces Metevior will or will not report. Then I read the statement from Steven Watkins. He shakes his head, paces a couple of times, stops right in front of me, and says, "I will send units to bring Allard in and place her on administrative leave immediately."

I follow him into the precinct, I am not sure why, other than my connection to him, this case is sealed at this point; no one knows the information from Steven went through me. This will be the first time since being employed by the Seattle Police Department that I have had anything to do with charges being placed, accusations, or reprimands of another member of the force. When we arrive, Glenda at the front desk, who only deals with internal issues at this time of night, eyes us as we walk by and knows something catastrophic will happen shortly since Chief Stewart may work late but isn't generally here at 4:00 am.

I make sure he has a copy of Steven Watkins' file; assure him I will not contact anyone else about this matter and proceed to my third-story office to make a list of complaints I have witnessed on Allard for my own files. She has only been with this division for a short time. I cannot think of how she could have all the connections to make Watkins' story true, but after thinking, she would only need one point of contact to sell the product. Maybe between Connely, Watkins, and the streets, she found that contact, but high-level dealers don't usually seek out anyone in the police department to acquire drugs. Maybe it is a connection remaining from Portland. This story isn't lining up with any actual cases I have ever solved. My first thought is to call Metevior, as I have thousands of times when cases just don't make sense, but as I recall, Metevior and Allard are on shift together. I know he will be relieved tonight that he is not the one to report about her deeds, but I will never tell him I was the one to point the chief to the head of her trail. There is a small piece of doubt in me, but could Metevior have been involved in this all along? I have known him for over two decades and want to believe he hasn't gotten into anything under the table, but does anyone truly know anyone?

After my list is complete or the incidents I have witnessed, I file it with my other notes on unsolved cases. I feel no one needs to read it until Chief Stewart asks for it. It will be information he will funnel down the pipeline of accusation, but Allard will know I have been interviewed. The story from Steven Watkins has my signature at the bottom of the page as the interviewing detective. Why do other coworkers put us in that position? Allard and I work differently; she let him sit for a few hours before the interview, and I met with him as soon as possible. Maybe she needed time to collaborate her story and warn contacts, but I do not need that time with me working above ground. I do hope the time she yelled at me on the bus comes out, it shows her character, how far out of it she travels when angry, and how she would treat a total stranger.

Even though I had come in the front door with the chief, I left out the back exiting through underground parking and walking up the hill to 5Th Avenue to retrieve my cruiser. A couple more hours until I am officially off the clock. It is 5:00 am, the sun has not risen, and the air is starting to carry a crispness as it blows up the hill from the sound. The early morning Sounder trains are arriving, and I think of Jill just a few blocks from me, sleeping at Hector's, and wishing her happiness, but I miss her and add her to my list of people I need to contact because they are important to me.

I return from my early morning daydream when I hear my name being called from down the hill. I see it is Metevior and know that Allard has been taken in for questioning and released from her duties at least for the moment. Metevior looks relieved as he approaches, almost back to his amicable self. He nods yes, and I know they have her, but he tells me anyway, not knowing I am the cause; he doesn't give out any information. I only have one question. "Do you know what Allard has against Metro?" He looks at me and says, "Something about oranges. I don't have any idea what that means." Metevior says he is going home to rest and returns to the parking garage to retrieve his battered Honda; I see exhaustion all over my friend from the duties of the past few weeks. He turns and says as we part ways, "They pulled us over. Surrounding our vehicle." Then walks away shaking his head.

I drive to the property on N 145th Street with the key from Steven Watkins. This might not be exactly above ground, but I don't plan on entering, just knocking to see who else may answer, since Little Mel doesn't generally live solo. I will go there to notify the next of kin of his whereabouts, thinking back to the past two visits, approximately nineteen miles south of here, and a few months apart. I wonder what transpired for him to go from there to here. I turn east onto 145th, and several houses down on the left, I see an A/C unit in a bedroom window hanging close to the ground, and call it in as a possible burglary, but do not enter. I knock on the front door, knowing for sure it is the right house. Donny's truck is in the driveway. I see the flannel with the mustard-colored suede patches on the elbows strewn across the front seat. I wonder how long that flannel and Melvin Scriptnor will last. He may be in the ICU, but I feel that I can be of assistance in the protection of his house.

Patrol officers arrive, and after they walk the perimeter of the house and ensure everything is locked up, I open the door with the key I had been supplied with and would have never used except in this situation. I help clear each room of the 1970s house that reminds me of Mrs. Johnson and the furniture she left me in her duplexes. I focus on the bedroom and unplug the A/C unit to close the window, as it was just shoved in there and not attached to anything. I see a pen that has SPD printed along the barrel, a credit card and piece of ripped denim attached to a screw on the window frame. I flip the card over with a butter knife I find lying on the lace-covered vanity and see it, says Serene G. Allard in the silver raised lettering. Now I know I need to locate Raven since she is the only one remaining of the group who had relocated here. I quickly check the address on the tax assessor's site and see the house is in the name of Mavis Scriptnor. I conducted a background check on her and found no records, including traffic violation. I am on the fence about the credit card, pen, and denim, so I leave them for the moment, unplug the A/C unit, and lock the window. There doesn't appear to be anything missing; the report says A/C must have fallen out, the window is closed, and the house is secure. The only person to tell would be Little Mel, but he has not woken up yet from the shooting. I take pictures of the credit card, denim, and pen, leaving them there and the curtain open a crack so I can check on these articles from time to time.

I get back in my cruiser, relieved that there was no damage to Little Mel's house and hope no items of importance were stolen. There is no way to be sure of what Allard was looking for or if she found it. The burglary tells me Allard knew Steven Watkins was alive before the shooting, but why didn't she say something and reveal it wasn't him in the tent? There are too many variables in this story at this point. I know someone will rule out a few possibilities soon. Then I wonder if Allard will be released or held. There is proof, and then again, there is no concrete evidence besides her credit card, pen, and ripped denim. Knowing I must act before she is released, I pick up my phone making necessary call to the chief not wishing to reveal this to anyone else yet and he can make the official decision of who needs to know but the items inside may be the key to hold her in custody, so we don't need to watch her or our backs at least for a while.

24

Vernon

I DIDN'T HEAR RAVEN as she stepped out Friday morning for work, wishing I could have talked to her before our weekend apart, but she was probably trying to be as quiet as possible after our many miles and night out. Today I need to leave early and hopefully pick up Raven's backpack down on Jackson Street. If I remember right, there isn't any parking close by. The day cannot go fast enough for me to get there. My curiosity is overrun with possibilities of what is in the backpack. I wonder what the process is when something is received by them. I called to ensure what I am looking for is being held. The agent who answered the phone was hesitant to give any information. I told him I work for Metro Transit Police, and it belongs to my cousin. He still hesitated to ask me about the contents, I said I hope money, keys, a wallet, some clothing, and paperwork. He agrees to let me pick up the bag with my promise of showing ID and a company badge if I am who I claim to be.

Now, with his hesitation, I am concerned about picking it up and wonder if I should send Raven or at least give her the option. After looking at the hours of operation, I see she will not be off work in time, and the mystery of the contents will remain until Monday. I will leave early, pick it up, peek inside, and hide it in my Jeep during my shift, then call Raven after work to see if she wants to meet up to take it.

This job is becoming monotonous, up and back, north and south, downtown core and Aurora Village. Many of the same people, but then there are the ones I see on the streets. The young girls and boys who I know are supposed to be sitting in their upstairs bedroom, in a nice house owned by their parents who love them, but instead they are here on the streets of Seattle. I wonder under what conditions they arrived here. I see the young people, too strung out to gain employment, or even to keep a phone number for an interview. I don't think we as humans are supposed to see these sights every day, as it penetrates our spirits and views of the world. There is no way to block it all out, the driver may focus on traffic and not see all that I do out of the windows that line the sides of the bus. I think about the window man and wonder how he ended up in the front apartment for the world to see and know that I need another job. I don't wish to dodge Allard for years to come or even one more day but have been known to not quit because of others' actions. I need to remain tougher than her, she will not win this battle. I just hope no one gets hurt and involved in her careless moves.

I head out a couple of hours earlier than usual to retrieve Raven's backpack, easily find paid parking on 2nd Avenue S, cross the street from the entrance, and feel a twinge of guilt having not mentioned anything to Raven about the possibility of her backpack being found.

I try to convince myself it is because I didn't want to disappoint her if it hadn't been picked up, but deep down, if I am honest, it is my curiosity that has taken over. I want to know if there is any validity it the accusations from Allard, and the backpack may hold the clues since it is my only direct link between Mel and Raven.

I enter the brick building, looking at myself in the reflection of the rounded glass doors, tossing both scenarios around in my mind. Guilt is still at the top, but curiosity is ruling every other option out. A young man sits at the counter. By his voice, I can tell it is not who I spoke to earlier. He barely looks at me, not taking his job seriously. I describe my item, show my Oregon driver's license, and Metro badge. He records the numbers from my credentials in the correct boxes online, I sign, and he hands me the gray backpack with a key chain attached to the zipper pull, a raven. When he picked it up, I noticed he acted like it was heavy but didn't anticipate its weight. I feel fortunate to have possession of the bag and leave. The young man clears his throat. I think he will call me back, but I don't want to wait to see, so I just say, "thank you" quickly without turning back and leave.

I return to my Jeep, and I am torn between opening the backpack and leaving. I see a row of tents across the way and decide to go to the bus garage and open it. There, I may be on camera, but safer than here. When I pull out, I see the place Muncer and I met by Lumen Field a while back, time has been moving so fast with all the extra activities, I am losing track. Just as I make my way up Jackson Street and turn south onto 2nd Avenue, my phone rings. It is Detective Muncer, suddenly I am fearful of anyone knowing my possession of the backpack, and I wonder if the young man whom I thanked on the way out had needed something else from me, and I didn't stop. I wonder if I should let it go to voicemail and then decide what to do, as I hesitate with these thoughts, the decision is made for me as the phone stops ringing and the voicemail alert goes off. I pull into the bus garage now with two items on my mind and curiosity running rampant. I listen to Muncer's message, only asking me to return his call, that is not helpful. I hang up, retrieve the backpack from the back seat, and open it. A silk flowered blouse, not something I think Raven would wear, a birth certificate and passport for Melvin Script-nor, a ratty old, faded men's tank top and swim trunks, an Agatha Christie paperback book, and a few stacks of money. I carefully take each item out, counting the money as I go. I am surprised that just over $17,000.00 could fit in the bottom of this small backpack and wonder why Mel was giving it to Raven if he wants her to come back. This looks like escape money to me, but why include his passport and birth certificate? She couldn't pose as him, or was this connected to a plan they had concocted? Just as I was thinking about this larger web of crime or whatever it is, a bus driver recognized me. The one who always has a story comes over to talk. I get the money covered with the book, and blouse by the time he is under the carport, standing next to my driver's window, but he sees the passport and swim trunks and starts talking about his memorable trip to the Bahamas twenty or more years ago. My mind is not here or on his story, but that doesn't stop him from telling it to the end. Then he turns, saying he will be behind the wheel tonight, on a route unfamiliar to him. Me knowing I need to hide this backpack and get ready for my shift, wanting to start my vehicle, leave this place and wait for Raven to get off work so I can give it to her but I feel the safer option would be to call her when I get off and see what she wishes to do with it so she is not out on the street with Enzo and all this cash.

I had completely forgotten about returning the call to Muncer when my screen lit up again. I switched the phone from Bluetooth and answered, "Metro here." Muncer told me that he couldn't divulge all the information, but Allard had been brought in and questioned overnight. Now with Mel in the ICU, Steven Watkins, who was one of the unidentified faces from Mel's property, Donny, Mead, and Stephanie Thomas dead, Don is in jail, and Raven is the only person left to locate. I ask again if she is wanted. He hesitates, remembering my last call on this subject, I imagine and know I need to reveal all this information to Raven and let her make the choice of an interview if she chooses. With my conscience on high alert, I think Muncer knows I am guilty of something, just not what. I then remember Muncer hearing Allard on two occasions asking me how I was connected to the crimes on Aurora and make sure he knows I don't have any connection to her or anyone else in this city.

I ask why they made the decision to bring Allard in. He says, "I can't divulge the details, but there have been accusations made against her." Muncer wishes me a safe night and hangs up before I can relay the same to him.

It takes everything in my being to get out of my Jeep and walk across the parking lot, past the maintenance garage, other coaches and board the outgoing Rapid Line E. I have all night to watch the streets but the only two left on my radar are window man and the individual sporting a blonde curl top.

Being Friday night, I know something will happen, but all is quiet on our first trip north. It feels strange to know I don't have to watch my back for Allard's visit tonight. I don't think the feeling of that has worn off, and I remain on edge. Maybe I can continue on this route and make a difference. Just as I was in thought and involved in the turmoil of multiple events that have transpired since my hire four months ago, one season almost. I look out the window, seeing the transfer of leaves from summer coloring to autumn, red on the maple tree with hints of purple as the sun sets on another day. I hit the floor of the bus while still in my time of reflection, taking up the aisle, holding onto the post at the base of the seat as bullets break out the bus windows, the sound of the remaining shots reverberates through the nearly empty coach. I am trained for this, maybe not by Metro but by the United States Army, even with my three tours in Bagram, Afghanistan, I have not had any rounds come as close as here. The danger of Allard gone, I hope, and now this. It was the window behind me that was shot out on the opposite side before I hit the floor. I turn and look up to see a young man sitting slumped over in the seat, blood on the floor running from his right arm. I notice he is trying to speak, and his uninjured hand is pointing to the inside pocket of his puffer coat. I have already heard the driver call for help and hear multiple sirens in the distance coming towards us. While I am still shaking, I think I should obtain a safer occupation. What if I had died tonight? Who would have given the backpack to Raven, without her name attached to it? Mel would have gained possession if he survives.

I hold the bleeding, wounded arm of the teen while we wait for SFD to arrive. I am doing all I know how to do, the driver is still on the phone, probably making a report and arranging for a tow truck and another bus or whatever drivers do in this situation. I realize I am on my own with this boy, someone's son, whose life is in my hands, and I hope he makes it so he can help at Ethan's Edge. With everything going on, I had forgotten about Kernal and being on the fence about my commitment to the program. Time is moving slowly. I don't know what else to do in the four minutes it takes for the medics to arrive except tell this bleeding boy about Ethan and how he can help with the program when he gets through this. He points to his pocket again, and I find a business card. I can hear the young man say, "call". I pull out my phone and am prepared to ask for Marsha Williams, but she answers midway through the first ring with her name and adding Charlene's Place. I stutter when I tell her I have a boy here with this card in his pocket, and he has been shot but is alive, putting the phone on speaker so she can relay what she wants to him. Seattle Fire and Police enter the bus, I see the other six passengers have gathered on a garden wall adjoining the sidewalk with trailing purple flowers. This is something I focus on since it is normal, unlike the fragments of glass lying in the seats and aisleway. She yells out in tears, "Where is my Darius?" He tries to respond but is in shock and weak. I tell her SFD will be transporting him to Harborview, and it would be best to meet them there. I hang up, take a picture of the business card, knowing I will keep up on this case, wipe the glass off my seat, and sit back as the officers file into the bus to take a report from me after talking to the passengers outside. The first thought that crossed my mind is that there had not been rain for days, and the people were all able to stay dry while giving statements. Maybe I am in shock, my life could have been taken, and I want off work now. The police report is complete, I exit the coach, walk north to the bus stop a block or so up, take the next southbound bus to the end of the route, get off, walk to my Jeep, and get in. Possibly I should have talked to the driver, but I am now here at the bus garage. I don't know who to call to let them know of my absence since I have not skipped a shift prior to this, but I am leaving now.

My entire being is still shaking more than when I left Aurora. I text Raven and ask if she would like dinner. Her reply is a call. I can hear the surprise in her voice and the tremble in mine. She tells me she is at a friend's house waiting to pick up Enzo, but I can visit with them, or she can meet me out front as long as I can get her to Enzo at 7:00 pm. I detect the hesitation in her voice because I am acting differently, but I agree to come up and meet her friends; again, my curiosity is taking over. She gives me the address, and it is not far from here. I find a place to park, worrying about my Jeep and its contents, deciding to bring the backpack with me rather than chance having it stay on the street in Pioneer Square or anywhere, for that matter.

From my vehicle to the address Raven has given me, I have seen four people in the entryways of shops that have closed up for the night, all in various states of stupor from substances I have not sampled. I am relieved when I arrive at the brick building with large wooden, glass, and gold trim doors. The glass brought me mentally back to the scene I had just left on the bus. I buzz apartment 207, Martinez. Immediately, they buzz me in, and a woman answers the door who looks familiar, but I cannot place her. Raven sits at the old wooden dining table and gets up, hugging me, looking down to see her backpack in shock. She asks, "Where did that come from? Why are you off work early?" I tell her there was an issue on the bus, she says, "Mel?" All the while, I am aware of Jill watching our back-and-forth broken conversation without any answers. I tell them both about going to the lost and found to retrieve the backpack, but not how it got there. Raven, with her street smarts, knows there is more to this story but is smart enough not to let on that she has former ties to a questionable group. Then she asks again about my early appearance. I ask to sit and tell them about the shooting on the bus, just as a man enters the kitchen, rubbing his hair with a very old, threadbare towel. I assume this is Martinez from the name on the entry buzzer. Jill introduces him as Hector and tells me I probably saw her brother, Jeffery, tonight during the shooting. Then I remember Raven mentioning Jill Muncer. I tell her he has been helpful in a few situations but wasn't present at the call tonight. I ask Raven if she would like to go to dinner. I didn't care where I just needed out of this place with the backpack and was counting the minutes away until I could escape. Raven did not need to unzip the backpack; I think she sensed that, since the last place she had seen it was the night she escaped from Mel's, it may contain something not right for this setting.

I take the backpack from her before we get to the bottom of the stairs. On the way back to my Jeep, I tell her we can eat, but I would like to do so in my vehicle so we can talk privately. Raven is concerned and immediately asks if we are ok. I tell her the whole story of seeing the backpack a couple of days before Mel was shot and called it in for the next bus to pick it up, didn't know if they had been able to pick it up, then forgot to see if it had been retrieved. "I picked it up this afternoon before my shift and was going to call tonight, then the shooting happened, and here I am. Yes, I did look in it. I needed to know what I was hauling around. You are going to be ok." We drive down 4th Avenue to Burger King, Raven peeks in the backpack, pulls out the swim trunks, blouse, sees the money, puts the trunks back over the stack, and pulls out Mel's passport, looking at his picture with sadness. I know they have known each other for a long time, and he was there for her. She says, "It would not be a good idea for me to visit him now. Thank you for bringing my money." I do not know him, but I hope he pulls through. Knowing I will check on him and Darius soon.

She gives me her order; we pull in the parking lot and eat. Both of us are silent. I am thinking of Darius Williams, I imagine Raven is thinking about the money, her future, and Mel. We eat and realize it is nearly time for Raven to get on the #40 to meet Aleene and get Enzo for the weekend. We will not be going back to my house; that thought always sits wrong with me. How quickly a way of life can change. I ask if she would like me to meet her where she gets off the 40 and drive her to Evelyn's. She is deep in thought and says she would like that and for me to take the backpack for safekeeping, at least for the weekend, as she peels $500.00 out of it. I tell her there is $17,000.00 in there, her eyes nearly come out of their lids. She knows this will get her through the process of setting herself up and filing for custody. I cannot see clearly where that leaves me in her picture, but my goal was to help her, and that is what I am doing.

At 6:30 pm I drop Raven off at 3rd and Union with no discussion of our plans other than for me to meet her 7:05 pm in Freemont to take them to their weekend accommodations. Raven is doing well I think, staying with me, keeping up on her end of the bargain with Enzo, getting a job and commuting. I have not seen any frustration from her, she appears to be doing what needs to be done to get it together.

I pick her up, we drive in silence to Evelyn's house, she asks me to come in, we take Enzo, his weekend supplies, and Ravens' two backpacks in. She tells me Evelyn will not be back for a couple of weeks and wonders if I would like to stay a few nights. I think of Gus and feel sad, knowing I could never move unless it is to a place like this, on a lake where I can bring Gus, my wild pet. We agree to meet tomorrow for a movie, and then I will come back to stay Sunday night. She looks at me and knows Gus is on my mind. Raven turns and sits looking at me like she has something hard to say, then tells me, "Jill and Hector will have a room to rent in a couple of weeks, and I need to stay in Seattle. The five-hour commute on the bus has to stop. I am going to make sure I see you. I want this to work, but it all has to fit together." Just as she tells me this, I think I could work another shift, different days, or another job to accommodate her schedule, but don't know if we are that far into whatever it is we are creating.

I know she needs to prepare Enzo for their evening together, the little guy who moves between homes with ease. I wave at him and hug Raven as I prepare to leave. She hands me the gray backpack, minus the raven, which she has placed on the one she currently carries, and Enzo runs over to hug my leg. I have never had anyone who I felt needed me, but I know they do in a world that can be cruel. Before I leave, Enzo lets go, grabs my hand, and takes me to the window to see the lake and ducks floating out a few feet.

I get in my Jeep with the backpack, drive home, uncertain of my future with Raven, but will let it play out to see where it ends. I get off I–5 at Gravelly Lake, stop at the store for worms, get two containers, one for here and one for the Lake Washington ducks. I return home, and Gus greets me at the edge of my parking space. I finally relax after this violent and uncertain night.

It has been a few weeks since I have taken time to unwind and enjoy my view by myself, which I know is the easiest route to take. Since I am home earlier than usual before dark, I notice most of the neighboring boats have disappeared from the water, the leaves have turned, and autumn is upon us. I reflect on the various lakes during my journey from Afghanistan to here and cannot believe the turn of events in the past few months. In my prior life, I never knew a slew of people. I used to live in an unsavory area of Miami, but that was a view from my window and a trip to school. I didn't leave home looking for trouble or travel through areas as vile as N Aurora. I have nearly completed my military training to live in modern-day society, but where I have been placed for work is worse than anywhere, I have been stationed before. Tonight's shooting has set me back a few steps and made me think about taking another position somewhere else, but then I think about Darius Williams and Raven. If I hadn't been there for Darius, would he have bled out and died? Where would Raven be if it weren't for me? I am sure she would have found a way to make it work, but she wouldn't have had her backpack or a place to stay, at least before now. It makes me sad she will be staying in Seattle, but at least I know where and with whom.

Saturday morning rolls around, and I still am not positive my body has internally stopped shaking since yesterday, my mind being on high alert. All of my military PTSD counseling is geared towards what I have already been through, not what I am going through presently and in the future. My text alert startled me at 9:15 am. Raven says Enzo is not feeling well and asks if I mind skipping the movie. Honestly, I am relieved to not drive back into the city for a day or two. Not that I want Enzo to be sick or not see Raven, but I need to get used to staying here alone again and also have to unwind before my next shift in thirty hours.

I decide to look through the backpack again since I was interrupted at my last inspection by the over-informed driver and did not check the side pockets or front zipper compartment. I find an old pacifier in one side pocket, the other being empty, a packet of ground-up crackers, baby wipes and a tag with a key attached. The tag looks new, as if it had recently been placed there. I take a picture of it and ask Raven if she knows what it goes to. She quickly responds, asking where I found it. I tell her about going through the front pocket of the backpack and take a picture of the pacifier, sending it to her with a reply of please throw that away and don't let Enzo see it. She doesn't know what the key goes to, but says she doesn't need it, even if it is to Mel's place, she doesn't want it. I figure with a new job, contemplating her custody case, and the uncertainty of a place to stay long term, the mystery of a key is a bit much to add to her plate. I ask if she wants anything else in the backpack besides the money. She says the passport and birth certificate should be returned to Mel, but she is scared to be seen with him or at the hospital. I make certain she doesn't want the backpack or its contents, unload the money, stash it in my fireproof safe, wishing I could deposit it in the bank, but know anything over $10,000.00 is tracked, and where would I say it came from. Plus, if Raven needed it in the spur of the moment, I have immediate access to it.

25

Detective Muncer

SATURDAY NIGHT, AT ABOUT 9:00 pm I receive a call from Metro. He says he has information for me but wishes to hand it to me personally. He states he will meet me anywhere. We agree that I will meet him at his house. When I first agreed to this arrangement, I had not pictured where he would live, but after he texts me the address, I see I will be on a road trip tonight. It is good to get the cruiser out on I–5 once in a while after all of my city driving.

After getting off the interstate, I wind around a few roundabouts and almost miss his driveway while seeing a boat launch and taking in a slim view of the lake. I text him while turning in, see his Jeep parked at the bottom of the hill with Metro emerging from the side of a small house. I get out and stretch, telling him, "I had no idea you escape every day to this place." He laughs, saying, "We all have secrets."

We take in the view of the lake from the front lakeside. I sure hope whatever he has was worth my drive, but I am glad part of my Saturday night won't be spent in the city. He tells me of his military service, three tours overseas, and the VA slowly releasing him to society. He doesn't think shootings like last night are helping his recovery, but he will continue on with his job.

He pulls out a gray backpack that lies in a puddle on the table between us, looking nearly empty. I sense he is recalculating something. It may be whether he should have called me, revealed his hide out or the story he will tell me, but this is where we are on both sides of the backpack. He carefully unzips the smaller front packet, showing me there aren't any items in the side pockets, just the two zipper pouches. He has left the nearly ground-up crackers in a baggie that the key was wrapped around, held by the tag that says BL–2. The numbers have no significance to me or him. I know they will connect to something; otherwise, he wouldn't have called me here. He opens the top zipper and pulls out the blouse, tank top, book, swimming trunks, and a passport with another piece of paper folded inside. I open the passport and am surprised to see Melvin Scriptnor's name with no travel history and his birth certificate. I ask, "Where did this come from?"

Metro proceeds with the story, stating only facts as if he is reading a bullet point presentation.

VC: I saw it at an abandoned bus stop on 145th and Aurora

DM: How did you gain possession?

VC: I saw Mel and the backpack two or three evenings in a row before he was shot, just pacing. One of those nights, the backpack was left at the stop. I called it in to be retrieved and sent to the lost and found.

DM: When did you get it from Jackson St?

VC: Yesterday, before my shift.

DM: What do you think BL–2 means?

VC: I have no idea. I hope Mel pulls through to let us know.

Just then, there is a quiet knock at the door and a strange noise, Metro almost flying out of his chair, saying, "I almost forgot Gus." He opens the door, a duck waddles in, Metro gets a container of bait from the fridge and stands just outside the doorway feeding Gus worms, so the dirt doesn't drop inside this house that looks unlived in, everything in place except for the girl's sweater on the rocking chair and slippers to the side of it.

I stand to leave just as an older male approaches, out of breath, asking if everything is ok. "I know when the police are here. Are you or the girl in some kind of trouble?" Metro introduces me to Mr. Owens, the tight-shipped landlord, and explains we are colleagues from work. He asks what we both do. I show him my SPD badge, and Metro tells him of an adventure while working as Metro Transit Police. Mr. Owens rubs his head, saying, "I had no idea. Guess I am in good hands," as he walks around the garage back to his home.

I ask Metro about the girl; he tells me she was just in town a few nights. I know there is more to that tale, but this piece of the story was delivered first, so I will file it like the others. Truthfully, I don't expect Metro or the girl to give me any trouble being as he turned over the backpack to me and didn't have to.

Thinking about the possibilities of BL-2, there are not many apartment buildings lettered that way, but I would suspect the 2 is for the second floor of somewhere. It is a mystery to be solved. I will start with asking Steven Watkins, then Mel, if he wakes up. I don't know the status of Allard, but I wish to steer clear of her. I can't even talk to her being as she is being held downtown. I hope this key is not connected to her and just something Mel had in his backpack.

I thank Metro and wish him a good weekend. Congratulate him on a peaceful hideaway, not revealing any of my secrets. I wait to blast my stereo until I hit American Lake Park. Then travel north back to my territory with newly found mysteries and being thankful I am a detective. Tonight brings light to my music, I usually have inspiration from my cases, but I will write when I get home. Words form in my head as I drive.

There is no other choice but to return to the precinct in the hour between today and tomorrow, have the guards bring Steven Watkins to room three, since room four is currently occupied with a scuffle going on. The interview rooms are mostly unavailable tonight. Stories, factual and dreamt, floating through the holding cells, ones that will convict, others become free due to what they know, some told are figments of imagination.

Watkins enters looking wide awake and the same as our last visit a couple of days prior, except for his change to an orange jumpsuit. I can tell he is surprised by my late-night visit. There is worry in his eyes. Does he wonder what evidence I have discovered? Is he ready to confess to more? I am sure the first thing on his mind is whether Mel is currently alive. I pull out the key, and there is immediate shock showing on his face, but he quickly replaces it with amusement, which doesn't fit the question or setting. He denies ever seeing the key, knowing the meaning of BL-2, and says he needs sleep. I know he has knowledge of where the key fits, but he is not ready to bargain.

To make this easier on both of us, I request the guard, knowing this is a waste of my time. Frankly, I am angry that I have driven over one hundred miles tonight. Watkins knows the answer and will not divulge any part of it. There are possibly only two more people who know the answer, and both are out of my reach.

My next stop is to head up the hill to Harborview, hoping to see Naomi. Somehow, I need to find out Mel's condition. The midnight hour is not always the best time to seek information. Although it is in the early morning hours, I take my chances entering the ICU with the key in my pocket. I can tell Melvin Scriptnor is not awake from the monitor I see at the vacant nurse's desk, and if he doesn't come around soon, he may never see this side of the soil, stopping at a state of vegetation. I begin to wonder what the people in the comas are working out, which way they want to proceed. I hear warning bells from a monitor and follow the sound to Mel's room. He has rolled his arm sideways a bit, and his IV is crushed under his elbow, but is he now aware this has happened, or anything else? The nurse tells me visiting hours are over, so I show her my badge, she looks at me, wishing my exit, but tends to Mel, not asking if I am family or if Mel is involved in a case. I ask if she has seen any improvement in his condition, and she smiles, saying his stats are improving. I thank her and leave before she instructs me to do so.

My next stop is the ER to see Naomi, one of my stabilizers. I walk around the nurse's desk, and a few nurses and doctors recognize me from previous visits and probably wonder which patient is attached to my late-night visit. Without a reason to be here, not seeing Naomi or wanting to inquire about her whereabouts, I leave, stop in the hallway, and text her, knowing if she is with a patient, it may be a while before she can reply. She responds when I make it to the elevator, saying she is home, and it would be good to see me.

With my lunch hour about a quarter of the way over if I calculated right after leaving Mel, I hurry to my cruiser parked on the west side of the building and drive the few blocks from the hospital to James St. Parking is at a minimum this time of night with everyone already tucked in their homes sleeping. I find a spot blocks away and run like I seem to always be doing, only this time to somewhere I wish to be. Naomi meets me downstairs with a soda. I am grateful not to have to waste time climbing the stairs. I see tiredness on Naomi's face. She looks at me and says, "I am supposed to be at work right now, but we lost or someone did, six tonight. They were all gone before they were brought in. I don't know what they thought we could do except take them downstairs. There is no reviving the dead. What do they want miracles from us in the ER?" Discouragement covering Naomi and the steps we sit on.

I have never seen her like this before and am not sure if I should have stopped or need to stay for support. We sit as we do in the cafeteria, side by side and nearly asleep, but realize our strength and determination to continue is what keeps this city going, no matter what choices other people make. Some pass through, but we do our best to bring them back from the jam they have pushed themselves into.

We sit holding our thoughts with the season changing in the beginning hours of this day, the bars are closing. I can tell from the escalation of noise on the streets nearby, just east of here. I know my lunch hour is nearly over but take these last few minutes and hold the only person who truly matters to me. We part with Naomi standing on the sidewalk watching me walk towards I-5, where the cruiser is parked. I am wondering if all my efforts are worth it, and do I need a normal life with office hours. Then I know I could never be that person; I am Detective Jeffery Muncer, defender of the night.

Half a shift to go, N Aurora and music are on my mind. I drive by Mel's house; nothing has changed that I can see from the street. Now I have many regrets about what I could have done while in there, but there is no going back now, legally. Of course, if I had seen tags like the one in my suit pocket, it would not have had meaning at that time.

I circle the block, turn north on Ashworth Ave, and make my way to N 155th to make my return trip to Fremont and home to work on files. I drive down to about N 100th, and a man is in the road yelling at a nonexistent vehicle. I pull over, not positive I would like to be involved, but I need to determine if he needs me, patrol, or medics. At least he is not horizontal, he keeps yelling over and over again, "Acura, Acura, silver, Joey's". I calm him down for a second until he starts back up again with his mantra. I ask for his name and receive the name Jake before his spiel about the Acura, then Simmons. Where does he live? He points to the apartment with the light on, front door open, just off to the side of the southbound bus stop. A male comes out of the stairwell asking Jake what is going on and Jake can't place his words in the proper order announcing, "Silver Joey Acura, the Acura gone." The male looks into the parking area for the building seeing his vehicle is gone and I realize this is Joey and his Acura has been stolen. I show him my badge, ask for his ID, and Jake's. Jake says he doesn't need any ID, doesn't leave here ever. He stays in the window for the lady, but Joey pulls a wad of keys out of his pocket with tags, tags identical to the one in my suit jacket. I do not reveal this fact until Joey returns with his ID, then ask Jake to return to his apartment and lock the door for his safety and I return to my cruiser to call patrol to make a report knowing on an early Saturday morning they won't show up before I learn about the tags from Joey.

He quickly returns with his wallet, his registration stating he doesn't leave it in the car and has a picture on his phone in case he gets pulled over. Not that I don't care about this man's car, but I need to know about the tags, and Joseph Carlisle is the man to tell me. He turns his head with an uncertain look and asks where that key is. I tell him someone found it and gave it to me. I don't think he believed my story, but that is the truth. He doesn't need to know it was in Lakewood. He says, "BL–2 means basement, laundry 2," and leads me through an open door into the laundry room, machines spinning, the odors of laundry products mixed in the damp air, lint hanging from the overhead pipes, and puddles forming on the floor like most low-budget laundry rooms. In the rear, almost behind the last dryer, there was an odd-sized door, and the key fit. I open it, turn on the light that is surrounded by years of cobwebs. There was nothing in the room except a small blue bin on the only shelf with a few plastic bags next to it in a stack. Joseph inquires about the patrol officers, his vehicle, and the reason for us being in this room. His eyes light up, and he wonders if the key is connected to the theft of his vehicle. Just then, the officers show up and take his report. I stop to check in on Jake, who answers the door saying, "I have stayed in the window, blonde curl, tall blonde curl." Jake doesn't have any other words tonight, but I will return to find out what else he has to say on another night.

I do not understand this night or if the theft of the silver Lexus RX is connected to anything in my investigation, but I believe I am closer. The next step is to return to my studio and get these words out of my head, onto paper, and add the beat.

Metro

(Verse 1)
Yeah, I'm ridin' through the city, no fear in my eyes,
Crossin' county lines, elevatin' for the buys,
Seattle rain, let it wash away the doubt,
Space Needle high, On the sly no need to shout.

Confidence drips from my words like a waterfall,
Built this from the ground up, watch me stand tall,
Ferry on the waves, I'm glidin' through the tides,
Every struggle faced, only makes the stride.
　(Chorus)
Crossin' bridges, coming lookin' back,
Winning ain't a dream; I'm livin' on the track,
In my zone, see the fire in my veins,
Boom Bap rhythm, let me take the reins.

(Verse 2)
Echoes of the past, they're a student of the game,
Old school vibe, but you know I bring the flame,
Lyrics hit harder than a thunderclap,
Got the city on my back, yeah, that's a fact.

My crew follows me, we roll deep and stay,
On this journey of life, we think we never fade away,
Channeling the legends, I'm feelin' that embrace,
With every word I drop, I'm leaving my trace.
    (Chorus)
    (Outro)
From the corner of the block to the top of the game,
Seattle's in my heart, it ain't never gonna change,
Crossin' county lines, I'm a king in the fight,
With my story on the mic, I'll shine through the night

#Seattle Strong #DJ Muncer #mun det J

In a Seattle State of Mind

Light the night it's time.
It's time, we roll, this shifts begin.

Straight out the dungeons of rap.

The ball drops deep as does my ways.
I never getting away, 'cause to getting away is the friend of strays.
Beyond the walls of rats, life is defined.
I think of rain when I'm in a Seattle state of mind.

Hope the protocol got some stall.
My peeps don't like no dirty fall.
Run up to the call and get the recall.

What more could you ask for? The sly ball?
You complain about streets. Do something.
I gotta love it though - somebody still directs the protocol.

I'm rappin' to the bridges,
And I'm gonna scale your ridges.

Mountains refrain

Uncouth, green, single, like a siphon
Boy, I tell you, I thought you were a hyphen

I take the streets, no dash on cards

Goin straight to the prize found in shards

I can't take the streets, can't take the fan.
I woulda tried to undercover, I guess I got no can

Seattle is a state of mind.

Younger me, contemporary.
I was kicked out without no arbitrary.
I never thought I'd see Union, University, Pike, Pine or Cherry.

A stunning ferry is quite the dictionary

Waves, waves of words

No reason, no system. It's remains arbitrary

Thinking of rain king of rain

On my mind pain, justice obtain
   #Seattle Strong #DJ Muncer #mun det J

26

Vernon

SUNDAY NIGHT I ARRIVE at Evelyn's house with enough clothing to stay two nights. I can't let myself get entwined in this situation any further until I know the time is right. I pull in, Raven is in shambles mentally. She is not even constructing full sentences, her thoughts falling out before the words are formed. She needs to file for custody as soon as possible, is what I understand.

Raven blurts out, "Albatar was here with Aleene. I didn't want to see him. He has not tried to help with the mess his parents created. I had it under control without his help, now he is on leave and will be attending Enzo's third birthday party tomorrow with Rubio. I celebrated Enzo's birthday with him this weekend, but I was not invited to the actual party since Rubio isn't aware of my involvement. Albatar can leave." Our evening is tense, but I didn't forget to bring the worms, and that seemed to calm Raven down for at least a moment.

On Monday morning, Raven leaves for work, and I call Carl about my commitment to Ethan's Edge, Kernal, asking to involve Darius Williams and inquire about free legal help for custody cases.

Carl asks, "Is Darius Williams the son of Marsha? What trouble has he gotten into, and how did you become involved?" I give him a brief summary of the incident on the bus and tell him what I promised Darius while waiting for the medics. Carl's voice changes as he feels for Marsha, one of the shelter's own staff, asks if Devon was with him, and agrees that Darius could be involved. His dad was an overactive gang member, his mom came here after his dad was killed, frightened for her and Darius' safety. This will show him another way before it is too late. "Glad Devon was not involved; he is Darius' cousin, and I believe he is trouble. Stop by anytime today if you have time, and I can give you the information on the legal network. Just curious, are you going through a divorce?" I tell him about my friend not using Raven's name in case the connections are too close.

Early afternoon, I stop in to pick up the legal flyer from Carl and ask what steps I need to take to become part of Ethan's Edge and take the paperwork for fingerprinting to be completed, since I will be working with minors. I stop at a café, get breakfast, and then drive back to Evelyn's before realizing I cannot get in. I leave the information for Raven under the doormat and text her. I don't expect a reply so soon, but I don't know what time her lunch is. A smile suddenly appeared on my face as the thought rolled through my mind that maybe we can have lunch tomorrow since I am in the neighborhood.

I pull into the bus garage early and get to my route, see another MTP member already on the coach as Alfred the scheduler runs across the yard to me saying since the shooting happened and I had left they weren't positive I was coming back and figured it would be better anyway since I am a floater to send me to Rapid Line H. He takes his hat off and runs his fingers through his short crew cut and his thoughts return to me he comes back saying something about, "Calm my nerves a bit to not be in the same area so soon." I don't know what to think about that. I had mentally worked through the incident over the weekend and think I am fine now as I board the other coach heading in the opposite direction. I guess it all pays the same. I just hope I get to see window man again. The other route does not start here. I suppose I will have to take another bus to get to the start of this route on 3rd Avenue and Pine Street. They quickly realize their mistake of routing me away from here. They use a courtesy van to transport me today, but say I need to make my own way tomorrow. Perturbed with the decisions being made for me, I turn to him and say, "Why don't I park here tomorrow and go back to my normal route?" I don't know if it was my tone, that I am almost a foot taller than Alfred or he is simply jumpy to start with and used to being in control, but he starts to walk away, gets what he figures is enough distance between us and says, "You have a great idea. Go back to your regular schedule next shift?" I watch him hurry with his short legs, carrying him back to the safety of his office, wishing he would work on his communication skills even though I don't have any.

I take the ride in the courtesy van with the driver, thinking Alfred must have given him a warning about my attitude and condition of

PTSD and the shooting. He silently takes me to the beginning of my route as I wonder how I will get back to my Jeep tonight, but that is hours down the road. The route seems ok, some sketchy housing, a few parks, gangers at the bus stops that don't board. I am not sure what they were thinking about my mental health before assigning this route and the shooting but placing me in an unfamiliar area is not helping.

We round a bend on Delridge Way, I don't know the cross streets yet since it is my first day. That is when I see who I think is Darius, and another teen is placing a large package wrapped with paper and twine in his backpack on the radar as he looks around like he is guilty before even being spotted. A group of three males stand in front of him, one pushes him onto the bench, so he is seated again without choice, and the bus takes off. I don't see anything further, but I wonder how Darius got out of the hospital so soon, remembering Carl's fears and wondering what his business is at this location. That scene didn't look good. The bus returns on our next run through, and Darius is at the stop headed in the direction of Burien, a place I have not been before today. He boards, looking behind himself, carrying the true meaning of watching your back. One of the three men I had seen at the bench runs up to tell him not to get on. I can see fear in his eyes. He tries to hand over the backpack, but the man grabs him, pushes him onto the curb partially under the bus. I see him lift his face with mud and grass in his mouth, blood forming on his upper lip. He is clearly a young person stuck in a sticky predicament. The bus is not able to close the door or proceed on the route. I take a picture with my phone of the man standing before walking up the aisle, exiting the bus, and say, "Darius, you need to come with me," sliding the backpack off his shoulder and dropping it to the ground in front of the aggressive man.

I realize once I am closer to him, it is not Darius, but there is no hesitation in this young person to get on the bus and obey my orders. He gets on, sitting in the seat directly in front of me. I know by some strange coincidence this must be Devon. I see him text and read over his shoulder that it was best to get on the bus since he knew my name, and you have your product. No harm done. I can't believe how speedily he allowed the ganger to think his name was Darius and put him in danger again.

I don't say anything for a while, then ask why he is involved with those up to no good. "Does he know if I saw what happened, so could anyone else? The police or other gang members." He hangs his head and says, "I am only trying to survive. They picked me to do stuff, this wasn't his choice. Why did you call me Darius?" I figured it wasn't right to give up that information, but look at him and ask, "Does Devon fit better?" He is nervous to be with a stranger who knows his name but isn't letting on that is who he is and remains deep in thought. I wonder where he will get off the bus, and I ask if he needs help. He looks at me like I am crazy and whispers, "Haven't you already helped enough?" I text Carl and ask where teens can go when in trouble, hoping for a reply before Devon exits the coach. It is late, and I don't expect an answer from Carl after business hours.

27

Detective Muncer

I WAIT UNTIL MONDAY night, give Steven Watkins a chance to think about the key and decide if the information about where it belongs will help in his departure, even though I am aware of the lock the key fits, I don't know why, although I suspect Allard has her hands in this mess. The guard brings him out of his cell to room 1, my least favorite. He looks like he hasn't slept since our last meeting a few days ago. I open up the conversation right away with, "How do you know Jake?" His eyes change with recognition, then he acts as if the question didn't affect him being true to himself, but I can see he wonders how I know Jake, as silence becomes heavy in this small room. He responds with, "Jake who? I can't recall anyone by that name." I know he is lying and wish Mel would wake up, or even stranger yet, wish I could talk to Allard. Then I have the idea of contacting Metevior about the key.

Metevior has been distant the past few weeks, like his last assignment with Allard has altered his train of thought and eagerness to be a detective. He has always been the one I talked to about my cases,

184

but now it seems like he doesn't care. I feel fortunate that they didn't select me for his assignment and feel for him being placed in that predicament. If it had been me, I may have retired, especially after seeing how a role like that has transformed my friend. With a partner, which I haven't had since being a patrol officer, you have to be able to trust them and not always second-guess them.

I feel fortunate that Metevior is on duty tonight, maybe we can gain back some of the ground of our friendship that was covered while he was put on the mission of capturing the deeds of Allard. We meet up in my pseudo-office on the third floor at 3:00 am. He brings in a file, lays it on the table, and leans back like it offends him, and he doesn't want anything to do with it, and mutters, "These are all the stops she requested; no one else has seen the information this early in the investigation. I still, after all that extra riding with her, have no idea what she was up to." I ask about the key, Jake, and the three-story yellow building that connects them all. He hears on the street that Jake may not look like he is on the ball, but he follows directions and knows everything that happens in that complex or the surrounding area. I believe in all my years on Aurora, there has only been one encounter with him, but I feel we should ask him more.

Metevior doesn't know what Allard had been up to, but I look at the carefully detailed list of extra stops, and Mel's residence was not one of them, which she could have done on her own time. He gets up, sidetracked, and says his heart isn't in this job anymore and leaves. I hope my oldest friend in the department doesn't retire, but it is a possibility I have to face. This one case could have caused an above-board detective to change his dedication level. Technically, how can he come back to work? Anyone he is involved with will think he is there to scrutinize them.

I call Rubio, knowing it is his night off. He always keeps the same shift, working or not. Says he is glad I called. "I am in a conundrum; life has me all wrapped up, and the reins are getting tighter." We meet down on Spokane Street under the West Seattle Freeway, at 4:30 am. Just as the commuters are starting to revive and head into town for the day. When I pull up, Rubio is pacing, obliviously, there before me, with enough time to fret over whatever is traveling through his head. I wonder where he had been and gotten himself into.

He stops in front of my grill. I was hoping we could sit in one cruiser or the other with the cooler air of autumn crisp this early morning, but he is a man who doesn't wish to be caged. He looks at me and blurts out, "Albatar is in town. Don't get me wrong, I love to see my son, but he and his mom had a birthday party for Enzo this evening. They already had the speech memorized, and the roles laid out for each of us. Aleene will be free since she has put her time in previously, Albatar already extended his contract with the military, and cannot have custody. We should never have taken Enzo from Raven. Aleene convinced me Raven was an unfit parent due to her need for a child once Albatar had left. She always desired perfection, and no one could be a fit parent to her grandchild except her. She will never admit she made the wrong decision and now feels ensnared. They want me to commit to three years with the little guy. I love him but don't wish to be a full-time parent again with my overnight work schedule. On top of that Tiffany Brobowski wants me to share a residence with her and her daughter's tot, a nanny and our lives. She doesn't want to live at my house which would fit us all so I would have to sell the only place where I am content. I am happy now with my life as a free man, coming home after work, relaxing and with life being uncomplicated. I don't mind having days, even committed ones, weekly with Enzo. He is the greatest little man but not full time." Then he paces some more, it isn't as if I actually have any expert advice or an opinion on his dilemma except, I cherish my freedom and think of Naomi. I feel guilt roll in since I should have checked up on her the day after I saw her last and didn't. I am not good with commitment either and know I couldn't do full time, let alone with two children, neither being mine. Rubio's troubles are above my experience. Maybe when my family left that did something to me and I don't commit to anything except loyalty to friendships and my occupation. This doesn't make me hardened it actually brings compassion when needed. I have always made sure my circle was small and when I am off work usually no one is in it.

Rubio goes back to his cruiser, I know we are not done. I watch as he retrieves an envelope from his visor, he saunters over to me then leans on the car. He is weary from the mental load he has shared with me. I feel compassion for him but also gratefulness for my decisions of keeping my ties at a minimal level. He tells me Tiffany gave him the tickets for a fundraising steamship ride on the Virginia V out of Lake Union. "There are four tickets, are you still seeing that gal from Harborview?" I know this will be good for Naomi and me to do our part in saving a ship instead of people and spend some actual time together. I tell him, "Thank you. Are you going with Brobowski?" He turns to me with regret in his eyes and says "yes, we will be there right after looking at a rental close by. Imagine me in the city, I live south under the planes." He removes two tickets from the stack, hands them to me, turns away and I think I heard him say over the traffic noise, "see you Saturday." It was getting hard to hear with the volume of traffic exiting off I-5 and crossing to Harbor Island. Rubio gets in his car and circles back to 1st Avenue, waves and is on his way to somewhere on his day off with the heavy load of his story shared.

I place the tickets in my glove box, take the onramp of northbound I-5 and decide not to text Naomi this time of day even though 5:00 am is probably more appropriate for her lifestyle than 5:00 pm. After thinking about the tickets and knowing it would be the best decision to attend this event. I never prefer being up at noon when the boat ride starts or at least not away from home and stuck in a crowd but am a smart enough man to know this will have to happen. I will text Naomi tomorrow.

On the way home I think of Jake and his words the other night, who was the lady he was talking about? Why does he stay in the window? What is his story prior to this? All items I will find out tomorrow. Thoughts to end my day just as a call comes through on the radio about a Lexus RX hitting a pedestrian and leaving the scene. Male 5'9", blonde curls on top, black and white flannel shirt and jeans, 2nd and Spokane where I had left. The call is picked up by patrol officers. I will read the report when I come on duty tonight before my visit with Jake.

28

Vernon

THE REST OF THE week is chaotic, I don't know what has happened with Devon, although he is not mine to worry about. When I returned home to Evelyn's house on Monday night Raven had already made an appointment to begin the process of filing for custody.

I have made an appointment with Carl to start fulfilling my time in Ethan's Edge, which I feel since I work full time would be best done on a weekday in the morning. I will be Korn's main contact and volunteer once a week, but he will work with different leaders on his other shifts fulfilling his community service hours. While I am on my bus routes that they change around I will look for places of graffiti to cover.

I am ready for this week to be over with the promise of my route back next week. Each day I have been given a different route. Even though Alfred said I could return to the E Line. Beacon Hill, West Seattle, the U District, Bellevue, Renton all places and miles behind me. I just want to get back on Aurora not a statement I thought I would make but it has become true, there are mysteries to be solved out there.

On Monday after work, I go back to my place which seems quiet. I think back to all my lake adventures since leaving the Army and am thankful for this place of solitude. All the people I am involved with and need help are external, not that I don't care but once my help is done will I even see any of them? Will I know Enzo by the time he outgrows his car seat? At least I know Raven doesn't have plans to reunite with Albatar. I will have to wait and see where the twist of time takes this situation.

Friday night with my shift change today I meet Raven after work for dinner. This is the fourth day since I have seen her, and I am relieved she is sitting here in my Jeep. She tells me, "Aleene is willing to meet anywhere close to get Enzo at 7:00 pm, it doesn't have to be on the 40. The time is all wrong. I get him when he is almost done for the day being as he gets up at 6:00 am." With me being free to roam anywhere as long as it is in the USA, I wish I could fix this situation by just driving off with the two of them but do not know what to say or do to her remark being as my life is uncomplicated except for the bus routes I do not want.

We eat dinner, discuss purchasing some live bait for the ducks but do not easily find any in the city. Then head to the Metropolitan Market purchasing some weekend items for Raven and myself. Shopping together but for separate homes. As we load the groceries, hers in the back seat, mine in the rear compartment, I stop for a second and kiss her knowing this will be the last time we have alone for who knows how long. We stop and hold each other as someone sees our empty cart roll away and offers to return it to the store. It was a moment, a stress reliever for both of us who are out in the city on our own taking care of tasks and ones we care about each day. We decide to have Aleene meet us on the corner of 2nd and Mercer. Raven starts to get out to meet her, I squeeze her hand, and I know our undivided time is up being torn between my thoughts and knowing Enzo and Raven need to be reunited. Enzo's care and safety are much more important than what is going on in my head at this moment.

Saturday Raven has agreed to go on adventure with me, reminding me Enzo will be with us. I think Enzo will be the happiest about our adventure. I arrive at 10:00 am, watch Raven pick up the dishes from breakfast and take Enzo out to the front lawn to feed the ducks since I brought more bait from the corner store by my house. The lady who owns the store always asks, "Big fish?" I laugh. It has been our point of humor to me for a few months. I will take a picture of Enzo feeding the ducks and show her next time I stop.

We load up, Raven has not asked where we are going. I just say to bring a coat; she also grabs Enzo's train blanket. We pull into the parking lot of the Virginia V steamship for a ride, the tickets coming from Metro Transit Police due to my help with Darius during the shooting. With these things on my mind, I look back and see Enzo has unbuckled himself and is climbing over the console into Raven's lap. In his excitement opening the door, he doesn't even know he is getting on the ship yet.

We get out with Enzo leading the way. I hand the tickets over to Raven who is almost as surprised as her son. We board, getting a seat up top near the front. I am grateful for the warmth of the sunshine as summer is closing. The ship fills in a matter of a few minutes and we take off. It is a relaxing afternoon and when the boat has docked, we are free to walk around a bit and tour the steam ship. Just as we turn the corner, I hear, "Metro," as Raven pulls on my arm and hides behind me. She is too late since Rubio has already seen her. Enzo takes off out of her arms wanting Pappy. I know the decision of being here today could jeopardize Raven and Enzo and my credibility. These are not thoughts I had prior to this moment and pray for the outcome of our outing to be positive. Muncer introduced Naomi and Tiffany not realizing Rubio wasn't aware of Raven having Enzo on the weekends.

Rubio is looking ill with a tint of gray under the surface and is confused saying Tiffany and him just signed a yearlong lease on a property close by so they could take Enzo. I feel Raven tensing up and see the fear in her eyes as she walks in front of me saying, "That is not necessary. I never wanted Enzo to be with Aleene or you. I have been taking him for over six months now on the weekends and in two days Aleene will be served with custody paperwork." Rubio sits at the closest table, turns and speaks with an uncertain voice, "Why this second? Why not yesterday?" Having never met Tiffany, I can still see the deflation of her demeanor. A happy woman twenty minutes ago but the uncertainty of her carefully planned life now may have fallen apart. Rubio gains composure takes Enzo off his lap holding his hand and walks across the wooden planked ship deck to Raven. He picks up Enzo, hands him over, and hugs Raven with much more meaning than the occasion of a boat ride would hold, saying, "Call me."

We were in the parking lot loading up and hadn't spoken since the encounter on the ship. I am waiting for Raven's response, not wanting to influence or interfere in her situation. Just as I open my door waiting to get in until Raven buckles Enzo I hear, "I didn't know you had a baby." It is a male voice I don't recognize. Raven turns and smiles, as the man introduces her to Willow then I make my way over after Raven makes eye contact with me and she introduces me to August, her boss, and Willow who had just taken the same cruise as us. He asks if we saw Muncer. I ask, "August from the name on the sign?" They all laugh, and he says, "I get that a lot."

We say our goodbyes, see Muncer and Rubio with their seat mates exit the ship. We stop at McDonalds so Enzo can have some dinner. Raven is silent most of the time but pipes up almost at the end of our meal. "Rubio probably should have known all along about Aleene's deception since I have been keeping Enzo on the weekends for over six months. It was strange to see August there too and meet Willow. I have heard about her around the warehouse. I don't think anyone except Hector has met her since they are both in some club."

I am not sure how to feel about my deception with Muncer but am expecting a call soon. I wish it was now to get past this point, but I will not make the first move in this situation. He knows where to locate me. He will make contact when he needs another piece to his story.

29

Detective Muncer

WITH BOTH NAOMI AND I off this weekend, having additional waking hours in the middle of the day on Saturday has disrupted my usual weekend routine. After the boat cruise Naomi and I had dinner at a place she loves downtown and went back to her place where we fell asleep watching TV. We slept through until Sunday midday, changing the balance of our Monday schedules. We are now trying to regain control of our schedules, launching another week starting tomorrow.

I can feel the weight of the weekend after returning home on Monday morning. Naomi and I have never spent that much time together, but it all went well. I suppose we have not attempted to test the territory of an entire weekend together because we are solo people. Maybe next time we will go away somewhere.

After returning home I know someone has been here and Jill is the only other one with a key. I see a note on the kitchen table saying she was sorry she missed me. Should have called. I text her and ask if she is ok. She replies with a smiley face. I don't know what she wanted but don't feel the smiley face fits the scenario. She will get a hold of me when she is able to talk freely.

My first stop tonight is to read the report on the stolen Lexus RX, then up to talk with Jake to find out who the lady is. After that I need to talk to Metro if it isn't too late to find out how he ended up taking Raven and Enzo on the cruise. I know sometime overnight Rubio will contact me about his situation even though I am not of any assistance with his dilemma.

I pull into parking for the precinct, go to my office and retrieve the report that includes camera footage of the pedestrian crossing 2nd Avenue, carefully stopping for traffic as he walks under the West Seattle Freeway and then I see the Lexus parked behind a semi-truck just outside a fenced business with his lights off. Just as the pedestrian, a homeless man carrying a backpack that looks like it has tent poles sticking out, gets to the northside of the bridge ready to cross the west bound lanes of Spokane Street the Lexus pulls out at full speed, running the man over They then leave the stolen vehicle and run towards 1st Avenue. The camera loses him then. I see a mop of blonde curls flop from side to side as he runs, something else to add to the file. People without experience don't run at that rate of speed. My guess would be he is employed nearby or has stashed his own vehicle in the area.

I see from the report no prints were found, it had been stolen for a few days so possibly parked in a garage, the owner, Joseph Carlisle, was called to retrieve it with a now broken windshield made from the man's body at impact.

I travel to N Aurora knowing I would not need to make a call to Jake and could just stop in anytime. I don't think he leaves the grounds of his complex at all.

He isn't in the window as I pull in, nor is the Lexus. I knock on Jake Simmons' door, he answers immediately. Me knowing he was on the other side of the peek hole and had seen me pull in. He asks me to enter his premises. I am not entirely comfortable with that but know this is where he is free to talk and no one else can intrude.

We chit chat a bit about the weather and other trivial matters then I question him. He seems happy to have someone to talk to, even me when he realizes I am the police as he asked to see my badge when he opened the door. He smiled and touched his heart which was an odd reaction to a badge but now I know the badge has other sentimental values in his life.

DJM: How did you get this nice apartment?

JS: My dad owns the building, and this is my space here. I see the bus and have cameras in my TV. I got to pick my apartment.

DJM: Can you show me the cameras in your TV?

Jake gets up, walks across the room, pushes a button on the wall and a big screen TV appears with a piece of paneling concealing it. He turns it on and shows me the parking lot, front and back of the building and the bus stop out front. I am surprised at his ability to operate this complex system. He rewinds the footage back to the night of the theft and says, "See this is the time we became friends. Joseph's car gone with curly man." Sure, enough there goes the Lexus with a mop headed man peeling out of here. The windows tinted only showing a shadow of the hair.

JS: I keep my window clean to see. She doesn't want me to look at the parking lot while she is there. I am scared of her but do what she says so she doesn't hurt me and still talks to me.

DJM: Who is the mean lady?

JS: Allred, Allred. She looks at me with a red face and when she yells her eyes turn red. Do you think that is why they call her Allred?

DJM: What does Allred do here?

JS: She does her laundry fast. Runs in, runs out. Funny wig fell off once. I saw it on the camera she didn't want me to watch but I turned it on and had a mirror turned so I could see it and still be in the window. I am smarter than her.

DJM: Have you seen Allred recently? Was she always alone?

JS: She is gone, I think. I hope but miss her. I need more window cleaner if she comes back.

I lay my card on his table by the window seeing his spray bottle is nearly empty. I ask if he wants me to bring more window cleaner. He smiles and says he will get some, a ride from dad to his favorite store. I put a $20.00 bill on the table and tell him to buy an extra bottle, thank him for his time and leave. Outside I look for the cameras but cannot locate them. They are carefully hidden, so no one is aware of their existence or for their safety, so they are not tampered with.

It is only 11:00pm, I know Metro is about to end his shift. I place the call; one I know he is expecting. He answers on the third ring. I can hear the hum of his tires on the interstate, aware he is already headed south to his hide out but ask if he has time to talk as he drives. He says, "Sure I have been expecting you, wasn't that a nice boat ride?" I agree and go into my police mode not knowing why but it is part of me after all these years. Not being capable of separating my job and acting like a human being.

DJM: How did you meet Raven?

VC: On the bus

DJM: I know now why you asked if she was wanted.

VC: You told me she is not, and I wish to help her regain custody of her child.

DJM: I am sure Rubio would like to talk with her if you know where she hangs out.

VC: I will arrange that if she is willing.

DJM: You know you have been a tremendous help to us, and I don't want this to change anything.

VC: I am glad because you are not someone to be on the wrong side of, we need each other on the streets.

I hang up with the assurance from him that he will let me know either way if Raven is willing to talk or not. I go back to the precinct and pull up the report of the night Don Montgomery was arrested, and the female was on the bus. Was Raven named in that case? Was there even an issue beyond disturbance that night or did he just have warrants out for the prior crimes related to the ODs?

30

Vernon

THE WEEKEND FLEW BY with the surprise of meeting Rubio. Raven seems as if she is relieved the secret of her having Enzo on the weekends is out in the open. I ask if she wants a ride tonight after dropping Enzo off at Aleene's, she agrees then changes her mind. Says she will get there.

I hear a knock at the door, surprising me since no one ever visits and it is only just over an hour since Raven and I talked. I see a car headed up the hill looking like Muncer's, but the color is off.

Raven suddenly starts with, "You'll never guess what happened. I was dropping off Enzo and Rubio texted me while Aleene was right next to me. I wasn't going to be the one to tell her we saw him over the weekend, and I guess he hasn't either since she didn't let on. I texted him back when she crossed the room and told him I would call once I leave here. I leave Enzo, he doesn't ever appear phased since this is what he is used to, but it is the hardest part of my week. While I am still in turmoil, I call Rubio who I hope will help with my custody case. He is about a block away, was planning on paying Aleene a visit but thought he should talk to me first. He offered to drive me here. I hope you don't mind we had lots of conversation on the way, and I didn't tell him who I was going to see. He is not going to tell Aleene he knows about me having Enzo for some reason. I assured him I would file for custody as soon as the law allows. I don't know what he is up to but on Tuesday or Wednesday Aleene will be served with paperwork from me."

With Evelyn back in town and Raven staying with me another week I pick her up on Monday night at Charlene's Place in south Seattle. She had an appointment after work at a free legal clinic. She gets in the Jeep with a manila folder, papers ready to file inside. She says, "The original plan was for Hector to drop them off at lunch time since he knows the process but then August heard about it somehow and is driving us to file them. By the time I see you tomorrow I will be on my way to having Enzo back full time." I see this is what she wants but is also a heavy load. I ask, "Where will you two stay and where will he be while you work?" She looks at me fearfully having just crossed this hurdle, knowing there are many other speedbumps to cross and other people who are in the same predicament and manage. "Something to ask at the next meeting," she quietly responds then looks out the window facing away from me. I assure her I will help in any way possible, feeling bad that I may have just burst her newly acquired bubble. This is a learning experience for me to and I just learned to let Raven take her own steps and to keep my thoughts to myself.

We were almost to South Center, and I see an Audi Q5 fly by barely wedging between two cars then cutting off another. I recognize the hair, blonde, curly. This is the third time I have seen him, now I am positive it is a man. I can see the vehicle two lanes to the right of us get off at the SeaTac rest area. I signal, get over two lanes and tell Raven about this guy who I don't know what he is up to but am looking for a license plate. She quickly pulls out her phone to type in the information: blue, Q5 Audi, no license plate. I see the driver is not in the vehicle, so I get out my phone, walk over and take a picture of the VIN before he returns. We park facing away from the Audi, he returns to the likely stolen vehicle and proceeds south. We cannot follow too close since it is later at night and there isn't much traffic to blend in with but keep an eye on him. He gets off at Portland Avenue in Tacoma, crosses over and takes the next left back onto I-5 north. We stop following him when he changes direction and gets back on I-5 south to home. Raven is already yawning since she leaves at 5:00 am so we go in, turn on the music and she is asleep before I change my clothes.

My thoughts are on the blonde man, the probability of me seeing him again was slim. I figure the only reason I have seen him is my frequency traveling the major thoroughfares. First, I spotted him on north bound Aurora pulling out of a driveway at a high rate of speed. He wasn't driving an Audi, then the next occurrence was on foot N 47th, the west side of Aurora, the night I had the meeting with Muncer and Metevior. Now the sighting tonight. I will ask Muncer about this guy if I ever have a private meeting with him again. I am not making contact with him he can initiate that from now on.

I sleep waking at 3:00 am with my stomach growling realizing I did not have dinner. My schedule is off and with most of my life balancing on uncertainty I am not comfortable but happy that Raven trusts me enough to stay here. I can't help but wonder, though, if she wishes she had kept Mel's key and stayed there since Mel is gone, Steven is locked up, the house is vacant, and the commute is many hours less. I am happy her money is hidden, and she is safely tucked in here.

31

Detective Muncer

IT HAS BEEN A week since the steamship ride and seeing Rubio. Sometimes we go a month or more without contact. I was wondering when his text would arrive but wanted to give him space to redirect his life.

He wants to meet at 4:00 am on 2ⁿᵈ and Spokane again. His last text says he has a plan. He is at our destination before me. Thankfully he is in his cruiser. I pull up next to him facing the opposite direction. He seems amused this morning, early for most but late for us having been out all night.

We discuss Mel, the burned-up tent, Allard and the weather. Rounding our way through conversation and winding around to the pressing issue of his move and custody of Enzo.

After having exhausted the trivial issues, he blurts out, "That house was mine before we got married and I was going to give it to her eventually. I am relieved that I didn't. She has deceived me this time and probably more. She knew I would have to move and rearrange my entire life. I told her, but she didn't care. She just wanted to be free of the mess she unnecessarily created. I am not setting foot in the house again until it has a for sale sign posted on the lawn. I stopped to tell her about my progress on taking over the care of Enzo, but she just acted happy. She does not know I am onto her scheme. There wasn't even a mention of Raven from her. Not that she had ever talked of this before. I asked if she was positive Raven didn't want her child back. She just looked at me as if I was crazy, placing her hand on her hip, her classic pose. It makes me wonder what she is trying to do to me after all these years helping her out by letting her live in my house. The one I had before I knew her. The house I left after I had the affair, and she said we were done. I packed and left. She is still punishing me. I have never asked for rent all these years but now things are different. I will see Enzo when Raven has him and the house will be for sale as soon as the custody hearing is final or before if that will help Raven's case."

I ask if Raven knows about the visitation schedule and what he will do with the other residence and Tiffany? Rubio rubs his chin as if in thought, "Raven will let me see Enzo, maybe keep him on my day off. Tiffany, I haven't told her any of this yet, but I am not moving in. I will not leave her to handle the cost of the lease, but she will live there on her own as I will do by the airport." He finishes just as I hear a call come through his radio. Pedestrian hit at 30th Avenue SW and SW Roxbury St, a neighborhood we are familiar with from our first meeting over a shooting that began in King County the south side of the street and ended in Seattle City limits on the north side. This time the pedestrian lays in the middle of the road, an Audi Q5 sits running, still in drive, and being held in place by the curb. The driver has vanished. Rubio and I are enroute.

We arrive and patrol officers from SPD and KC are present. In cases like these it needs to be determined which jurisdiction the incident will be handled by. The victim is one I recognize from the Duwamish encampment; his name slips my mind but talk to patrol about ID. Patrol says city camera footage has him dancing in the street before the impact. I access the frames needed as the SUV idles in front of the school and as the victim draws closer to him, he inches out in the Audi, punches it and then hits him at a high rate of speed. Another premeditated case.

The Audi has been reported as stolen, towed off as evidence. I return to the precinct and pull a list of stolen vehicles. The Audi was stolen two days ago and used today for this heinous crime; the same system used for the Lexus. It would be impossible to watch every stolen vehicle with approximately thirty a day taken in King County but maybe we will get a lead if enough eyes are on it.

I text Metro, sending a screenshot of the footage from Roxbury that has the suspect running from the vehicle. He immediately texts back about his three sightings of this person. This is just two of us and Rubio on the case in a city but it's a start. The distinctive hair is what caught Metro's attention.

32

Vernon

RAVEN HAS BEEN STAYING with me. Hector and Jill are taking a while to clear out the extra room. I imagine Raven is becoming tired of her long days and the longer she stays the worse it is for me. I get used to her being here, even though I enjoy my solitude and have never lived with anyone except Birdie but that wasn't real. She just came home, fed me, and slept. I never shared my life with her. Somehow it feels like when Raven is here, I open up a little but then shut down knowing she will be leaving.

This morning the house is quiet. I never used to be up this early but can feel the emptiness of the space after she leaves.

I show up for my first day with Ethan's Edge at 9:00 am. I have agreed to help Darius even though he has light duty restrictions and Korn is my official case. There are a couple other groups ready to go too. We wait in the alley behind the shelter, Carl is present and asking questions, "Do you have my number?" Yes, we all pull out our phones to calm his nerves. "What happens if a property owner refuses services?" Answering in unison, "We call you." "Do you have all the equipment?" We open the back of the van, lawn mower, paint, shovels rollers and brushes are neatly organized. "Are you ready to be sent out as representatives of this organization?" Just then a teen runs down the alley in a puffer coat, he is breathing so hard he can't stand but I can make out his breathy words, "Sorry I am late." I was not aware that Devon would be showing up today but willing to take him on my crew if he wants to work.

Carl pulls him aside and has a private conversation with him. While the overconfident boy waits in front of the van with Darius looking at him like he is trouble, Carl approaches me asking if I will be responsible for him while he is out there, reassuring me he is a handful. With the situation put like that I am hesitant and ask why he is here, and did he need these community service hours for some new trouble? It did seem odd to me about him showing up without my knowledge but of course I don't know how this system works yet being my first day. Darius appears nervous and Carl doesn't know why Devon has appeared. How did he know of this morning's happenings?

We agree to take him along, drop a couple other crews off at houses with equipment and stop at 89th and Aurora to clean up graffiti that has been placed there recently according to the store owner. As we are applying coats of paint to the cinderblock wall with various colors of spray paint bleeding through, Devon keeps looking over his shoulder. He is a child who always watches his back undoubtedly from his actions and associates. This action has caused Korn, Darius and me to be unnecessarily on alert, me wishing Devon was still in the alley or anywhere except here. Just before we load up Devon takes off behind a closed business and comes back around the other side looking guilty. He states he just had to take a leak, but I know there is more to the story and am not comfortable with him under my care if he lies about his actions. I look up and a 4 door maroon Volkswagen Passat pulls out of the fenced off area Devon had just visited. Our van arrives right on time to take us back to the shelter, I get in knowing Devon was either selling or retrieving drugs and there is either product or cash in this van connected to it. Korn is grateful for my involvement in his freedom and thanks me repeatedly. I assure him I am on board for him through the completion of this program as long as he complies. I do not confront Devon but wait until everyone has signed out and talk to Carl about the disappearance of Devon and the Volkswagen. Carl says, "I am familiar with his kind. He used us today to be an alibi for his actions. Whatever he did he will say we can all vouch for his whereabouts." Carl walks off then stops shaking his head and apologizes. I am not needing an apology, just am making sure Carl know his instincts are right and to let him make the decision of what happens with Devon next time.

I check my phone and see I will be late to work if I don't leave now. As I walk out the back door, I hear Carl make a call saying, "Darius what are you into now." I know Darius doesn't need this program and has agreed to participate before he gets into any trouble but even after being shot, he may still precariously remain on the edge of freedom and prison life.

I pull in with minutes to spare almost forgetting my lunch in the Jeep. Alfred approaches me and says Beacon Hill for you today, route 36. We need you there, hop in the courtesy van and we will drop you at Pine Street, and pick you up at the same location at 10:00 pm.

I am not pleased with this decision since I was looking forward to keeping an eye out for the maroon Passat, but you never know what will happen on new routes. We travel south through downtown, up by the VA where I started this insane journey, over by Evelyn's and wonder how far Raven has to walk carrying Enzo on Friday nights. Our longest stretch is on Beacon Ave where I can catch slight glimpses of Lake Washington, which reminds me to stop and get some worms for both sets of ducks on the way home. We slide into The Othello Station with no incidents, wait and make our return trip to downtown. On 12th Avenue right about where it turns into S Charles Street, I see the top of a blonde's head just briefly as he ducks into the wooded area of Jose Rizal Park. I have no idea if this is the blonde we are looking for in connection to the thefts and assault on a few people, but I shall keep my eyes out.

We continue down the hill to downtown and on our return trip I see him on the opposite side of the street slowly walking on the no parking strip and casing out vehicles, trying door handles. I snap a moving picture as fast as I can and text it to Muncer with a location and description of what I had seen. Immediately I hear sirens in the area but then they stop. On our return trip twenty six minutes later the strip of cars is there, one spot is empty, and blonde man is nowhere in sight. SPD had the area surrounded but I suspect blonde man is off with another vehicle. I expand the photo to look at the line of vehicles and see a gray one is missing but cannot make out the model from the motion of my photo. I text Muncer this information, the rest of my shift is quiet. I stop at the store for the worms buying three containers this time, one for Gus the other two for Evelyn's house.

I walk in and Raven is asleep on the couch, this is the first time I have been at peace all day.

33

Detective Muncer

I RECEIVE A CALL at approximately 10:00 pm from Rubio. He is not speaking coherently, switching from police lingo to civilian talk, mixing street slang in the mix. I cannot imagine what would have him so rattled. I stop his words after the third time through and ask, "Did Albatar call you? Is he ok? Where are you? Who was shot?" He is short with me, like I should already be aware of his problem, but I know his irritation with me lies with whatever situation he is in and not me. He almost screams, Albatar called, police are all over the alley, my CI called. "I am on my way to 59th, Aleene's, she is gone. Taken out in the alley behind her house. Albatar was watching Enzo so Aleene could go to the grocery store for a traditional breakfast before Albatar returns to his unit tomorrow afternoon. Now she is gone. I should have known, taken the mysterious note more seriously. I started investigating Tiffany's daughter's murder last week and the next day received a note under the wiper of my cruiser saying, "You don't know what you have opened up. Close the case NOW."

I meet him in the alley along with homicide and SPD patrol officers who continue to glance at Rubio. Word spreads among them he is not SPD and who the victim is. Albatar continues to look out the window on the back porch, I picture Enzo inside.

Aleene had been inside of her vehicle, just backing out of the garage when she had been shot. Rubio leans over whispering, "They were thorough in their research on me. Aleene didn't even have a part in the investigation, nor is she technically connected to me." He walks around not revealing information to anyone about the note except me. The note being stored in his glove box. It wasn't turned over yet because he wasn't positive of the connection. Now he slowly walks down the alley, retrieves it from his car, takes a picture of it and hands the daunting piece of paper over to the officer in charge who is questioning everyone. So far, the only evidence they have is a single shell casing that sits just outside of Aleene's car. She ran over it and crashed into the neighboring collection of dumpsters and trash bins since the bullet struck her while she was backing out. With the rain pounding down there are not any skid marks in the alley suggesting someone was in a hurry.

Rubio leans on his hood in the rain and begins to purge the story he had been told a few weeks prior, just before he signed the unwanted lease. "Tiffany Brobowski's daughter Novah had become increasingly wild after her child's dad had left them. She had met a new guy at one of the after-hours clubs. He introduced her to their system of living, she wasn't accustomed to their ways, nor did she wish to conform. She wanted out and threatened him with the information of her mother working as a police dispatcher. The Cartel did not take kindly to that connection and Novah never made it home to Tiffany or her two year old child. I met Tiffany shortly after that during the investigation that has not yet been solved. Last week I asked around and this is where it has taken us. Aleene paid the price for Novah's actions."

Rubio turns and walks back to his cruiser without receiving input from me. Out of respect to my friend I wait for the medical examiner to leave and then knock on the door to talk to Albatar.

It takes a couple knocks for him to open the door, I ask what he knows. He says all he heard was one shot but wasn't sure if it was a firework. I am standing in front of a young man who doesn't know his mother is deceased and am suddenly angry at Rubio for not talking with his son and delivering the news. My mind tries to convince me that I should have never stayed and knocked if I knew he was not aware of this death, patrol could have delivered the news. Then I dig down to my true self and realize this is a young man who needs direction on what to do with Enzo since he is leaving in a few hours, I think.

34

Vernon

I DON'T THINK I have slept this soundly since I was in grade school. I wake feeling off but warm and content in the covers. Suddenly there is a knock at the door, without looking at the clock I envision Raven on the porch and locked out having forgotten her key. I spring up wearing nothing but my gray plaid pajamas and find Raven sitting on the couch with a blanket wrapped around her, seeing the clock on the wall behind her says 4:16 am. My first thought is I think Raven is going to be late catching her bus.

I look out not recognizing two of the three males on my porch except Enzo. I wish to return to bed but know I cannot leave Raven here alone to deal with these two men who I am not comfortable with coming to my home in the middle of the night. If it wasn't for Enzo I probably wouldn't have answered, they could take their problem somewhere else. I open the door a crack, Enzo smiles and opens it further with his arms out trying to get to me. I take him leaving the two men outside while I contemplate shutting the door, knowing that is not going to be the solution nor bring a conclusion to this unwelcomed occurrence. Enzo runs to his mom, the only content person in this room. The two men enter against my better judgement and the younger one tells Raven, "Let's go. My plane leaves in a few hours. We'll get you a ticket and we can get married there." Just as he gets to the get married portion of his story Mr. Owens walks in and says, "Vernon, I told you this is a quiet place, not one for multiple visitors at 4:00 am. You will need to vacate." Trying to save my residence I turn to Mr. Owens and inform him I am working on an important case, police business. He looks at the other two men who I am only guessing one is Albatar and the other Rubio who has not said a word yet, but he does flash his badge. Mr. Owens walks out shaking his head and in waddles Gus ready for worms. I assume this morning can't get any stranger, the police come to my house to deliver a child and a man to propose to the lady on my couch, so I go the refrigerator and pull out worms for Enzo and me to feed Gus while they negotiate in the house. Letting Raven know I am just outside the door but being confident she can handle this early morning negotiation.

My phone that hardly ever rings is notifying me there is a call. I guess this day is becoming more out of the normal. I answer it in my room, as I pass through, I see Raven still on the couch and pinching the bridge of her nose, shaking her head no, as if in disbelief. The screen on the phone shows Muncer on the other end of the line. Without anything to lose I answer, telling him of the bizarre visit and proposal happening in my living room as we speak. He is shocked by those actions and says, "I am not sure if I should tell you or not but Rubio and Albatar are in a predicament in regard to Enzo. Albatar is leaving today. Rubio told Tiffany he is not sharing a house or nanny, and Aleene has been murdered. I suspect they are there to figure that out. How did he know where you live?" That is more information than I have ever received at 4:00 am and I answer with, "Did you call because they were here?" Muncers changes his tone from aggravation to sympathetic. He says, "This actually doesn't have to do with you, but I needed your opinion. Evelyn Wells was found dead in her yard this morning and Raven is her emergency contact. How do you think she should be notified? I can come there, have patrol call her later, or show up at her work." I tell him to hold on and retrieve Raven leaving Rubio and Albatar in the living room. I hand the phone to her, pick up Enzo, and stay close in case she needs me. She has just been informed of another death I think, not knowing if she is aware of Aleene's passing and now this.

Raven inhales so long I wonder if she will be ok. I hear thank you for calling and she hangs up. Enzo has not been over here before so everything in my bedroom is a toy. I keep him in there for a while looking at a book with lake birds in it. He likes to point out their colors and beaks pretending to give each one an imaginary worm.

I can hear Raven's voice becoming increasingly agitated as she tells Albatar he has never contacted her since Enzo has been born and she wishes to never see him again. The first words I hear Rubio say are, "What should we do with the little guy?" I peak around the corner as Raven opens the door and points out, leaving Enzo secure with me.

After they leave, she apologizes for their actions and thanks me for all my support of a place to stay, rides, friendship and everything else and says she will be staying at Evelyn's from now on since the house will be vacant. I am shocked by her sudden departure since the plan was until Friday. I turn and ask if she is ok, she looks away pinching her ear lobe and says, "I need to text August about work today." This was not an answer to my question but now I know she is committed to her job and journey. She gets up and texts August, I assume. Clearly, she has missed the bus she regularly takes. She pulls out legal papers from the front of her backpack and brings them to me. It is the newly filed custody paperwork she then says, "This may be the last thing Aleene received before her accident." August texts back "Please come in, I need you today. You can bring your child and we will figure it out. There are extra orders. Today might be bumpy but the other days can be pieced together."

Raven starts to pack up her stuff realizing they didn't leave anything of Enzo's. I offer to take her to Walmart, the only 24 hour clothing and food store open at this time of the day. Then drive her to work, I am thankful for the car seat and want to know more about Aleene and Evelyn but now is not the time to ask. I also wonder if I will have a place to live when I come back, or will there be an eviction notice on my door? I guess at this point all that matters is that Enzo is safe. I do ask, "Will you be asking for Enzo's toys, bed and such." She says, "I hope to never speak to either one of them again. Since the original custody order didn't have either of their names on it, they were not included in this case so they will have to file for visitation separately if they wish. Rude they have been since the beginning. Only doing what works best for them."

We find breakfast in Walmart and make sure lunch is covered for her and Enzo. I drive them to work, go to the bus garage, pull in under the carport in my usual spot, set my alarm, lean my seat back and go to sleep wishing I had gotten something to eat before coming here but sleep is what I need now. My shift starts in seven hours so it will be figured out by then. Rest never felt so good.

On my shift I receive my usual route and watch everywhere for the blonde curly headed man and don't have success today but do see Devon on my third trip north up on a street corner on N Aurora. He has some other players with him, they are bouncing around, looking in every direction. A sure sign they are avoiding trouble or looking for customers. On my third trip south, I can see across the median dividing the lanes Devon is still there as a gold Mazda pulls out of a hair salon, a fact collected after the incident. The gold Mazda fires into the group of teenagers on the corner. I see Devon go gown along with one other of the five gathered, the other three scatter. We proceed south getting the passengers out of the line of fire as quickly as possible, but I suspect we could have stayed there, and the gold Mazda shooter would not have done any harm to us. I switch to the seat across from me to get a better angle of sight and see he sped off northbound turning a couple blocks up. I only have the view out the side window since busses do not have rear windows. I don't see the driver call it in since we were not involved but hear sirens in the distance and could picture the lights as they reflect off of the buildings traveling to the scene. Devon, who I spoke to and worked with just a few days prior, may be dead or out of commission for a while. I am not sure I need to but do not ever mind being another set of eyes on the streets for Muncer. I text him with the information

I have. He asks if Raven is ok. That is what I respect about him; he cares about the city and its people.

On our return trip the crime scene tape is in place, a couple officers are on the side by the bus stop but there are not any victims in the taped off area. I picture them being taken off under the best circumstances in an ambulance and worst, the medical examiner. I am not positive who was taken away in which fashion but know someone didn't make it with the amount of blood I see running off the curb into the gutter matching the color of the no parking zone.

My shift ends, the day started eighteen hours ago. Raven will not be there when I return home. This night feels strange to start with then as I pull out onto 2nd Ave, I see police lights behind me. I signal as I change lanes, obeying every law, stop in a parking lot and notice the police vehicle is an unmarked SUV. As soon as he gets out, I see it is Metevior. He blurts out as if holding his breath, "Do you know how fast you were going?" Without a noticeable inhale or exhale he continues, "That is not why I pulled you over. This is off the books, but Allard wants to speak to you. I don't know why on earth I am helping her. I didn't have your number and couldn't ask anyone. So here we are with the only means of communication I have." He hands me a card with her number, not the one she used to have. Then says, "She is out on her own recognizance now, at home with an ankle monitor. I don't know what she did, what she wants, or how the hell she got out, but this is where my part of her story ends. This stop never happened."

I know this day has been one of the most active ones I have ever lived but at the top of my list of pros and cons, I am comfortable knowing Raven stood up for herself with Albatar and is safe. I feel for Devon and his family and hope Darius wasn't one of the others on the corner, but we can only control ourselves. Raven texts that she has day care set up thanks to August and hopes I sleep well, leaving a heart at the end of the message. I drive home and fall asleep after giving Gus a few worms. Having forgotten before this but after laying down I realize there was not an eviction notice on my door.

35

Detective Muncer

THIS WEEK HAS BEEN endless, the pedestrian hit and runs are escalating. Chief Stewart called a few of us in for a meeting. I am now the lead detective on this case of mental madness. Twenty to thirty vehicles stolen a day in King County, a vast area with Seattle being 83.9 square miles. I am one person on this full time, my other cases taking less priority. So far, the vehicles are stolen two or more days prior to the crime, always left at the scene like he singles out a person while not with a group and waits for precise timing. There have been five pedestrians hit; the only consistency is they have taken place in high crime rate areas. The first three were people involved in something on the street, of course we can only guess about that. We are positive the driver is not a customer of the sex or drug trade. Last night the person hit with the gray Nissan stolen from Beacon Hill was not part of any street activity. She was a tourist, lost and had stopped to ask directions to a group of young males on the corner just prior to a shootout. She was targeted when she left just around the corner and out of sight of city cameras.

I stopped at Harborview just as the body arrived, without ID, wallet, or any other identifying items except a hotel key belonging to a low budget room. I suspect this is someone from out of state who booked a vacation on a budget and made the wrong stop. At the scene there wasn't anything missed, I went back after forensics was long gone to scour the bushes, my attempt to identify the woman was futile. Frustration rules me as I know the city and SPD are relying on me to find this blonde curly headed person. It is as if this female did not carry a handbag or anything else. Maybe she was told by the young males it was a bad area and didn't wish to be a target, so she turned the corner to get off Aurora. No matter what her reasoning or who she is that still doesn't give us any information on the driver.

I don't know why I stopped at the morgue except to talk with the ME of comparison on all five victims. The other four have been identified. This one has a couple small tattoos probably from a former life she lived, but nothing else, no jewelry or other identifiers. She reminds me of a missionary with a plain skirt and blouse and flat shoes we only found one of at the scene, suspecting the other is stuck somewhere under the vehicle that hit her, or someone picked it up to wear.

I stop in at the ER seeing Naomi running into a room holding IV bags and change my mind about needing to know who was brought in from the shooting just a few hours ago. That is not my main case anymore but would like to know these things. That is just in my character. Clearly there are other victims, criminals and people with common illnesses who need immediate medical attention. I will go to the cafeteria and take my lunch break alone then return to the

ER or just get the report from the precinct. I was hoping to visit with Naomi tonight but that might not be possible, living our lives impromptu.

I opt for the cafeteria which, to my surprise, is crowded for 3:00 am on a Thursday. I station myself at a table having my back to the wall and a view of the only entry door. Just as I am ready to leave in walks Naomi. I hear her laugh before I see her, she is with a young male med student, they sit with her back to me. I then think I don't know much about our time apart, could there be other people she goes on actual dates with? It appears she knows this person well. I can sense the familiarity between them. On the occasions she comes to the cafeteria with me she is not laughing. At this moment I wish I was the person in front of her and the one being the source of her laughter but realize we have a relationship where we transfer our nightly burdens to each other not the amusing parts. I don't mind being supportive but wish for more. Then it hits me I have never tried for more, been truly supportive and Naomi hasn't asked. I sit at this table by myself analyzing our relationship and know I need to be all in or step out. Giving myself this ultimatum I get up from my vantage point feeling guilty for spying on them, I turn the corner, round the support pole in the center of the seating area and hear her laugh again. She rises, the young man comes around the table and gets behind her to push her chair in. Knowing I have never done that for her with her being so independent, I increase my step to talk with Naomi before she leaves, if only for a second. It is like she can feel me approaching, she turns seeing me, places her hand on the young man's arm asking him to stop and introduces me as her boyfriend to her nephew, Archer. She tells me Archer was saying he never sees his girlfriend anymore. I was laughing while telling him of our first date at Green Lake. The picnic where we fell asleep. Suddenly I know I am all in and not walking away. Archer excuses himself and I take Naomi into my arms kissing her like never before. She is surprised by my actions and as I say I am all in, we know it is time to walk different directions. I delay our separation for a few more minutes and decide to walk with her down the long corridor dodging the floor polisher and return to the nurse's station to look at the white board holding the list of initials, condition and room numbers I may need to inquire about or cross reference to the report I am going to pull up when I leave here.

I walk out of Harborview a new person and wonder how many other people have made life altering decisions before exiting these automatic glass doors. I drive down the hill to the precinct, head to my pseudo office on the third floor, and pull the report from tonight along with the seventeen stolen vehicles. These are only from the past twenty four hours. For some reason even though it is only 4:30 am I feel a need to talk to Don Montgomery. I research for another half an hour placing each piece of evidence on the board, color coding the papers so I can take them with me. That is one of the only drawbacks of this office, maybe I should talk to Chief about relocating here since it appears no one ever uses this office.

I enter the jail interrogation area and talk to the guard; inform him I will be in room 4 and need to speak with Don Montgomery. I know there is not a specific reason to see Don, especially not this time of day but my intuition tells me I need to do this now. Don files in, sits without saying a word, he appears amped up. I have never seen him with this much energy, and he looks at me and states he is a morning person, anything after noon he is too tired to notice. That is how he is managing his time in here. Up before the rest, reading, and in bed before lights out. He asks, "Did you get him, I mean her, no him? I don't know why you are here but figured you wanted information on a recent arrest. I was there that night in the woods you were looking for me, but I didn't kill Meade or roll her down the hill. I saw her being pushed over the edge onto Westlake. I knew it wouldn't look good for me being present at the crime scene, but I loved her. I didn't kill her." I turn to him with doubt covering my entire being and question why he was present at the scene. Before he has a chance to reply I tell him what I heard, he had a long time relationship going on with Meade that no one was supposed to know about, but they were on a date the night she was murdered, everyone knew, and he supplied her drugs after his long awaited visit to town. The ones that possibly killed her, with all victims having the same deficiency causing green fingernails. Don gets up from his chair and backs into the wall, suddenly cold from the reality and his touch of the concrete wall. He yells, "No, no! I didn't kill her. I loved her, that is why I followed her. We were supposed to have a date, and she changed at the last minute telling me something important was happening. I know she belonged to Little Mel's crew, was one of them above all else but when it was too much for her, she would hide out at my trailer. No one suspected our secrets. I don't know the guy she met that night but have been trying to find out. I am being charged with her murder and the others all over western Washington, but it wasn't me who added the different ingredient to the mix. It was Donny and that is why Donny died too; it ruined a good man. I tried to save him, but I was too late. Everyone said wait and since I was only a visitor at Mel's compound and not a resident, I didn't have much say about Donny's transport to the hospital. I was only good for getting side jobs, occasionally selling product and working. Manual labor, I about ruined my body for the meager amount of money I made through them. I lost everything helping them, so I tell myself, but I was sort of accepted by that group."

I sit back and think through what he had said, knowing he was wanted and that is why he fled back in January but why would he return? I ask him why he left suddenly. He responds with, "I had to hide elsewhere. Mel and his crew were going to kill me or at least I thought they were. Maybe it was paranoid thinking. The drugs and reality all mixed into one and then Donny's death tipped my mind over. They said I laced their product, but I had only stolen it out of the woodchipper the night I took Donny to the hospital. It was already tainted but I didn't know anything was wrong. It feels not right to be talking to the police about this but what do I have to lose now? I did do those things but surely didn't kill anyone. I just thought this was my big break when Donny called me for a ride to the hospital. I knew, as his friend, he wouldn't want me to leave the product in the garage adjacent to his room but to keep it safe or at least that is what I told myself as I loaded it into his truck. My conscience told me something different, but I went with the guise of being a good friend and if Donny didn't make it, I would be on easy street. At least for a while."

I ask if all this information is correct, if he is willing to meet with a sketch artist to give us an idea who was with Meade on the night of her murder? He looks up with hope in his eyes. He may be partially telling the truth or not, but it won't hinder my investigation to get a sketch even if he has created a tale to make his sentence shorter. With as many charges as he has racked up, I don't think he will ever get out.

Not wanting to put too much hope on Don Montgomery and his knowledge I ask one more question. "Why were you at the tent when it caught on fire?" He replies, "That's easy. I was delivering the last of Donny's product to Watkins, Steven then Connely, Joe showed up and tried to get his hands in the pile. Isn't he supposed to be on methadone? It was getting a bit crowded in the tent, so I left, or they thought I did. I waited in the tree line within hearing distance. In and around the tent there was Joe at the door, Steven inside who came out when the lady cop arrived shining her flashlight around the area, not helping anyone to be discreet. Steven acted like he was getting into the tent once the cop left but backed up after looking in and laid next to it on the tree line side. Joe walked off as soon as the lady cop arrived, not wanting to be involved. Someone else, I had not seen before mind you, I didn't live there or hang out much, but this person didn't look like they fit in clean, green bandana, chino pants and slip on shoes like they wear in southern California walked over right as the lady cop had turned to leave and lit the tent on fire. I didn't know anyone was inside, the lady cop kept going but I bet Steven Watkins knows who the person was."

I knew there was a reason to pay Don a visit this morning. I ask if he is willing to meet with the sketch artist on this case too. He agrees and asks, "What will happen to me with my charges?" I tell him, "Lets meet next week after the sketch artist appointment and we can work out a plan. I may not be alone with cases of this magnitude. The tainted product alone killed many and you did distribute it and flee. What do you think the lady cop wanted?" He rubs his chin and says, "She made us all swear we had never seen her, but she was up to something in the Duwamish Encampment. She didn't buy anything but whoever was in that tent heard what her and Watkins were discussing. She always wanted information on higher level dealers and not your average corner boy. Where is she now?" I reported, "I honestly don't know." I thanked him for his time and information. We agreed to talk next Wednesday. He stood, thanked me and waited at the door to be released, having the full weight of what he chose to reveal in the open. More connections made this morning, other pieces settling into place. I rise after he leaves, taking my notes and head home to my studio.

I text Jill asking if she wants to have dinner in the near future.

36

Vernon

OCTOBⱻɾ 2025

THIS WEEK HAS FELT harsh. It has affected me like no other since being in Seattle, possibly my entire life except before I joined the Army when the officers knocked on the metal door using their flashlight. That sound has echoed in my head since they notified me of Birdie's death, my only living relative.

I do my best not to make connections with anyone but last week being my first time at Ethan's Edge and trying to help Darius after his incident on the bus, Devon after pulling him away from the drug dealer on Delridge, I thought I was helping. I inquired of Carl if Darius was with Devon, and he verified he was at home. This brought on much needed relief that maybe I had helped getting one on the right path. I also texted Korn to make sure he is keeping out of trouble. He is hanging out in the park with his girlfriend Ringer and is safe, a relief to my mind.

I was hesitant to take on this role after talking to Carl and hearing the story of why Ethan's Edge was started. No matter how much I wanted to help save Devon, maybe it wasn't his choice to get shot but it was his choice to be out dealing or crossing over on the gangers. Technically he was with us last week but was not on the roster. I still wish I could have helped him.

Work has been stressful too, being on the lookout for the usual crimes and safety of my passengers. Not to mention, looking for the blonde curly headed monster who runs people over has added stress. Now the lady has been hit by him, he isn't just going after people who generally hang out on the street but picking anyone he sees and plowing into them. Muncer tells me over twenty vehicles a day are stolen. How would anyone police that and be able to trace the vehicle that may commit a crime?

I think my mind is in a ranting mode ever since Metevior gave me Allard's number. I don't want to talk to her nor will I, not today. If I don't call soon, I know she will pop up on a route, no matter which one I am on. I feel she knows everything and still has control of my life.

I get off work, call Raven who I know I am not acting normal with and that is not my intention. She has so much on her plate at the moment. The tone of her voice tells me she is happy to hear from me. I am quiet and she asks if I am ok. I do not want to leave my burdens on top of hers and assure her I am just tired.

She briefly touches on the top stories of her life. Work is good, Enzo is loving his day care set up with Allison and Patricia from work. They are able to keep him on the days they are off taking care of other family members. The custody paperwork is in limbo with Aleene's passing and will need a court date to modify the original filing. The house is in the process of being transferred over to her and she misses me.

We make plans to go to the pumpkin patch next weekend and as we are ready to hang up, she tells me she knows something is wrong. That is when I know I need to get this Allard thing off my plate before the weekend.

I hang up and call Allard. She answers before I even hear it ring, like she has been waiting for me or someone. I want to meet somewhere public, in the daylight, she wishes to meet now, in the dark. She has the ankle monitor and cannot go cavorting across town. I see her time in the jail hasn't curbed her attitude or her brass knuckled way to handle life. Not trusting being alone with her I ask how far she can go with her monitor. She says to the curb in front of her house or to the alley behind. I know the alley isn't happening so agree to meet her in front of her house on 11th Avenue W.

I wind my way through the city I am still not familiar with to 99. I know I will regret this meeting, with the two of us being the only attendees. I hope she has turned in her service revolver since there will be no witnesses. My thoughts wonder to scenarios of her creating stories of my threatening behavior being a detriment to her safety and this ends bad for me no matter what. GPS alerts me my destination is on the right in 200 feet. I pull over before I need to trying still to keep distance between her and me. I see her on the covered porch just beyond the wooden fence through the low hanging tree, the light shining through the blindless front window behind her. A decent tan house, white shutters, three steps, two black chairs. My mind wanders to anywhere except here. I think I am in the right occupation with my military training and before that growing up in a sketchy neighborhood, I have learned to take it all in and survive up to now. Observe as if your life depended on it, because it might.

Allard rises hearing my footsteps just as I kick a piece of gravel on the way to her gate. Somehow, she doesn't appear menacing and seems rather worn down from her recent untraveled road of awry events, but I know what lies beneath the carefully constructed cover. She is wearing a cream colored cable knit sweater and her usual jean jacket similar to Birdie's. She invites me up the stairs, we sit on the porch, I notice her jacket is torn. She has the control since it is her that has been able to rehearse and know the end results of our conversation for many days now, possibly longer. Without any niceties both of us are aware that is not what we are here for she starts in, "This started many years before now. I didn't know who my rage was propelled to, but it has been you all along. My dad was a cop in Miami, I did everything I could to get out and left Liberty City in 2008 for college, knowing I didn't want to place myself into law enforcement from the start after seeing what my dad went through, but here I sit. Somehow you are to blame." I look over and see rage in her eyes, her hands gripping the ends of the arms of the worn wooden patio chair, she pulls at the tie that is supposed to be holding the pink and white cushion in place. Running her statement through my mind I cannot figure out why she thinks I am the cause of any of her insane behavior.

She starts in again, catching her breath, "I wish I smoked or drank that would be appropriate for this occasion, but the cold night will have to be comfort enough. I didn't know you were involved at all in my fifteen year dilemma but when I returned after college dad left some files on the table with the names Birdie Edwards and Vernon Cannon listed on the first page. I finally knew you were the end cause of whom I had lost control over for so many years. The lady who stole my oranges, every day, was Birdie. Birdie Edwards and you probably sat at a table eating them. It was my mission to stop her, and she always won." She gets up pacing the length of the porch, I am stunned by her accusations but know she is correct, but I didn't steal the oranges.

She starts up again, "I know she stole them for years because I used to run her off a few times a week. In fact, if she had asked, we would have given them to her, there were plenty. We didn't need an entire tree full. My father was the notifying officer, I don't know what happened that morning, but I snapped since I had fought the battle with her all through high school and now on the day I return from college. Criminal Justice is what I studied; my dad was so proud. I am sitting outside reading a magazine, relaxing and hear the crisp snap of the picked fruit and movement in the tree. I suppose she had gone on with her thievery for another four years with my absence and felt it was fine."

She sits back down in the chair next to me, my keys in hand just inside my pocket, I am prepared to jump the porch rail and wooden fence and make a break past her allotted area and peel out of here but now I hope to hear the end of her story. Almost at a whisper she proceeds, "That hippie lady, Birdie as I know now, I wasn't aware of her name before her death. She looked at me surprised as she plucked two oranges off the tree, her daily ration. I hopped the fence, in pursuit, with her having the lead. She headed toward the water. We ran a considerable distance, she was fast, must have been the oranges but she rounded a blue vehicle parked at the curb, hopped from rock to rock entering the area of the beach and fell. I turned back as soon as I saw her go down. I wasn't there and didn't see anything so I couldn't call for help. You understand she stole for you, and I was the cause of her death because of you. This has been a burden I have carried for more than a decade and that is why when I saw your name I came after you. You." She was huffing, pointing at me with her accusations not able to catch her breath, breathing through her mouth. The late night air blowing steam clouds into the porch in front of her face.

I consider rising from this chair, getting in my Jeep and driving home but then think of the possibility of cameras, proof of text messages from me to her one containing this address, proof that I at least knew where she was and knew I must do the right thing for my conscience. I pick up my phone to call 911 and she hits my arm and shakes her head so hard it appears she may do harm to herself. My phone becomes airborne and lands on the bottom step. I bring her story to mind; she was the cause of my mother's death. Birdie, I miss her and need to stop at the grocery store on the way home for oranges and English muffins. I sit on the stairs retrieving my phone from the bottom step, looking back at Allard who grasps her chest and yells, "No, don't call anyone." I suddenly know I will have no part in releasing her from the misery she has caused herself, me and most of all Birdie. I go to the wooden gate and dial 911, then text Muncer to have a witness and friend.

37

Detective Muncer

OCTOBER 2025

I WAS JUST PREPARING to leave the scene of another hit and run when I received a text from Metro. He said he needed me now, leaving an address and the name Allard pops up on my screen his second message. I text back, enroute. As soon as I leave the scene and turn around to head to south, the radio always has chatter, but I hear a medical emergency on 11th Avenue W, female. I don't listen to the rest but hope Metro hasn't endangered himself being in Allard's vicinity or hurt her. I know she always came down unnecessarily hard on him, hoping they didn't come to blows. I can't imagine why they would be together but then recall the nighttime meeting I have had with him that were off the books. Maybe they were setting things straight. I bring myself back to the night of my undercover bus ride and her fury with him then with me a stranger, or so she thought. All I can do now is arrive at the scene whatever it holds, take notes and be there for Metro, hoping I don't have to arrest him.

I think of the vehicle, a gold Nissan, used in the latest hit and run. One that had been reported stolen four days prior. The driver and scene fit the same description, hitting someone, a sixth victim pushing a shopping cart full of their earthly belongings, minding their own business and then it was over. The victim precisely hit to kill, and their wares strewn across the road with onlookers thinking they have found treasure. Just like the other five, except this time the driver took off and abandoned the vehicle a couple blocks away instead of at the scene, and he did not have curly blonde hair but was completely bald. Do we have a copycat, or has he changed up his MO? These are all questions I ask myself and know Chief Stewart will want the answers to in the morning.

I see Metro's Jeep parked at the curb up on the right. I don't know whose residence he is at but pull in behind him, take in all the emergency vehicles on site, get out and walk two houses up to the address he had provided. Seeing him on the sidewalk with an SFD officer who is taking notes I know for sure he was a witness to something. An ambulance carrying a female patient, who appears unconscious, that I cannot see due to the paramedics working on her and a couple patrol officers linger over her in the area waiting for the all clear to leave. The scene is quiet and there may not have been a crime committed here at all. As I near the gate, I see the female being loaded into the ambulance. If I am not mistaken that is Allard on the gurney. Metro spots me surveying the scene and walks over, his first words were, "I know I shouldn't have come here alone but am so glad I did." I don't know what that sentence holds yet and hope that wasn't a confession since I like Metro and don't want to arrest him.

He asks if I will follow him up to the porch to make sure the doors are locked on Allard's house. Then he turns to me with a quizzical look on his face, "Do you think that is right to lock her doors? What do police do in this situation?" I see the ambulance pull away before I have any idea what has happened and if we will need forensics. I suggest we sit on the porch and Metro tell me the story. He looks at me and says, "She may die for oranges." I think back on what Metevior said, it was about oranges.

I sit in the chair and Metro tells me he can't sit in the other one after what he had just witnessed, it was the chair Allard had occupied, it is bad enough being on her porch. He takes me through the story that began a few days prior with Metevior stopping him and asked me to keep that quiet since no crime had been committed then proceeded to tonight and his call to Allard needing to get the encounter over with. The story that began in Florida nearly two decades ago and brought me up to today. He ends with, "Allard wanted to die but I couldn't give her that satisfaction. My call to 911 would be my gift to her after the fault she finds in me."

I walk through the house ensuring the windows and doors are all locked and ask Metro if he would like to stop at Denny's on 4th Ave for an English muffin and an orange to celebrate the commitment Birdie had exercised all the years to bring food home as she walked through the streets of Florida. Metro smiled. I could see a relief wash over him as we returned to our vehicles. I don't know what condition Allard is in but will check on her later.

During my meal with Metro, I tell him the story of my family and he gives me background on Birdie. I return to the precinct and retrieve Don Montgomery's file from upstairs, wind through the maze of hallways badging through and wait at the guard's station for one to return. I ask for Don to be brought to room 4. He types in the name and informs me Don Montgomery is no longer in custody at this facility. I recall our recent meeting, and he was going to meet with the sketch artist on two cases. Now I am being told he is not here. I check the file and see the appointment date with the sketch artist was two days prior, but the notes state Don Montgomery failed to appear. I ask to speak to the Seargent on duty, he is at lunch and no other information is available except the word confidential is stamped in red on the last page. I return with the file up to my office and check jail records for the days following our meeting. It appears Don, not being the sharpest tack in the box, traveled from cell to cell asking the Mexican gangs about each other's activities. They nearly took him out. He had a picture drawn in pencil that he created, was pulling it out of his pocket and asking if anyone knew the guy, thinking he was making his big break his own way. It was almost like a stickman drawing but they knew he was up to something, and it wasn't going to help anyone on the inside or the cause of their trade on the outside.

I know visiting hours are over at the hospital, but I could show up to find out if Don Montgomery is a patient and visit with Naomi. The guard at the ER entrance of Harborview says they are not holding him there. I know then that he has been placed in solitary confinement or in a hospital somewhere. Most of our cases are sent to Harborview.

Seattle Autumn Fallin'

(Verse1)

Rain slicked streets, the leaves are turnin brown,

callin' got cases comin' down.

Falling solving, code is my detective tool,

Running alleys, chasing those breakin' every single rule.

Untimely deaths, data points aligned,

Algorithm's hummin', try to leave no soul behind.

(Chorus)

Seattle's my domain,

Autumn's chill, but justice is the aim.

Burning tents, encampments in the night,

Gotta find the truth, expose it to the light.

(Verse 2)

Civilians scared, sketch artists on the scene,

Building digital portraits, sharp and keen.

Processing data, patterns start to form,

Predictive analysis weathering the storm.

From Queen Anne Hill to the International District

My neural network's lockin' on the culprit, listen quick!

(Chorus)

(Bridge)

Got terabytes of info, runnin' parallel.

No human can handle this, that's what I tell.

Unraveling the mystery, layer by layer,

This city's secrets, on either side of the law, I'm the only player.

    (Verse 3)

Seattle Autumn, skies are fallin gray

Another case dropped in my data array.

Silicon brain, aint no night time for sleep

Untimely deaths. Secrets buried deep.

Runnin' alleys, codin' as I creep

Got the city's heartbeat, analyze and steep.

Burning tents, drone and a digital scan

Encampments hummin, part of the city's plan

    (Chorus)

    (Verse 4)

No need for hunches, facts are all I crave,

Byte by byte, a city to enslave.

With logic gates and algorithms tight

Unraveling the mysteries of the Seattle night.

Sketch artists render, every pixelated moustache precise.

Trackin movements, payin the ultimate price.

For secrets hidden, in the rain soaked street,

Comin' for you, can't escape the heat.

    (Chorus)

    (Verse 5)

On the digital grind, solvin' , creatin' crimes, leavin' none behind.

Civilians sketchin' witnessin' the dread I'm breakin' down the data,

planted in your head!

Autumn leaves fallin', code is coming alive

Seattle whispers, I can make 'em thrive.

From the waterfront docks to the Space Needle's gleam

Justice fulfillin' the dream!

(Outro)

Seattle, Seattle, my algorithms bite,

Justice served, bathed in the digital light.

Word up. Seattle Autumn, we on the case!

Keep your secrets, I'll find your digital trace!

#Seattle Strong #DJ Muncer #mun det J

38

Detective Muncer

MONDAY MORNING STARTS WITH a meeting intended for day shift and me since I am the lead detective on the hit and run cases. We don't have any information to go off of. Everyone, including Chief Stewart, wants this guy off the street, not today but yesterday due to the urgency for the sake of our department and its reputation to protect the city and its citizens. The media is having a heyday with this story, not blowing it out proportions but it is the top story nearly every night for the past month, even though an incident doesn't occur daily the newscasts are on repeat filling any empty spot. I am sure as a department we are doing all we can, but we need everyone in the city to keep their eyes out for anything unusual. I went home after the meeting feeling defeated and overwhelmed with everyone directing their questions at me and I don't have any answers. I am no further along in this case than I was on day one.

About noon I receive a text from Jill asking if we can meet for dinner tonight someplace private or if tonight is not enough notice another day will be fine. We confirm for 5:30 pm at my place. I need to know what is going on with her after these past few weeks with her acting as if she needs to talk then becomes evasive.

It seems like ten minutes since I had stopped responding to Jill and I get back to sleep my service phone rings. Hazel being on the end of this daytime call tells me there has been a message for me from Randy Eason, who wishes to meet with me only, at the southeast corner of 47th and Fremont at 2:00 pm. He will be driving a green Toyota Sienna; says it is important, and he will be there whether I show up or not. I get up with the decision being made for me of being sleep deprived today, running on someone else's schedule, starting with the meeting this morning and hope by the end of this day I will have answers to something.

I leave at 1:30 pm, arrive at the intersection, not wishing to meet anyone I don't have any information about, but they only had plans to talk to me. As I circle the block, I see a male about 40 years old, slight build, wavy hair. Somehow, he looks familiar, but I cannot attach him to a scene or case. He walks around the van, opens the back hatch and sits in the rear compartment. His arms crossed, leg tapping the pavement releasing nervous energy. I pull up behind him and am comfortable with the fact he does not have many places to conceal a weapon. His t shirt hangs off him like he bought the wrong size. When he stands, I see his pants have the same problem as he inches them up towards his nonexistent hips. His skin is a sickly shade of gray.

He puts out his hand to shake mine introducing himself as Randy Eason. Then proceeds on with the story, "I think I have information you may be looking for. There is a high probability my brother Ricon could be your hit and run killer. I don't have one hundred percent proof. Let me tell you about him. Our family owns a repossession company, cars. Car lots hire us to go after the ones unpaid. Ricon, being a year older than me, was next in line to run the show after our dad was unable to operate it due to age and health. Ricon got himself all hooked up on pills, smoking them, even in our driveway. Dad turned the shop over to me. Ricon is clean now and has been for a few months but that doesn't mean dad will undo the decision of placing me in charge of operations. This is a bonded position, one of credibility and Ricon has not proven himself. We have had this business in our family for over forty years, dad built it from scratch. Lately he says he is detailing and flipping cars. There have been six or more in the past couple of months. He would bring one home," as he points towards Aurora and says, "nearly a block up there in the alley. I heard on the news you were the man in charge of this case and didn't want to speak to anyone else. I put this together in the middle of the night, my suspicion is Ricon is using my equipment, slim jims and such to steal the cars and parking them in the garage bay we only use for storage if the business that requested the repossession is not open when we locate the vehicle. An hour or so ago Ricon took off with the Toyota Prius, I don't know why he would choose such a small vehicle to complete his next assignment, but this is where we are."

I find the speech pattern and Randy's choice of words don't line up well. Just then he adds, "I have brain cancer and hope I put that story together right. I went down to get the license plate before meeting you, the vehicle and Ricon were gone."

Randy gives me his contact information including the address and making certain I know the garage access is in the alley. We make our way over there parking in front so as not to alert Ricon of our presence if he is here. The garage is empty, and tools are on the wall neatly stored including the slim jim. I thank Randy, give him my contact information, and wish him well not being sure what to include about his health.

Just as I walk through the side yard dodging ivy that is growing up the chimney and exit through the perfectly manicured gardens, I hear the radio nonstop in my cruiser and know it will be a long day.

I listen to the radio but am not tuned in lacking sleep and this is not my shift. Then I hear "Toyota Prius, 9th and Lenora, hit and run, left the vehicle at 9th and Virginia, one victim down and deceased, suspect on foot bald, white male, fled northbound on Virginia, fleeing behind alley of hotels, entered the free shower program area, exited through the back, chasing him eastbound on Boren, over I-5 to Plymouth Pillars Park and he is gone. Waiting on K-9." The chatter has gone nearly silent. I may not be there physically, they have it under control, I call Chief Stewart and give him the information from my meeting with Randy about Ricon and give him a recap of the incident that happened in case he had not heard. I return home and nap until Jill arrives with sandwiches, a bag of chips, and sodas from the deli up the road. Dinner never tasted so good. Jill seemed preoccupied then blurted out, "I lived with mom and dad, then Mexico, and you, now Hector. I feel like there has always been authority over me and I want to be free without hurting Hector. He doesn't tell me what to do but we are always together." I know there is a fine line to be walked here with my advice, being as I am not good with relationships, so I ask, "What are your plans?" I know Jill was looking for answers from me, but I don't have them. She replies, "Raven was going to move in with us but now has her own place and I think I would like to ask her about renting a room while still dating Hector, if he still will have me. I don't want to lose him. Maybe it would be different if it wasn't Hector's grandpa's place, but he is not leaving anytime soon."

I know the fine line between professionalism and family safety is becoming thinner but waffle between telling Jill about Raven and her previous circumstances and the Raven I know. I opt on not swaying her either direction and tell her to make sure she weighs any decision she makes by the end result. She says, "I will ask Jill if I can stay the weekend and then decide. Hector will be studying for his final exams the weekend I go." She seems excited when she says, "Hector will be a real detective," then looks at me realizing her choice of words may be slightly off and adds, "but not one like you." I am not entirely sure if that was a compliment or not, but I thank her for dinner and offer her a ride home knowing one then two hours of sleep will be all I get this time around before I start my long shift tonight.

I drop Jill off and ask if she is positive about going home, she nods yes and says, "I love Hector, I just don't know the alone me. Maybe I will take up a hobby instead of leaving." I wait until Jill gets through the enormous doors of the building, waves and starts her ascent up the wooden stairs. As I turn the corner on 1st and Yesler under the Pergola pushed up along the fence line I spot the back of a bald head sticking out of a new red sleeping bag. Both bald and new generally are not words that describe the population in that area, at least the ones who sleep on the ground. I circle the block, find parking at one of the few spots on Yesler, walk over and call him by name, "Ricon, it's time to go." He gets up, starts to run in place as if unimpeded except I was holding the belt loop on his freshly ironed blue jeans. He did not blend into his surroundings with his recently acquired sleeping bag. I know these pants have enough starch in them to last until he gets out of jail, which may be never.

I call this in as he sits on the now vacant bench, the previous residents fleeing as soon as they detected I was police. Ricon tells the story of his deep seated anger with drugs and himself. He had been in counseling for a while and was at the stage of assigning blame, so he has dug down deep enough to know it is not his dad or Randy he is mad at. It was himself and the poor choice of drugs. He goes on to say, "I ran them over so they wouldn't have to go through the process of getting free and seeing what they lost out on in the time they weren't sober or maybe not be free at all and live in misery. I helped them. Twisted mind."

39

Detective Muncer

NOVEMBER 2025

DON MONTGOMERY IS STILL missing, under protective custody somewhere. I hear the VA, Swedish, out of the area but no one will tell me where he is a key witness in two of my investigations. Chief Stewart informs me it is for the best that he remains off the grid. Meanwhile I know he has information that I need. Without him some of the facts could be missed.

Two weeks after my meeting with the chief my phone rings about 3:00 am from an unknown number. The voice on the other end is barely above a whisper. It is Don, always a wise crack, says he outsmarted the guards in that seedy joint. I ask where I can meet with him, maybe we can draw the sketches. I ask him this to let him know I feel he is a priority and still remains useful. I know neither of us can draw but I can get a description from him in the process. I grab a tablet and pencil on my way out.

We agree to meet at the on the dock at the Arboretum Waterfront Trail on Foster Island at 5:20 am. I don't know why he has picked this remote location, but I will be there and take him into custody after my interview. These are possibly the longest two hours of any shift I have ever spent. After repeatedly combing through the files pertaining to the tent fire and Meade's death, I drive through town thinking of Jill and her decisions. How I was not any help but didn't wish to influence her. If things went wrong after, these would have to be her decision. I know I need to interview Ricon Eason but that can wait until the end of this unexpected meeting. Ricon isn't going anywhere.

I pull into the parking area for Foster Island under 520, giving myself ample time to hike the trail and locate Don somewhere on the length of the bridge overlooking Lake Washington. I quickly change out of my required dress shoes into my runners. The morning holds a crispness in the air with winter creeping in, the sun rise has nearly begun, and I am going through the woods, across an isolated island to meet a serial killer who is in denial of his crimes. Who is the crazy person in this story? He is undoubtedly here to bargain but I will be escorting him back to the precinct with my information in place. The Chief will need to find a safe secure placement for him. I wonder if they are aware he is missing from whatever facility he was being held at.

I easily find him after a twenty-minute hike taking longer due to darkness. He sits in a self-made chair of sticks and small logs. His first words to me were, "I am a survivalist and lived in the mountains on my own. I owned property in the hills." I don't know how to respond to that so ask him, "What do you want the outcome from our meeting to be?" He looks at me his eyes on the water, points quietly and says, "Fish, oh ya, I don't track well since the accident.

My head doesn't process right." Then lifts his shirt showing his white thick scar from ribcage to the shadow of his dirty neck winding around the back and when he turns away from me, I can tell one side of his head is now concaved. The hair growing in many directions, he looks at me and says, "Don't tell anyone but my memory is gone. I only know a few things. If I was returned to the location where they did this to me, I would be killed. I will never be safe anywhere. I need your help."

My hopes of recreating the suspects are slimmer than I thought and wonder what I am doing here on this cold morning holding a tablet and pencil as the wind whips off the lake through my thin required trousers.

Don kicks the poorly constructed pile of sticks chair off to the side making sure it is in the bushes talking under his breath about not leaving evidence of his location and people tripping. He clearly thinks we will have a conversation here at sunrise and he will walk away. I figure this is as good of time as any to start my interview, pull out my pocket recorder and ask for his consent to record our conversation. He nods yes and we proceed.

DJM: Don where were you the night Meade Wells was murdered?

DM: I was there on 8th Ave where Raven was supposed to meet the cop man with information. She was out by the garage, I heard her side of the conversation while talking on the phone a few days before, arranging the location. I didn't know she was hooking up with the police, this took me by surprise. Going back that far my mind is fuzzy.

He stops and holds the dented side of his head, pressing too hard then realizing it is him causing his pain and looks up at me. I figure it is time for the next question. I didn't come out here to leave without some answers.

DJM: Don, I think you are doing well. Why was Meade at the location Raven was supposed to be at on that night back in January?

DM: They didn't know but I would follow them around if I saw anyone disappear because I knew they were telling secrets, tucked away in the garage behind the woodchipper or in the back of the house near the fence line. The lady insisted Raven bring food to her child on the same night as the cop said he needed information. Raven tried to arrange another time with both of them, but the lady and cop would not budge.

DJM: Where did Raven go and where did Meade go?

DM: Raven sent Meade to meet the lady with food. I saw them carefully picking out clothing so they would look identical only at the last moment Meade insisted on meeting the cop. She said she was not going be alone with that crazy lady. She had done that another time and couldn't answer the questions and Enzo kept asking for his mom. He knew she wasn't Raven.

DJM: I'll ask you again. Where did Raven go and where did Meade go?

DM: Raven was on the balcony at the fourplex with a man, I think. I am so confused, I loved Meade, she was the one for me. Now I am not positive if that was Raven or Meade up on the balcony. He had dark hair, shorter guy, lanky, wearing a flannel like the one Mel used with the sleeve patches. I was across the alley in the trees trying to watch when the man with the cart filled with aluminum stopped his journey right at the base of the stairs and blocked my view, while he watched the fight between Raven and the man. I needed to know who the cop was, that is why I was there and to see if Raven really met the cops away from the compound. I had a hard time believing that. Was it you she was going to meet? You showed up not long after her body was discovered.

DJM: Raven was meeting another detective not me.

DM: The man and Raven were fighting on the balcony at the picnic table, then I heard him say "You are not getting in the way of my plan. You are not meeting with any cops; this is my business you are getting in. I will lose it all if you spill the story, any of it." Once he stood up, I recognized him, don't know why I didn't know before. Steven Watkins had taken his hood off, then he pulled a syringe out of his front pocket. She stood to flee down the stairs, but he grabbed her arm and threw her under the table, and I saw the syringe he was holding up in the air, the half wall blocking my view of Raven. I assume he injected her because she never got back up. I sat in the woods and cried. If it was Raven or Meade that died that night, I loved them both. One as my girlfriend the other her sister.

Don sits down on a log and rubs the concave part of his scalp so deeply I am alarmed for his safety. He says he is not ready to draw or answer any more questions. Then pulls out a western silver lighter, lights an odd looking uneven cigarette, takes a drag and slumps over. He is clearly gone in seconds. I suspect he took a dose of his own tainted product on purpose after releasing his story but only a portion of it. He knew he could never return back to general population in prison after his antics before getting beat up. I see a note has fallen from his coat along with his cigarette pack. These are not items I am prepared to touch. I call this in, having ample time to think through the story I had just heard. I am unsure about revealing the tale recently told to me about Raven and Meade, knowing there is the fate of a little boy involved, Rubio's grandson. He thinks Raven is alive and doesn't have doubt. Neither Raven nor Meade had been convicted of anything except possibly poor choices. I believe the story should not be spoken unless the note contains more than was revealed to me.

Don lays on the uneven dew covered ground, dead brown fern sprouts lie under his body, the evidence of a former life in both species. The sun has risen in the amount of time it took him to tell his version of this complicated story. I didn't have time to ask him anymore details about the male and the burning tent, another story connected but separate from Meade, Raven and this scene here. The furthest thing from my mind was for him to make an escape route from this situation after transferring his burden to me. It was clearly premeditated; Don being done with his travels and life in Seattle. The morning is calm now with only me and what remains of Don Montgomery here along the shoreline of the lake. I listen to the waves lapping up along the pylons supporting the weight of the dock and think of Metro, his lake, Gus, Raven, Enzo, Aleene and her past life knowing the root of this is all connected. The chatter is what has killed a few, destroyed many others and my silence will cover some. I picture myself seeing Raven next time and will always wonder who she truly is. I hear the radios through the quietness of the morning coming up the trail towards me, patrol interrupts my cherished silence and is here to make a report, it being one I will turn in, written carefully omitting pieces of the story. The medical examiner shows up for transport, there is not a crime scene for forensics to inspect or preserve except the careful removal of the cigarette pack. The note that I had laid out with my foot and taken a picture of has blown away into the brush along the shoreline, nonexistent but may hold answers to my case, a secret at this moment between Don Montgomery and me. I walk the twenty minutes back to my cruiser and drop my runners in the garbage can. I drive home and piece together what I can. Then I think of Jill who may possibly be moving with Meade or Raven, fear takes over me then I realize I don't know Jill either, not the one who surfaced in Seattle less than a year ago, last February. A day to remember, add facts to my case, miss souls who have laid it all down for their cause. Don Montgomery was always on the hunt for his next big break and has had a cross country vacation, love, helped others while not doing what was best for him. A man in denial following his drugs, the only authentic priority. There are many out there like him, this brings back memory of Loretta Ethan's mom, both sad cases.

40

Vernon

I HAVE BEEN VOLUNTEERING at Ethan's Edge for four weeks now. Kernal has been keeping up his end of the bargain—showing up on time, volunteering for extra shifts and staying out of trouble on his off time. Once, when we had an assignment close to where Devon was killed, Kernal stopped and surveyed the memorial of dead flowers, photos, wet stuffed animals, and crime scene tape that someone surrounded the area with, placing Devons memory in a cocoon. He looked at me after and said, "Thank you." I knew Kernal didn't have much parental guidance, but he was appreciative of the guarantee I gave him to finish the twelve week program by giving him three hours weekly. Even Ringer showed up a couple of times and helped.

Carl is easy to work with, he even assisted in the funeral arrangements for Devon at City Square Cemetery. I had never attended a funeral before but felt I should be present at this one in support of his family and Darius. I felt I had a part in trying to save both these boys. Muncer was in attendance also, off in the background talking with an employee of the cemetery, surveying the crowd for suspects.

The one responsible for this early death and the shooting of Darius. Both victims Darius and Devon were shot with the same weapon, the connection being mistaken identity on Darius. The two boys being cousins are similar in stature and style.

Muncer told me there is a possible suspect on the loose. The night with Darius still remains the most frightening night of my life, the one closest to death for me. The single event that makes me reconsider my job every day that I board the northbound Rapid Line E and start the continuous loop for eight hours. One day I won't be doing this anymore but for today I will get on the bus wearing my concealed badge and act as a passenger in memory of all the Devons out there and try to prevent anymore from going down a similar road.

The funeral made me wonder what happened to Birdie after she had passed. I had technically just become an adult. I feel guilt now after attending this event. I should have had a service for Birdie on the beach. Surely, she had friends there or maybe she partied with tourists selling her homemade goods. I don't know because I didn't know her, there had been no way to crack the shell to her being. I should have made sure she was taken care of but what would that have entailed? I didn't have money, except the change and a few bills stored in the can and needed freedom, no matter what if I didn't leave or missed my appointment to tend to her, I am positive my outcome would have been different. The postponement of my enlistment may not have brought me here to this cemetery. With my mind flopping from the what ifs, I think maybe I should have asked my recruiter, but I just needed to leave on the date I had committed to. No matter what else happened Birdie was still gone, I couldn't have changed that fact. I have a sudden craving for oranges, more so now that I know the actual story that started over 3000 miles from here under the humidity and whispering palm trees. Maybe Allard and I were supposed to meet right here in Seattle to heal from that story in some way. Hers being a near death experience and my freedom.

I haven't seen Raven in a few days, we are communicating mostly through texts. Full time motherhood suddenly being placed on her has worn her down. Enzo, or any three year old, is a full time job. Of course, Raven has lost her sister, Evelyn and Aleene in a short period of time and started a new job. They were all close to her and each part of the structure for keeping Enzo safe. The custody case is unusual due to Aleene being deceased and no other relatives were named in the original file. Raven has been given temporary custody on a trial basis for six months requiring her to report for weekly drug testing. I wish I could help out more, but she is doing fine, doesn't appear to want help and with my schedule and hers not coinciding time is limited. She is asleep most nights when I get off work, so we have a system. If she is awake at 11:00 pm she will call or text. If not, I will see her on the following weekend. This weekend we are supposed to go to a movie just the two of us. Our first planned date, there have been other times together, but this is a conscience decision. She has made to be with me and has arranged for Jill to stay with Enzo on Saturday night saying Jill is a long story at this point. My worries are not with Jill, I am simply happy Raven has enough time in her life for everything and is including me.

I hear from Raven Friday when I am on my route still. She tells me Jill has made the decision to leave Hector and stay with her for a short while. She briefly tells me of Jill's Mexico tale, including the whole family being abducted. It is the same story Muncer told me at the diner, but I do not let on that I have heard it before. It is good to hear her voice no matter what the story is. I think of Muncer and his missing family, a solo warrior in the city, and can sympathize with that. Then Jill arrives and she needs her to show her where to put her suitcase. Not wishing to end our conversation Raven talks of her job, reminds me of our kiss on the corner of 8th and Westlake and says she has to go tend to Enzo and his bedtime routine. We make plans for Saturday and hang up on my third southbound trip just as I see a rather tall female outside of window man's apartment. She is slipping through the door with the stature and walk of Allard except she is wearing a large poncho raincoat and gray sweatpants on this evening where there are no clouds in the sky or any chance of rain. I have only seen her wearing the ankle length straight leg denim pants and a jean jacket before this. Every part of my being wants to get off at the next stop and watch his apartment until that person comes out, but I remain in place not getting myself further involved.

The anxiety I felt daily when reporting to my shift had disappeared on account of Allard being detained in jail then the lengthy hospital stay but now, she has obviously returned to the streets. I know that was her, I can feel it anytime when she is around. On my trip northbound I see the curtain is closed on the window facing the street with window man not anywhere in sight. The lights are off including his porch light. I picture her in there with access to whatever he controls which may not be much, but he has something she requires, or she would not be there. She is a user of people, and he will take what she offers in return wanting to please and being fearful of her simultaneously. I text Muncer who may need this bit of news. I cannot tell from his response if it is helpful or not because he has only texted asking, how long have you known Raven? How is she? I have a strange feeling about his questions and then being priority over Allard's escapade makes it feel off. I respond with she is good. I know this tells him I am still in contact with her. The police are definitely interested in her for some reason but not enough to arrest her. Then respond with I have known her since about August. Is there something I should know? He texts back saying he is just concerned about her wellbeing after the news he delivered and hearing of Aleene. I know there is more to the story but there is no one to ask that would reveal the actual truth so here I am waiting for it to unveil.

41

Detective Muncer

THE WEEK HAS BEEN long, it feels like we went through one extended lengthy season in seven days. The case of the burning tent, the extensive hit and run file to now I feel I have not had a chance to rest. Today staying home is my priority. I sit and think of my recent and final visit with Don Montgomery. I wonder why he planned to spill his story and end it all. His admission of facts was not concrete so bear no weight in my actual case only faltering concrete evidence in my head. Our talk reminds me of a jury trial when an item is brought to the front and that bit of information is stricken from the trial. The jury still saw that item and is reminded of an altering fact like is that Raven or Meade. He would have never been returned to general population anywhere in our prison system. He probably would have been placed in custody at Maple Lane as he had requested from the beginning, with a large portion of his skull missing he was considered disabled, if not insane, or at least his last action qualified him to be placed in that category. Although during our last interview he had the answers, was his inability to remember simply an act to stay out of the general population?

With the days becoming shorter, I prefer this time of year. The quietness after a long summer of activity on the streets, cases are finally being wrapped up and the heat has dissipated from the buildings and sidewalks. I walk over to my recliner; a place Jill had been curled up in during her first few days staying here. I sit and rest for what feels like hours, but it was only seventeen minutes according to the digital clock on my end table, when my service phone rings Agent Ford's name flashing across the screen. I answer immediately as the call feels urgent, this morning just as the sun has risen. Agent Ford starting his day and I am attempting to end my shift and prepare for tomorrow which I feel may be starting now.

His speech pattern is nearly animated from the beginning of our conversation. He spills out, "Jeffery how fast can you pack?" I am obviously behind in the storyline and wonder where I am traveling to. I know he doesn't make mistakes like this phone call, but it and his words feel out of place with my previous thoughts of sleep. The morning is opening up to a new possibility, I just don't know what. I hear him shuffling papers and not answering my simple question of, "why?" He comes back to me, still shuffling papers, as if he cannot find the sheet he is searching for, I hear typing in the background. "We are going to Oaxaca. Our flights are booked for 12:06 pm today. We have found your parents in separate facilities." My first thought is to contact Jill as he says, "This is between you and me at the moment. Normally I wouldn't involve any family members, keep the operation under wraps until all victims are safely in custody. I would just go in and retrieve the individual/individuals who have been missing and then contact next of kin. Don't let on to Jill where you are going, we don't want to tip off anyone there." Then he says something that surprises me, "I thank Jill for her help in this situation. We may not have ever gotten this far in the investigation if she had not given us the information, but we don't actually know her or her motives." I know Jill appears naïve but don't think she has any ill intentions, but Agent Ford is correct we do not know Jill and the actual story of how she left Mexico. I think back to why didn't she stop at the border and insist on talking to me, have them call Seattle PD? Now my doubt about her story has heightened as I pull my old backpack down from the closet and locate my clothing .

Agent Ford gives me instructions to meet him at his office, not to call into work or anywhere else to let them know you will be gone. "I will be waiting in the lobby for you at 10:00 am." I have only dealt with him in a professional manner on some cases, listened to his opinion and had a few meals with him but this situation is different. He is on a case I have thought would never come to fruition and he is in charge. I am always in charge; this will be a learning experience. I am not entirely sure his words have sunk in yet. My mom and dad, Margaret and Keith Muncer are coming home. I pack my hiking backpack to use as a carry on, remembering my trip to Tempe a few years ago and the hot days I was stuck there. I only pack light weight clothing, bringing a set of off duty clothes and call an Uber, leaving my cruiser at the curb. I wait outside watching the boats travel through the Fremont Cut and listen to the heavy sound of traffic on the Aurora Bridge and suddenly wonder if I will ever return here again. Will I be able to spend Thanksgiving with Naomi? I should have made plans earlier and a list. What about Everett and Micky? Why would I think all these thoughts? Because I have no idea what we are going into, only that I am on board. I assure myself that I will return on the same flight as my parents. My Uber pulls up, Jill had insisted I download the app after she bought her first cell phone. She loved the idea of getting a ride or food delivered.

I brought my badge, though I am uncertain if this is appropriate, but have left my service revolver securely locked in my safe at home and question whether that was the correct decision. This is the first instance since joining the force that I have been without it, and I feel as though a part of me is missing.

The driver takes me across the bridge and to 3rd Avenue as the app instructed him to. He has an accent; I am not certain of his origin and listen during our trip as he tells stories of his travels through the city at a right rate of speed. I do not share any of mine as they would not top his enthusiasm with my mind being in Mexico, a place I have never physically been. He drops me as close as he can to the entrance of the FBI headquarters since cars cannot enter 3rd Avenue on that block. I thank him, handing him a $20 bill as a tip as he looks me in the eye and says quietly as if to conceal his thoughts, "FBI man." I whisper in return, "Something like that. Thank you for the ride." I close the car door, feeling strange that I rode in the back seat and enter the empty lobby only holding Agent Ford sitting with his laptop open. He asks me to sit, and we look at topography. The pillared Oaxaca International Airport and surroundings, a mountainous countryside. He quickly locates the two assisted living facilities where my parents are staying, "mother" as he points to one and, "father," pointing to another, blocks apart. "I always familiarize myself with an area before entering any active scene. We will be meeting with the Federal Ministerial Police upon arrival and traveling with them to the locations. I don't know what shape your parents are in but from the reports I read your father is well enough to conduct karaoke and your mother leads a newly formed crochet class. The only pierce of information your father appears to remember from America is the word Jeffery, who he tries to get the nurses to call every night before bed since his arrival last month. They both speak fluent Spanish and do not communicate in English well according to the doctor's files that were released. Because of the information Jill released to us we may have uncovered many long awaited missing individuals in these two homes. We never had a reason to perform a search of elderly facilities until now. This will be an ongoing investigation, but your mother and father will be the first out before any other cases are investigated. I have our tickets; do you have any questions?" I shake my head no as I absorb the enormity of this flight. I do as Agent Ford does and grab my bag, still in shock that he has been working behind the scenes on this investigation. These are my parents but to him they are a piece of the American public and it is his mission to protect them which includes retrieval and confidentiality. He didn't let on to me about his progress in this investigation ever. I will not ask when he received the information. I am fortunate he trusted me enough to include me on this trip. I will be in Mexico, reunited with my parents who may or may not know me by the time I call in absent for my shift tonight.

I think of Agent Ford whose jurisdiction borders end on both coasts, east and west and in respect to mine I have a miniscule amount of square miles then my authority ends. I think of the line Rubio and I cross frequently to solve cases and wonder what new developments are happening with him. We pass through customs with Agent Ford showing his credentials in the leather wallet like pouch with a window, I flash my badge behind him thankful I brought it along and am positive security thinks I am part of the FBI. No questions are asked about me once he has been screened. We board ahead of all other passengers, are seated in first class and are quickly brought warm towels and water. They check our tickets and assure us no other passengers will be seated in proximity to our seats. I can hear other passengers boarding but see no one. We have one flight attendant dedicated to us. I can tell from his ease Agent Ford is used to this style of travel and imagine the many miles he takes across the continent to secure all loose ends to his cases. She quickly informs us that we will be having dinner in Oaxaca with our flight duration being approximately five and a half hours.

Once we are in the air Agent Ford pulls out his laptop and scans the files he holds simultaneously, I feel it rude to ask questions as this is his investigation. I try to read what I can without appearing to do so and pull a small spiral tablet out of the pocket of my suit jacket. I calculate not being able to think in the sequence I am required to at this moment and don't know why I am writing all this down using my phone to calculate years lost and current ages of my parents, Jill, Joshua and myself. We are one family but separated by miles and time.

I start with me born July 4, 1973. After performing with my band, The *Green Pyramids*, in Pioneer Square for so long I decided to become a police officer. One of my first shifts was Halloween. I felt like I was in costume, no one recognized me. Today my thoughts are coming out in factual spurts. The twins Jill and Josh graduated high school in in 2004, celebrating by taking the biggest family vacation we ever took to Mexico. I didn't go being so new on the force I didn't have vacation time saved up and it was their graduation. Within a couple of days all communication stopped with them, they weren't at the airport when I went to pick them up seven days after dropping them off. They had disappeared. Not knowing what other steps to take I reported my family missing to my Sargent who then opened a file with the FBI. I didn't know anything they asked except names and birth dates; I wasn't given a copy of their itinerary. People go on vacation every day and return but that wasn't the case for the Muncer family. I didn't live with them prior to the vacation so didn't hear the details of places they wanted to see. I look over on his screen and see the names of my family members, just another case file to the FBI and realize this is how other family members of victims feel when I am investigating. There are their names and dates of birth Keith A. Muncer November 2, 1952, Margaret C. Muncer June 24, 1951, Joshua E. Muncer July 18, 1986, Jill E. Muncer July 18, 1986, with the word in red located and another file number attached at the end to easily click on and switch over to.

I go back to my paper calculating without a computer. I use the pen, writing slowly, we are less than a half an hour into our flight and I need off the plane. What will I do for five more hours, I am not used to being cooped up anywhere and think of Steven Watkins in the jail cell. I write questions to ask him when I return to Seattle, if any of that matters to me anymore. This case that is all mine and not mine at all has taken over my day, possibly the rest of my life. I calculate dad would have just turned 73, a few days ago. I wonder if he celebrated this birthday or any others. Mom turned 74 over this past summer. I am having trouble picturing them with gray or white hair, just as Agent Ford points to his split screen interrupting my thoughts and reveals their drivers' licenses from 2004 and then scrolls to another screen with two people I do not recognize. These people cannot be my parents, they look like they are both over 100 years of age, tanned and they were in their fifties when I dropped them off at the airport. Not that it matters but I try to remember if they flew into the airport we will be landing at. Anything to keep my mind off the image on the screen. Agent Ford asks if I am ok and still on board, I nod yes and ask the current question on my mind about their airport arrival. He quickly flips to page one in the file and points to Oaxaca International Airport. I think I should close my eyes and rest the remainder of the flight but that is not me. I am not this person. This case has altered my thinking. All the other cases I work on are from the public, this is personal and is bound to feel different.

As we land, I see the mountains in the near distance and Agent Ford, always observant, asks if I am prepared and says something about the mountain ranges coming together Sierra Madre's. I think of my family and how we were separated during their vacation and now are being forced into a divergent version of us. I wonder if they know I am here, the FBI is here and suspect not.

Agent Ford automatically follows a corridor to a room labeled Federal Ministerial Police off the side of the one story airport acting like he has traveled here before. I want to ask if he has met with them on this case prior to today, but his answer would only quiet my curiosity and not make a difference, so I remain silent. I think of the people I meet at crime scenes and know I will take extra time, be more compassionate and carefully answer their questions because they do matter.

We step outside in the sweltering November heat, a dark blue, four door, Ford truck pulls up with Federal Ministerial Police insignia on the side. We enter the truck, Agent Ford does not waiver from his countenance as we pull out and he seems familiar with his surroundings. I follow his lead as we pull into a circular drive on a tall brick building resembling an upscale hotel. Agent Ford gets out, the closer we get to mom or dad I forgot to ask where we would be stopping first the more my body doesn't wish to move, and I feel glued to the seat. I know getting out is a necessity and as I walk over and enter the automatic sliding glass door that leads to the dining room I feel a mixture of emotion. We stop and check in; they unlock the security door for us to enter with looks of concern as if we are there for a surprise inspection. We are not simply local police but two jurisdictions at a federal level entering their facility with a warrant.

I turn from the desk after the security door is released and as if someone has answered my earlier question, I can hear my dad's voice traveling down a hallway to me singing one of his favorite old songs, Sweet Caroline from somewhere nearby.

It doesn't occur to me to allow the other agents to take the lead. I follow his voice down the hall and to a small gymnasium with shuffleboard courts on the floor. As soon as I round the corner and stand back behind the last row of seats taking in the new older version of my father, he says, "Jeffery" grabs his cane and comes down the three stairs and aisleway to me. He stands in front of me staring, neither of us know what to say or where to pick this story back up. He says my name again and I tell him Jill is safe in Seattle, his eyebrows furrow. He says, "Seattle, Jill?" Agent Ford tells me "Your family has received electroconvulsive therapy when they were in the factories, clearing some memories. That is why Jill has coped so well, and we do not know what your parents will remember. It will be a day by day discovery."

Agent Ford informs me of the next steps, "Your father will be cleared to enter the US, transported to the airport and met by another agent for questioning once in the country. The same system will be set in place with your mother. We need to leave your father with an agent here to be cleared and immediately go onto the next facility for your mother. As soon as we leave this location the Federal Ministerial Police will lock down the area to screen the remainder of the patients to obtain their point of origin. Once your mother is cleared, we will all meet at the airport and fly out tonight."

My heart is torn, they explain to my dad I will be leaving, he doesn't seem to understand why I am not remaining with him after our ten minute visit twenty one years too late. I try to explain to him about bringing mom back, but he looks at me and clearly does not understand. I then wonder where they will live once they are returned to Seattle and how their vacation and years away will affect my life. Agent Ford hurries me along as the other agents are already waiting in the circular drive out front. I squeeze dads' hand and reluctantly let go assuring him I will be seeing him soon and head out to the pickup truck to recreate the same scene with my mom.

We arrive at a similar residence a short distance across town. This one is two stories and made of stucco. There are already numerous Federal Ministerial Police vehicles and agents blocking the entrance. They part as we enter. Agent Ford and I are led to an office behind the reception desk. Everyone is speaking in Spanish, and I pick up a few words. Madre is the one I zero in on, behind us a door opens up into a dining area and there sits my mom with the federal agents, a sight I could have never imagined. I am relieved she does not appear to be harmed or alarmed and is telling a story in Spanish to the guards surrounding her as if they are all there for a social visit. I enter the room once I am given clearance. I see mom stop her story midsentence, switch gears and look at me then she says in unbroken English, "I can't believe you came to visit Jeffery." She gets out of her chair and grabs my hand, telling the agents I am her son that plays guitar, the one she was just telling the late night story about.

We quickly grab her suitcases, place a light sweater around her shoulders and leave through a door I had not seen before this moment. There is a van waiting outside, the plans have changed from what I had been told or imagined. This is different for me since I am generally the one who calls the shots. I open the van door giving mom my hand to help her up, she sits on the middle bench seat. Her suitcases are loaded in the rear compartment as she sits on the gray bench seat buckling her seat belt next to dad like they have never been separated and are going on a sightseeing tour. She looks at him with recognition and introduces herself then realizes her mistake and lays her head on his shoulder. He takes her hand and holds it just as I sit in the third seat. I cannot stop looking at them or make my mind believe only hours ago I was in Seattle going to sleep and now this twenty one year development has happened.

All these events have transpired, and it isn't even time to call in for my shift tonight. There are still two hours to spare. I will call from the airport before boarding our flight. Agent Ford is in the seat ahead of me speaking fluent Spanish which is not something I have imagined him doing and wonder how many other languages he speaks. Mom looks at me and says, "We are going home, where's the twins?" I inform her Jill is in Seattle, she doesn't ask anything else and appears to be taking a nap so I omit the missing information on Joshua.

Agent Ford informs me of the debriefing session that will be held once we land in Seattle that I can attend, "Arrangements have been made for your parents to stay at an assisted living facility downtown if you choose for them to be there or they are free to go but will need care as they unwind from this two decade long event."

I agree to stay with them during the debriefing and assess the assisted living facility then make a decision. We return to the airport, board the plane, wait for takeoff and I know this is the day I have been envisioning for many years but now that it is here, I am suddenly exhausted. I lay my head back and rest as I look over at the two adjoining seats holding my buckled in parents and know with time it will all be ok.

Once we are in Seattle, the interview process felt long and above my parent's capacity, but they just sat there answering what they could like children would but clearly not remembering everything. Their description of living quarters, factories and treatment is similar to Jill's tale of her stay. After the agents are satisfied with the answers we are loaded in another van and taken to their new home.

I haven't had a chance to visit with them at all and picture us all in a room there wherever there is and am happy this piece of the immediate decision has been made for us. We enter the adequate facility; the administrator and nursing staff taking the medical files from Agent Ford and leads us through the dining room. We take the elevator to the eleventh floor, walk down a long corridor to adjoining rooms 11 A-B. We enter the sparsely furnished room, the curtains on the floor to ceiling windows are open, the city lights are a sight from this vantage point. I know this place is upscale and just as I think I hope I don't have to move them again, mom says, "Seattle," as dad joins her at the window pulling one of two chairs from around the small dining table. They sit holding hands like me and Agent Ford are not present. Someone delivers their suitcases as Agent Ford shakes my hand and says he has other cases to wrap up. I thank him for everything he has done for me and my family. It is like he has been reading my mind; he looks at me and says, "I couldn't tell you before, but I had been steadily working on this. Now to try to locate Joshua." He turns to leave with a big smile on his face and I realize I will be alone with these two strangers, my parents. I text Jill and ask if she is awake with no immediate response. The nursing staff enters and introduces themselves as the night nurses. They walk over placing the suitcases on the beds and carefully put the folded clothing in the drawers, read the files, talk about medication and leave. Mom and dad say they are tired, and I ask what I can do. They say go home and sleep, we will see you tomorrow.

I take the carpeted elevator to the lobby with the unusual feeling of not having transportation and get ready to order an Uber, looking for the address on the building when my phone alerts me to Jill's text. I sit in the lobby and inform her about our parent's whereabouts, giving her the address and a short version of our escapade and assure her they are fine and going to sleep on the 11th floor and will bring her here tomorrow. I hang up, place a request for a ride on the app and wait outside not believing the journey I have been on since I last saw my cruiser. I ride home, am deposited in the same location on the sidewalk that I stood at nearly 24 hours ago, enter my residence, make a list for tomorrow night's shift and fall asleep like I have never slept before.

42

Vernon

THE HOLIDAY SEASON IS starting. I see the ads on each coach wanting everyone to donate or purchase this or that as I ride my monotonous route and wonder if this job is one meant to work at for a few years, if that, or an occupation to stay for many years and retire. I ask myself on the second trip north is this my destiny to ride back and forth every day, make sure people stay in line? I think of the other transportation industries, and they are no different. You start at point A and return.

I may become antsy since it is November, with no family for many years I have seen and heard about all the other ones coming together to celebrate. As of now I don't have plans to eat even a meal with anyone except myself. I make up my mind to cook an entire Thanksgiving dinner, the works, turkey, mashed potatoes, whatever else goes with the dinner. I think back and realize Birdie and I only had sliced deli turkey on Thanksgiving.

Then Raven has been so busy with Jill moving in, the custody case and now Rubio wants to file one, her work, then there are our conflicting schedules. We had a wonderful date last week but have not talked about any holidays. Maybe we are not that far into our relationship, I don't even know if she has other family besides Meade. I make a list of groceries to purchase for my meal, check out a few holiday suggestions online and am hopeful suddenly that I can start a new tradition this year.

On Tuesday I show up for work as usual, for some reason I am not into this job with all the happenings since the beginning. I know Allard is on the loose and may appear at any moment on my shift. I would prefer that we had parted ways on her porch last month but that may not be the case. Her hostility towards me is uncalled for and puts me on edge, she is unstable. I board the coach, scanning the area and know she would not be anywhere near this end of my route. She is more like the jack in the box toy I had when I was small, popping up mid route. This, at least, brings some humor to the situation. As we start our route, Alfred comes running out of his office with a lady wearing a reflector vest under her shiny tactical jacket. I am not sure if we have picked up a construction worker or police officer. After meeting Allard I am leery of anyone. She smiles and juts out her hand to shake within an inch of me, she says, "I am Shila, Shila Jarvis. I will be training with you tonight. I hear you get a lot of action on this route." Alfred pivots in the aisle saying something like I think that covers it all then gets off the bus.

I had not been told about training anyone or being watched. I do not like this arrangement at all and prefer to be alone in my quest of avoiding Allard. Shila wants to sit with me in my seat. Before we leave the yard, I am working undercover and do not wish to be seated with someone in some form of uniform. She laughs using a boisterous annoying high pitched banter. Her noise echoes through the empty bus. I know she will blow any cover I have and wish to not remain in her presence. I change seats leaving her across from my usual vantage point telling her it is best we are not seated together.

I glance back on our scheduled route several times hearing her laughter as she tells stories of being a security guard at a bank downtown to other passengers. At the end of my shift, I do not know who will be there, but I am not working with Shila again. She needs more than training, out here life can be dangerous, being certain of herself and letting onto everyone the authority she thinks she has, she will blow any situation and become a danger to herself and other passengers.

I return at the end of my shift; Alfred is just closing up his office. He says, "They sent her, she needs eight more hours of training, and she can be on her own." I ask if anyone has told her she is working an undercover position? He tells me no matter what Shila is on board with me for one more shift. I get in my Jeep, chalking this up to another checkmark on my list of why I no longer wish to remain in this position. Then I think I have forgotten to check the status of the curtain on window man's apartment. Last, I had seen a few days ago Allard had entered, and the curtain was closed on my return run. I am pretty amped up over Shila and know if I return home, I will not sleep. It is too late to call Raven, so I drive north to look at the curtain of window man. I know this is a sorry excuse to be out but feel it is urgent.

There is almost no traffic on a Tuesday night, I quickly get to the spot on Aurora where I need to turn around to go southbound. The barrier prohibits my view in this direction. I notice the curtain remains closed and I have an eerie feeling that Jake the window man is in trouble. He is no match for Allard.

I text Muncer making him aware of my observations. He doesn't reply until after I receive a text from Raven saying she had a fun time on our date and that Jill had moved back home with Hector. I do not want to pull over anywhere on this strip and be accused of being involved in anything or be seen by Allard, if she is in the vicinity. Muncer gets back to me saying he can meet me there if I wish in ten minutes. I travel south crossing the bridge into downtown, turn around and see Muncer pulling into the parking lot of window man remembering his name as I pull in. Jake, who lives at the apartment I had seen Allard at last Friday.

Muncer says he has been thinking about Jake too but has been out of town. "The reason I wanted to meet you was the BL-2 key you gave me fits a lock in the back of the laundry room. I thought you may have some insight." We go into the laundry room, and he moves a dryer that was cattywampus off to the side, pulls out a key and opens the door saying, "Last time I was here there wasn't anything except dirt, lint, and a small blue bin with baggies next to it. Possibly a drop point." He opens the door, and we see Jake sitting on the dirt floor up against a wooden support beam for the three story building with duct tape around his wrists, ankles, and mouth. His arms are barely long enough to stretch around the wooden pole. Muncer pulls out a knife to cut the tape, but Jake shakes his head so vigorously he would be injured if Muncer proceeded. Jake is not understanding we are trying to free him.

I find an end to the tape and let Jake know this will be painful as he looks at his arms that are no longer mobile, and a single tear rolls down each cheek with him trying to say something behind the tape. I manage to remove it from his face first without too much difficulty. I am thankful the part wrapped around the back of his head had been loosened from his hair with sweat. I ask if he is ok, he shakes his head no and starts to cry. His arms remain straight out, I carefully unwrap the tape from around his wrists, knowing he needs medical care after being here possibly all weekend and the better part of today and we will have a short window of time for answers to Jake's predicament. Muncer calmly asks him if we can talk, Jake shakes his head yes. "Who tied you up Jake?" He screams, "I failed her. She told me to stay here quiet, tell no body. I didn't tell, you came in and found me. Serene, so mad now. I didn't tell anyone about the man with the baby, he was here." With his admission of her name, I for sure know now that it was Allard who placed Jake in the basement over three days ago. He cannot stand since being placed on the floor for all that time, his legs numb, his arms overstretch around the wooden pole. He allows us to take his keys and look for Allard in his apartment. We wait with Jake until SFD arrive and the EMTs carefully load him on the gurney. We assure him we will lock up his place and meet him at the hospital. He points at me and says, "Who, bus? I remember from the window. Tape 16, 31, 44, 47, many times on the bus." I was amazed that all the time I was watching window man he had been keeping track of me. Documenting our lives as they meshed together with the catalyst being Allard.

We wait for Jake to leave; it is just after 11:00 pm. His front door is locked, the curtain still closed, I imaging Allard holed up in his residence. But why would she be here? Muncer looks over the camera system, seeming to be familiar with it but I don't ask how he knows how to operate it so smoothly and think of Mr. Owens, who knows everything that happens on the property and think his system must be similar. At this moment I miss Gus, think of Raven and wish I was not here but thankful I had gone with my intuition and called Muncer. Jake will be ok if he can stay away from Allard, everyone will be ok if we can avoid her, and she be brought in and held. Muncer brings me back to my actual location as he says, "Whatever she is hiding is on the tapes she has stolen." I look at him and say, "Let's check Mel's place, do you know how he is?" Muncer is in thought not answering my question that doesn't have anything directly to do with this situation. He locks the door, places the keys in his suit jacket pocket and gets in his car like I am not there. I know I am this far in and will follow remembering what Raven said a few months back. "Do you know what page of this story you are jumping into and is that where you want to go?" My answer then was yes and the same now. I jump in my Jeep not needing to follow Muncer, I know the way because I was there first.

We get to Mel's, the window has been pried open where the A/C unit lays on the ground. Muncer calls it in as a residential burglary since the last time he was here the window was secure. When I join him on the side of the house he says, "I did hear you. I don't know how Mel is but don't suspect he is here. If he is out, he has taken the truck, it is gone." SPD arrives, the house is cleared of any individuals, but someone has been in here, searching, the drawers and cabinets are all open, sofa cushions neatly stacked on the floor. Whoever did this had plenty of time and didn't want to make a mess. I walk to the kitchen and tell Muncer, "The ring of keys is gone." He gives me a look of how do you know that. To clear myself and Raven, I tell him of the night Mel was shot. Raven and I had come here to retrieve her belongings, and she had me wait by the door while she returned her key to the ring in the kitchen drawer. He gives me a look wondering why I was here before and hadn't said anything. Then he calls Harborview, inquires on Mel's condition, finding out he has recently woken up but is still in ICU. We know then someone else has the truck and the keys. I look around the bedroom Raven used to stay in since I have access now and I may learn something. I see the closet door is busted now and the attic entrance is open. Muncer probably didn't know about the difference of the condition of the door from his prior visit. He comes in, goes to the kitchen and gets the step ladder, just inside the entrance to the attic is the blue bin, full of baggies each holding a few tapes from Jake's camera. I don't know where they all are, but these must be evidence of what she is hiding.

I hear the among the chatter of Muncers radio a 1999 brown Ford truck has been left abandoned in the intersection of N. 62nd and Aurora. Muncer calls to have them secure the area and then he goes into Mel's bedroom and shuts the door to make another call. The house is small, silent and nearly vacant, sound travels so I hear him tell someone, "She is on the loose and near your house." I think of our meeting and without mentioning a name I know he has called Metevior from the location that night.

We secure the window, lock up and leave to our separate destinations, him to the truck, me to my home, a safe haven. When I get a block or two down the road, my first text of the day is from Muncer. "Thank you for the tip, couldn't have done this without you. Will go see Jake and Mel in a while."

I drive home and catch a small piece of music on the radio similar to the one I heard in the background the first time, I had called Muncer. As I listen to the song, I realize it is about crime, thugs, police and Seattle. As I pull in late Gus is waiting and so is Mr. Owens. He wants to know if I have solved the case. I tell him, "We found Jake. It is nearly done one more suspect to locate." For his peace of mind, I add that I am glad they are all in Seattle. I wonder what has brought Mr. Owens out at this time of night but don't ask that, just assure him I am ok and ask if he is. I think he knew I was late returning home and was just checking.

Gus and I have a good chat down by the water. Soon it will be too cold to spend a lot of time out here with him. I know he prefers that to coming inside. I wonder what my life will hold, and hope Allard and Shila will be memories of the past soon.

I go in after Gus gets back in his bed by the lake, take out my suitcase and pack, leaving out only the necessities. It has been eight months since I moved here. It feels like I should move on, of course not this moment but I need to be ready. I go to sleep with nearly all my belongings packed on the other side of the bed where I wish

Raven was. Life hands out conflicting scenarios. Raven is in Seattle. I want to be in Seattle, but Allard is there and now Shila and my crazy job. I fall asleep thinking of my journeys around the world and know I will be ok no matter what, I am ready.

43

Detective Muncer

JUST AS I SENSED all along Allard has been the one entering Mel's residence. After hearing about the truck being abandoned on Aurora, I run the plate myself verifying it is Donny's. Covering all bases I call Chief Stewart and Harborview to keep extra security outside of Mel's room. I don't know what connection Allard and Mel have but there was or is something in his house she has returned for on numerous occasions. I should have searched Jake's house for whatever she was looking for. When I pull up at the scene, I know to patrol it is just another incident, so I take over the case making sure the truck is carefully transported to our evidence lot for forensics to print. I doubt if Allard had located what she was searching for that she would have left it in the truck. I wonder why she or whoever was driving abandoned it in the center of the road and didn't pull into a parking lot where the truck wouldn't have been noticed immediately. After the flatbed tows the truck away, I call Rubio and tell him of the scene I had just left. We always have banter like a tennis match, my story, his story they are always connected. This one connects Donny's truck to Allard and Rubio thinks Aleene's murder.

Rubio tells me about his CI in Portland that hear news on the streets. Apparently, Allard has cut off her payments to the Cartel and the protection she had arranged for her cash donations to them has been lifted. None of that story makes sense to me except Allard being involved in something shady.

I ask Rubio, "Allard has been paying the Cartel money?" "Yes, when she was in Portland a gang paid her to overlook any of their activity and in turn, after the Cartel found out, they made her pay with cash and drugs to let the gang continue activity on the Cartel's turf. She was running amidst a few sides of the law and also in a circle. There was nowhere for her to escape. She was buying from some member of the Cartel there and then selling to the gang who then infiltrated and upped the price to sell to back to the Cartel. The Cartel found out this was the case, whether Allard was aware or not, so she had to come up with a considerable amount of cash, like almost $20,000.00, but then when she had given it to her connection to resupply the gang and gain her cash back the supplier supposedly burned up in the tent with the money. Now we know that is not true. Her supplier, Steven Watkins, sits in jail and did not burn. The money is missing, and the Cartel are after her. Possibly the gangs too. I have never heard of anyone on the force having their hands involved everywhere. I think she didn't have a choice in the beginning with the fear for her life then the multilevel situation escalated, and she is out there on the run desperately looking for the money. I don't know why someone with her salary wouldn't be able to access that amount.

It is a lot of cash but not too far out of reach for someone with a job. Maybe if she turns the money over once they will return for another installment and she wants out. So, she acts like she lost it or is simply mad someone has gotten over on her and taken the money."

I receive a text from Metro. Allard just got off the bus, the first stop over the Aurora Bridge heading south. I call this in, an APB issued, and the area is cordoned off. The tape is willy nilly, flapping in the wind from the traffic driving by with no purpose at all when I arrive. Allard is not in that area; she was only present for a second. No one knows for sure if she walked a few feet and jumped off the bridge into Lake Union until traffic cameras are checked or did she have an accomplice waiting? Why did she get off here? Even though it is located five miles away I call Harborview again asking for extra security on the room that holds Jake Simmons. I don't know where Allard is headed to next, but I want to ensure Jake and Mel are safe in their vulnerable states. After I clear this scene Harborview will be my next stop. On the way I make a call to Metro to find out what transpired with Allard prior to his text.

VC: She boarded somewhere and climbed over the seat from the rear taking the window seat as I always keep the aisle seat. She was nearly in my lap before I was aware she was even on board. She had to of been hiding under one of the seats and boarded at Aurora Village when I had my break.

DJM: She had been at Mel's, as you know. We found the truck abandoned on 62nd and Aurora. I wonder how she made it so far north in such a short amount of time.

VC: That is the only place she could have gotten on. I would have seen her otherwise.

DJM: I can't release information on who she is working with or who is after her but can tell you she is looking for about $20,000.00 at Mel's house. Also, there are more tapes from Jake's camera system missing. I have extra security at Jake and Mel's hospital rooms and am headed there now.

VC: I sure hope she can be taken off the streets soon. I cannot keep working if she continues to show up.

Metevior calls me for a ride into the precinct tonight. He woke up at 7:00 pm and got ready for his shift at 10:00 pm and his Honda Civic had been stolen. I stop at Harborview, drop off Jake's house key and check on Mel. He recognizes me right away and says, "I didn't do it" as I enter the room. I tell him how great it is that he has woken up and ask if he is well enough for a few questions. He hesitantly nods yes.

DJM: Do you know Serene Allard/Detective Allard?

MS: No, who is that?

DJM: A female detective with SPD.

MS: No, I wouldn't be hanging out with anyone like that.

Then he stops with a look of confusion and says "Tall, red hair, jean jacket?"

DJM: Yes, so you do remember her.

MS: She met Steven in the back yard once. I saw them through the kitchen window. He was only there a week or two tops. Then he shot me. So much for helping people out I should have learned from before.

286

DJM: Do you know if money was exchanged between Steven and Allard?

MS: Something was passed between them, but I don't know what. Then the next day Steven was saying he lost something and thought I had it.

DJM: What did he lose?

MS: Drugs or money. He just kept yelling that I knew but I don't use drugs anymore or want them in my house or on my property. I was very specific about that when he showed up and asked to stay. I guess since I have been admitted here, I am off Brixadi. That was the first thing I asked when I woke up if I had been taking my medication. I do not want to return to any drugs ever.

DJM: So, which do you think they exchanged drugs or money?

MS: I don't know. I never saw what it was. He said he left it there when he went to pick up my prescription and it was gone when he came back. I only went to the bus stop looking for Raven. I don't think anyone could have come in the house unless the lady cop came in then.

DJM: Thank you, if you think of anything else, please call.

I leave my card on his nightstand, keeping an eye out when leaving the hospital for Allard and head to Metevior's house to bring him in for his shift tonight. My first stop will be to pay Steven Watkins a visit.

I bring Metevior up to speed on the investigation, he says he doesn't care about his car or Allard. Today he will be putting for retirement starting January 1, 2026. The need for this case and another detective wrapped up in a knot has brought a good detective and loyal friend of mine to the end of his career. His words put a sadness on my day as I count down the days until he leaves but it also brings more fire from within me to locate Allard and solve this complex case.

Some parts of today have made me not wish to remain here either but this is where I am and Allard needs to be off the streets for the protection of herself and the people of Seattle, Portland and everywhere in between.

Steve Watkins was called down to be interviewed again. He walks in looking as defeated as I feel. Metevior is a large piece of this department, and he cannot retire but I know deep down there is no way I can stop him. Steven sits on the opposite side of the table from me, picking at the worn spot, pulling up small slivers of wood. I ask him to stop, he keeps pulling up the strips. I figure this is a battle that will not matter and allow him to continue. He looks at me but remains silent. I am not sure which question to start with, there are so many loose ends still left unanswered.

DJM: Where were you the night the tent caught on fire?

SW: I was in the tent. Allard arrived and made me get out, then told me to get back in but we all now know I didn't.

DJM: Why did Allard come to see you? Did she do that frequently?

SW: She came with money for the buy. I had been helping her out with purchases, like I said. Recently it had become more frequent but once I lost total custody, I told her I wanted out and had no need for all the cash I had previously needed. She kept coming back and insisting. She acted like she was in charge, but I could see fear in her.

DJM: When and where were you supposed to meet her?

SW: Later that night, by 1:00 am I was supposed to bring the fentanyl to our meeting spot, but I couldn't get a hold of my guy. It was like he vanished.

DJM: Who is your guy? Where were the drugs going to be deposited?

SW: Whoa. I will never roll on my guy. I think he knew something was up, he had suspected something was off for a while and was there watching me. He knew I was getting the money at 11:00 pm and wanted to see who the buyer was. I ran with the money. I didn't know anyone was in the tent until the next day while watching the news at Little Mel's house. My supplier was in the tent listening all along and the last think he heard, right before his death, is that I was meeting the cops. I couldn't have set the tent on fire because I was in the woods.

DJM: Thank you for clearing that up, Steven. Where were the drugs going to be deposited?

SW: The drugs and money were usually exchanged in a room behind a dryer at a three story building up on Aurora. I would meet my guy nearby and pick up. I had a key and so did Allard. I don't know where she got the keys from, but she made all the arrangements. I just went to pick up cash or drop off what she had ordered. After running to Mel's and not being able to get ahold of my guy I tried a couple other places but no one else had that quantity on hand. Plus, I don't know many high end dealers. I was only a recreational user not a dope pusher until she showed me a way to help raise funds for the attorney. I was so stupid to believe her. I should have gone to court on my own and would probably have my baby now. I was clean and would have gotten myself set up. Mel had been going to the bus stop for a few days trying to locate Raven, who was long gone. He took her backpack and that is where I had hidden the key to the room since I had been staying in Raven's old bedroom and found it there. I wasn't aware he had taken the backpack anywhere and saw he came home with the it one day and I was furious asking if he was trying to get me killed. He didn't know the key was in there but what had happened to the money? It was no longer in the backpack, the closet or behind the dresser drawer. It had vanished. I demanded Mel give me everything that was mine including the money. He tells me the lady cop I had met in the back yard has it. I didn't know how that could be possible and had nothing to go on being scared for my life. Allard is frightening. I took the key, looked in the laundry room but the blue bin was empty, then went home. Mel did the same thing the next day, taking the backpack. I was still furious about the money and met him at the bus stop, then I shot him because I did not wish to remain free if I couldn't come up with Allard's money she would kill me. That is the end of my story.

Well now we know it was an unknown dealer in the tent, possibly with the product to be exchanged but not who it was.

My last thoughts before hitting the pillow are my parents are in town, Seattle, back here. It is so hard to believe after all these years. I am meeting Jill at 4:00 pm to take her to see them.

44

Vernon

AFTER MY ENCOUNTER WITH Allard, I have decided to look for another job at the end of the year, just over thirty days to go. I pull up the calendar on my phone and calculate twenty five more shifts being grateful for Thanksgiving and Christmas, my paid days off anyway. I cannot continue on with her harassment. I feel it is starting to affect my health. I think she is at every corner. After looking at the surveillance cameras we see she boarded the bus at Aurora Village and hid under the side facing seat behind me.

I did talk to Raven about Thanksgiving. She suggested I cook there; we could invite a few people. Maybe Jill and Hector since they are all back to being a couple now. I don't know who else. We shop the following weekend together buying some of the food and the rest will come from a potluck, we think. My heart is not in the holidays for sure this year but am willing to give it a try with this meal.

I wake up one night standing in my bedroom in the middle of an episode, clutching the handle of my previously packed bag having woken from a dream of Allard popping up from under the table at

Thanksgiving requesting a plate. Nothing was this bad before I was reintroduced to civilian life. As I sit on this cold night and feed Gus, I laugh at the absurdity of one individual creating this much havoc for so many and costing the city a great deal of money. I guess I truly don't understand the motives of others.

The next day I arrive early for work, as requested. Alfred meets me on the dock and introduces me to a man in a suit named Stan. Stan invites me into the office area and tells me Shila will be riding with me for the remainder of the week. He can tell I am agitated with this decision. Then adds, "I am from the union, and this won't be like last time she rode with you. You will stick by her and show her the ropes." I immediately ask, "Are we not supposed to be undercover? The last time she trained with me she wore police gear, was so loud some passengers had to move and then she told stories about being security. She was trying to blow my cover." Stan looks at me quizzically and says, "Exactly why she needs training, and we are assigning that task to you."

I board the coach with Shila who is more silent this time. I hope she is scared of me since she went to the union and ratted me off because of her actions. She sits in the seat across from me and doesn't say a word. I don't know how or wish to start a conversation with her. I am scared if she starts talking it will be like kindling on a fire, so I remain silent.

Part way up Aurora, on our first loop, a young gentleman boards the bus and comes back to sit with Shila. They had clearly continued the discussion they were having earlier today. She tells him he shouldn't follow her to work, she is working. No, she will not make a delivery on the bus, she only does that in the yard by Toppler Tower. He can make the deal. I knew this girl was trouble all along. The young male gets off at the next stop pulling her hair on the way out. She looks straight ahead knowing I heard that entire conversation. Then turns to me and says, "Tell anyone you want they won't believe you."

She gets up, rings the bell, gets off the bus and sits at the windowless bus stop. I know she has taken the package and will be meeting their contact in moments. I don't feel this battle is worth fighting and by the time SPD pulls up the drugs will be long gone, and Shila will be just sitting there holding nothing, making me look like a fool.

On our way back through she shows the driver her badge so everyone on the bus knows she is Metro Transit Police and boards, sitting across from me. She looks at me and says, "Tell anyone you want they won't believe you." In my futile attempt to not interact with her I point to the cameras. In her unladylike way she says, "You are the one who is supposed to be training me if I am not acting proper." I am ready to let loose on Shila when the male who was with her boards the bus again a few stops up and sits next to her. At least when she is with him, she leaves me alone. He insists she take the bag he is holding, and she is just as determined to not hold onto it, saying she already made one stop for him. He remains in the seat with her to the end of the route and as we proceed back northbound. When we get to about Westlake Center, I observe a young male jump off a construction barrier and throw himself into the window where Shila and her accomplice sit. She is acting like she is a victim. The driver and I call 911, the male who smashed the window is determined to retrieve the package Shila had placed in her construction vest and pulls out her badge with one hand and pulls him the remainder of the way through the broken window laying him on the seat like she is arresting him. He reaches into the pocket of his burnt orange puffer vest, pulls out a pistol. I jump on top of him knowing my life means more than this mess, being reminded of my twenty five shifts to go. He fires two shots with his free arm shattering another window with one and the other penetrating the front of Shila's tactical jacket. Immediately, I release him to tend to Shila's wound, but I can see her construction vest beginning to not be able to hold the amount of blood that she is losing. I have no way to save her and think of Darius and his fears. I tell the male she was conversing with to remain here, but he kisses his fingers, touches her head and runs to the front of the bus. The driver refuses to open the door for his escape, but he breaks the seal and runs into the city. The shooter is long gone, his weapon and drugs lay in the puddle of blood underneath me. I didn't see him go in the process of trying to save Shila. This happened for no reason, for the drugs but they remain here, covered in blood. A passenger from the front of the bus who must be stuck in place from shock whispers, "He was fast."

45

Detective Muncer

NOVEMBER 2025

I AM NOT USED to being awake at this time of day battling traffic from Fremont to SODO then back downtown. Jill will be off in ten minutes. I hope I calculated this trip so I will arrive before she comes out of the building and will be waiting for her. I know she didn't want to go to work today but I told her what the nursing staff told me before leaving last night. With them being on the memory care ward they prefer we leave them a day or two so they can get used to the schedule. Jill finally calmed down once I convinced her our parents needed to settle in and go through evaluations earlier today.

I watch Jill depart work; she flies out of the rear door kissing Hector in passing as she runs to my cruiser. I watch her with the mind of her older brother, and she is six again heading off to kindergarten and I am nineteen secretly watching her go to the bus stop since she was a big girl and didn't need anyone. I protected her from afar for many years then she was gone. We never lived through the part of our lives when Jill was a grown up and able to be on her own. She was a schoolgirl, now she is forty years old. Jill hits my arm and yells,

295

"Jeffery I waited all day, let's go." This brings me back to my current location and the predicament before me. Being as this is the first time I have seen Jill since my round trip journey with Agent Ford. I tell her what he said about the information she had provided being the reason they were able to find our parents and possibly many other missing individuals. She looks at me and says, "In Mexico they used to take me to the doctor. I would stay there hours in a dark room, then they would bring me back to my apartment to sleep for a couple days. I don't remember what happened before I would return to my bed." I tell her of the possibility of electroconvulsive therapy. She says she had dreams of home, when she was a child now and in Mexico.

We pull up at the curb. Jill suddenly tired and overwhelmed, wanting to be dropped off at the front door while I find parking. The traffic is at high volumes being rush hour and it feels like it takes me half an hour to return to Jill even though it has likely been ten or less minutes. The world remaining in slow motion with the congestion. I walk up and Jill is nowhere to be found, entering the building I spot her in front of the bank of shiny metal elevator doors. She is ready, turns and smiles at me hitting the only option of up. We enter the plush mirrored car, I tell her, "11." She pushes the button and as we ascend, we both know moments from now our lives will be changed.

We stand outside of the room with the nameplates Margaret Muncer and Keith Muncer. Jill enters first and sees mom. I had forgotten to tell her how much they had aged. She stops the second she gets in the door and turns to me asking, "Are you sure?" then proceeds into the room without waiting for my reply. I see dad come from the other side of the room, he looks at me and says, "Jeffery." I point and say, "Jill". Dad lights up like I remember when he would be really into something. Like the time he had gotten the Holley 350 dual feed dual pump carburetor for his blue Chevelle that had the V–8. I sold it to one of his friends not wishing to be responsible for the upkeep. Plus, I didn't have a garage. This brings me back to thoughts of all the items I sold of theirs and the bank statement that arrives monthly with the slight increase from interest. I never invested their money because in the beginning I thought they would return and need the funds to pick up their lives. I did sell their house and contents because I couldn't leave it vacant for fear of vandalism. Now I feel fortunate to have saved all that money for them. I didn't draw on their life insurance because I didn't think they were gone, just missing.

Jill, mom, and dad are seated by the window. The last beams of daylight bounce off the windows of the buildings. As night sets in the automatic lights begin to pop on all over town. I can see an office worker across the way on her way out, gathering her green coat and briefcase. I am anywhere except in this room. Dad brings me back to this spot and says, "The cooks are excellent here. What a nice place." I am grateful they are secure and look over to see mom and Jill talking like it has only been a day or two between their visits. She tells them of her job, of Hector and about watching Enzo. I wonder if it was Meade or Raven who left him with her and realize it doesn't matter at this moment. What matters is my family is almost complete. I think of Joshua and have hope, picturing him here on a future visit. I have not been this content in over two decades and suddenly wish to fill Naomi in on my travels and our newfound long lost parents.

Jill rises with the city lights behind her, mom says, "I always dreamed of living downtown." We all hug, knowing it is late, Jill and I do the reverse trip out. She waits for me on the scrolled concrete bench by the doorway to our parents. I retrieve the car, Jill tells me she was wrong about wanting to be away from Hector, she realized that after her girls' weekend away. She loves Enzo but would never want the responsibility of a child of her own or with Hector. I wind through town with most commuters off the road, drop her at Hector's house and drive around the emptying streets finding my way to Naomi's before she starts her shift. The quiet time of the night, for me a moment of peace, I have always been solo but now a part of many circles.

Naomi is surprised at my unannounced visit and asks if I am ok. I nod yes, walk in her door without being invited, hug her and sit down. The relief of being somewhere comfortable has washed over me. I am glad I came here and did not return home or to the precinct. Maybe twenty years of stress has rolled off. I tell Naomi of my last three days and ask if she would like a ride to work. She says, "No let's walk, it's a nice night and we can enjoy this moment longer." We walk down the five flights of stairs, and I am ready for my cruiser but take her hand once we hit the sidewalk and proceed several blocks south to the ER where she checks in. I walk across the parking garage to the park on top. I see the Smith Tower and notice a man with a Springer Spaniel. He approaches me and says, "No one is ever here this late. We come here every evening to say goodnight since my wife passed in that building. I know it is late but for some reason I can't go back home tonight. Glad you are here." We sit in silence, I think of Mel and Jake contained in the unlit rooms behind me. I don't need to go in to see them, bid the man and his spaniel a good night, and walk back the five blocks to my cruiser.

I return to the precinct and use different photo editing software to decipher Don Montgomery's note. The more I tamper with the photo it becomes less distinct. Had it become wet from the dew on the ground and was already blurry before I had possession of it? All I can make out is I loved Meade, and she shouldn't have gone to do Raven's job. Everyone is gone that I loved. I don't know if that carefully written cursive is Don's actual handwriting, or someone wrote it for him, but I will stop here since this collaborates with the report, I will turn in. I thought it would have revealed some more facts needed for my investigation but looking back on Don he was a simple man who had boxed himself in a corner, couldn't find his way out after digging the hole so deep and didn't want to die alone.

46

Vernon

NOVEMBER 2025

TODAY IS THE DAY of my volunteer service at Ethan's Edge. Kernal is late, the van is ready to leave, Darius is here but hasn't been the same since Devon was murdered. He confided in me recently that they thought he was Devon once and shot him. Asking, "why couldn't that happen again? It isn't just one person that had been looking for him, it was a gang that he had crossed, not me. They are still out there, no one has caught them. I stay away from that stuff. I am scared to go out. This is the only place I go; we are in a group, but they know about this program too. Devon made them aware when we were up on Aurora that day he was with us." I see tears forming in his eyes ready to spill over and make a mental note to talk with Carl about Darius just as Kernal comes racing down the alley on a BMX bike apologizing for being late, some story about his dad needing help. He put the bike inside the back door of the shelter and hops in the van, taking up conversation with Darius, who is not into talking. We head over towards Ballard and cover some graffiti on a bridge, that takes most of our time with the porous surface made of concrete.

Darius has come around by the time we are done, and I see him and Kernal have formed some sort of friendship. They plan to meet at a park tomorrow with Ringer and one of her friends so Darius can meet her.

Today was Raven's final hearing for custody, with Aleene gone they sped up the process. I asked if she wanted me there and she said it would look better if it was just her and she could prove she had a residence, transportation, day care, and a job all on her own. When we arrive back to the shelter I talk to Carl about Darius' fears and update him about Kernal and them meeting the new girl. When I get back to my Jeep, I see I have a message from Raven, she is off work and just leaving the courthouse with Enzo. She has been awarded full custody and wonders if I would like to meet for ice cream. My first thought is of last night with Shila and am so thankful this Thanksgiving Eve that I am alive to celebrate this step in the journey I have become so invested in. I tell Raven, "oh ya we are having ice cream." I don't care if I am late for my shift but probably won't be. I think that job is too much as I picture my packed bags on my bed and am also thankful for landing here and getting through my PTSD episode alone the other night. I agree to meet Raven and Enzo at Seattle Bay Creamery. Enzo is in a happy mood; he sees the water and tells me of our boat trip, remembering weeks before and wondering if we are going again now . We make plans to ride The Great Wheel over Thanksgiving weekend instead.

Raven orders while I entertain Enzo. I don't care what she gets, just that we are all here on this November afternoon with the cold wind whipping off the water into the restaurant every time the door opens.

I don't mention my nearly fatal incident from last night and listen as she tells the story of the judge while Enzo says, "Papa." Raven tells me Rubio walks in during the case, she was worried he would cause trouble, but he just sat. Enzo ran to him, and he proceeded to the second row so I could see them and held Enzo while the judge finalized the case. "Rubio will want to see Enzo but is not filing a custody case and has set up a college fund for him with the sale of Aleene's house. Well, really, his house. I am glad this day is over, and I get to celebrate it with you." Raven looks exhausted, I think I am too and will take the day off and watch the ducks on Lake Washington as Raven asks if I am going to work or would like to come over. I call in taking a personal day, happy that my twenty five is now twenty four. I am off tomorrow for Thanksgiving. Jill, Hector, Muncer, Naomi and Mr. and Mrs. Muncer will be attending our dinner. I am interested to know what the Muncer parents look like after meeting their children. I hope I can cook. We stop at Metropolitan Market on Mercer St. This whole trip would be easier with one vehicle, but this is how it is today with both of us driving, and I am reminded, we are two separate people but will come together tomorrow as a family with all our friends. It will be nice to get to know them all outside of the professional life.

Over the holiday weekend Raven, Enzo and I take a ride on The Great Wheel, Enzo doesn't seem to be bothered by heights. We get on a ferry and go to Bremerton reminding me of my first few weeks here testing out the system. So much has happened since then. I know Allard is still somewhere out there and if I remain in my position she will find me. I am not as jumpy about that as I had been.

Muncer texts me on Saturday about the time Raven and I return to her house. He asks if I have time for a phone call. I tell him in five minutes I can talk. I see Raven has a look of concern and ask her, "what if he asks about the money?" She says, "really it is Little Mel's." "So, we tell Muncer it was there if he asks?" She nods then says, "we can't start our lives out on a lie." Then shakes her head and leaves the room. I follow her, she turns and apologizes for being too presumptuous with her words about us. I hold her and say, "that statement was not off at all. We can't start anything on a false note." Just then my phone rings with Muncers' name flashing across the screen, breaking up the moment. He asks how we are; I know his question of the money will be next. He says, "I just wanted to thank you for Thanksgiving and having my family over. That was the first in twenty one years." I respond with relief, "we enjoyed every minute." Then tell him of our adventure on the waterfront today and the custody battle over. He says, "you know they still haven't caught whoever shot Aleene." I think of Enzo's grandma, a lady who missed her son so much she took another into her home. The last couple years of her life she was torn and unhappy. Such a sad ending to her life and that Enzo, who spent so much time with her, will never see her again all because Rubio, although not his fault, had been asking around about the murder of Tiffany's daughter, Novah. Muncer and I hang up with no mention of the cash. I am still in thought about the senseless acts happening daily all the way from Birdie to Shila.

Raven comes in, I shake my head no, she is cutting up leftover turkey for sandwiches and starts to laugh. Then says, "Someday I will go see Mel, but not today."

We eat and make the plan to return the money but try to follow the trail of it. Raven says Mel doesn't have that kind of money unless his mom left it to him. Steve may have had it for his custody battle, someone may be looking for it or something else if Mel's house was broken into. "For now, only Muncer and Rubio know where I live but wouldn't suspect the cash would be there, if they even know about it. I ask, "Raven what would you want to do with it if you truly end up with it?" She says, "help someone, somehow." We eat our dinner and notice Enzo has left the table and is asleep in the recliner with the footrest up, looking rather grown up. We clean up the kitchen and quietly go outside to feed the ducks a bit of turkey. Somehow this seems wrong with them both being birds, but they are happy and dancing in the yard. I think this is somewhere I could bring Gus but not today. Tomorrow I am going home to unpack at least one bag before I go return to my route on Monday. Fulfilling day twenty three but not before I put in my application to SCL and give proper notice to Metro.

I have not decided whether I will continue on with Metro if I don't get hired right away but I don't suppose so and think of Allard, of who the two unidentified victims of the hit and run are. Shila's on the loose, Devon and his gang member friend that were both murdered and wonder about the man in the tent if he has been identified or if there is even a way after this long. I have really gotten drawn into the police work of this city and feel I am making a difference but at what cost. I have made the concrete decision tonight and haven't told anyone but will apply to Seattle City Light over the weekend before I change my mind. The life of crime, no matter what side I am on, can be addictive but where can coming this close to death so many times lead to, it is senseless. Eventually I may not be spared, and I want to be here for Raven, Enzo and Gus. I smile as I sit out here alone in the wooden porch chair on this cold night while Raven puts Enzo to bed. I think I have it all figured out, at least eventually it will all be good. A new job that I am better qualified for, a comfortable life and a place for Gus. Raven asks if I will be sitting out here all night freezing. I look in and picture a Christmas tree in the front window. With Raven being on the same train of thought she says, "I know where the Christmas decorations are." We haul them in from the garage, she opens the festive totes and admires the collection of blown glass and silver metal ornaments. We agree to get a tree tomorrow, decorate it and I will stay one more night. We fall asleep on the couch after our long weekend, both content with words unsaid.

47

Detective Muncer

MANY TEMPERS ARE STARTING to flare up as Christmas draws near, maybe it is the neighborhoods I am working in and poverty levels. The money spent on needed or frivolous products instead of presents that may be expected to be purchased and are not. I heard one guy tell the lady next to him, "I have six people in my family so three months before December when I get my food stamps, I just go to the grocery store and buy a six pack of Hershey bars, six apples and a six pack of soda. I can't afford presents, but I brought something to the family." His seat mate nods as he tells the remainder of his unwanted holiday tales. Then she adds, "I like trimming the tree the best. This is my stop, excuse me."

I think listening to the snippets of real conversations is my favorite part of this job. People reveal what they wish to portray. Some act all tough when all you can see is fear on them, others may be sweet until someone rolls over their toes then they kick that person when their foot was in the aisle all along to be stepped on. I see senseless acts of aggravation placed on the general public every day. With everything looking calm and the recent turn of the calendar I pull out my phone to count the actual shifts I have left on this route or some other as I am still continuing to be a floater. Counting today, December 8th, seventeen trips are left on this route. I should have made a more thoughtful plan and chosen my last date as December 30th. I look online in the portal and see I have two days of PTO and will take one being my last day to spend New Years Eve with Raven and Enzo. That is how I would prefer to celebrate anyway.

A few stops in, on the way north but still in the downtown corridor, Allard boards through the back door as you can do in the ride free zones. She is wearing a brightly colored crocheted poncho. I can see she is carrying a small weapon through the open slit lined in red yarn that gives access for your hand. I imagine a snub nosed 38 is what she holds. She walks on, me sitting a couple seats back from her entry point. Stopping in the aisle, she looks me in the eyes and shakes her head no to indicate I should not do anything except scoot over to the window seat when she stops at the edge of my seat and moves my ankle off my knee with hers, dropping my foot to the floor. My boot makes more noise than needed and brings attention to us as she smiles at the other passengers looking at us, knowing something is happening but not their business. They are just not sure what is going on. I am positive they are not aware a renegade detective is in their presence and the possibly of shooting me exists. Now I wish I had given notice sooner, just not showed up for my shift today, anything except to be here at this moment with Allard. I think of Raven, the money, all the people from Thanksgiving. No one would believe this scene being played out.

She looks at me and smiles, her usual sarcastic grin that appears calm, but I am aware of what lies underneath. Her gun firmly planted in my left side still held in her poncho. I look at her and say something about that being made with single crochet. My life is passing before me, remembering Birdie with her hook making items to sell at the beach and know I have brought up the only person of memory we both have, and I should have stayed silent. Sitting next to this insane woman who hates me I picture myself in the same predicament as Shila, minus the construction vest and tactical gear. I think my thoughts are odd as I sit here in possibly my last moments when she tells me, "I am going to meet Jake. He loves me, unlike you. Although, I don't need you." I do not have any reply to that. I just hope I can get Jake assistance between her exit of the bus and arrival to his door. Knowing he will see her on camera before she gets there. I speed the time up in my head so I can get to the part of this night where I can be free and call for help for Jake. She sees I am not present and plotting my next moves. Then she almost yells and realizes she is out of control and quiets down with me wishing the driver would get a clue and call 911 since I am his protection and if he was paying any attention at all, he would know there is trouble by my facial expressions and the lady almost leaning on me. That is not something that has ever happened on my route, he should know. Her words startle me with the depth of anger in them, "Why did you save me? If I died that night on the porch we wouldn't be here. Again, you are the cause of your own troubles." I am furious with her words but know she will place a bullet in me if I make any moves. She sits silently as if she is planning or rehashing the next steps of her deranged evening.

She tells me goodbye for now, in the same second, I have comfort in the possibility of her departure but dread of any moment in the future which includes Allard. She asks me to ring the bell as the bus nears the next stop. The one directly in front of Jake's apartment. I reach up to ring the bell, she pushes the gun into my ribcage further, directly aiming at my heart. I know I will have bruising if I don't die tonight. My mind is all over, anticipating her departure and my death in the same thought. I find myself wondering if the gun so close to my flesh and my jacket pooled around it will make the shot quieter sparing the other passengers. Just as that thought hits my head she rises. I can still see the barrel of her gun, but she turns and goes to the front of the bus to pay as I dial 911 on my cell phone, keeping it low in the seat so she cannot see I have moved and am signaling for help. She walks down the passenger side of the bus next to my window with her weapon still visible, looking me in the eye. I stop talking to the dispatcher and remain silent keeping eye contact with Allard, so she isn't aware I am on the phone with my ear bud in place. The dispatcher asking for my location, I do not have an address but know the cross streets. After Allard has walked a few more steps north I return, giving information to the dispatcher. With the bus being full of holiday shoppers and commuters a couple passengers have caught on that there is trouble and have alerted the driver. He does not leave the stop like normal but keeps looking in his oversized rearview mirror back in my direction. Just as I think we will be taking off, I hear two shots ring out echoing between the side of the coach and bus stop with newly replaced windows. I am torn between looking out or hitting the floor. There have been too many scenes such as this.

I see Allard on the ground, lying askew on the grass and sidewalk, her hand holding the weapon now fully out of the poncho. The shots did not come from her weapon, but a male who ran north on Aurora and disappeared into the shrubbery. No one is paying any attention to him. I didn't see him come around the back side of the bus before he fired his weapon. I only have a scant description of his backside and the hood he wore. I exit the bus with the thought of danger disappearing with the male on the run and Allard unable to fire her weapon. Jake runs out of his apartment screaming, "Serene, I am here for you," as he throws himself on top of her bleeding body. I try to convince him to get off of her as SPD arrives. He pulls something from his pocket. Life is in slow motion. I see it is a ring, like from a vending machine still in the clear plastic container with a red lid. He carefully opens it, says, "I love you Serene. We will be married." Then attempts to place the ring on her finger, not caring which one. He wipes his tears away, but his hands are covered in blood. When SFD arrives they ask who the victim is. I want to tell them Jake is the truest victim here but point to Allard instead. My voice is frozen, Allard is gone from this earth. Jake needs a friend. At this moment he is sitting on the bus bench alone. I approach him and ask if he has other clothing. The officers, make their report, I call Muncer who is already enroute, and he asks if I can stay with Jake until he arrives. I am not comfortable out here with my bus being long gone, but Jake wishes to wait with Allard's sheet covered body until the Medical Examiner retrieves her. Once she is on the gurney, Jake asks to see her face and newly ringed hand one more time before they take her away. He stands on the sidewalk repeating the words, "Serene forever" and touching his heart. Then he asks me "Where is her shiny badge?" I tell him it must be downtown. Jake recognizes Muncer's car as he pulls into the apartment parking lot and runs over. With the scene cleared and tape around the only bus stop on the strip with windows we convince Jake to take us inside. He showers and changes his clothing as we sit at his kitchen table like Jake had done so many times before.

My phone rings as we sit there, it is the bus driver saying a man is on board asking for me. I ask to speak to him. The driver passes the phone to him, he responds with, "I am looking for Vernon F. Cannon." I ask what this is in regard to, he tells me of business in Montana and says he works for an attorney that I was not paying enough attention to catch the name of. I recall the trip Birdie, and I took to Montana when I was very young and the fun we had. It was our only vacation. The post card from that trip sits framed on my end table. Then as I come back to this conversation having no idea what business he has with me he is saying, "two hours to Bozeman."

We agree to meet at the bus stop out front of Jake's since he is on the bus, and I am here already. Muncer stays inside with Jake as I meet the supposed attorney, that I do not have any idea why he would want anything to do with me but obviously has gone to great lengths to track me down.

Marvin Riley gets off the bus. What I didn't know upon my first and only meeting with him is that the course of my life would be changed forever. He hands me his card, now seeing he works for Premier Land and Law Franklin, Montana. We sit in the cold windy bus stop, and I think of how tough someone would have to be to to ride the bus in all seasons. The next thing he shows me as the wind blows through his papers is a will. One that includes my grandfather and grandmother's names, Joris and Evelyn Edwards. I am in shock to hear of them and now know where Birdie got her last name from. I don't read the will as I am thinking about the family I had until recently but never was able to get to know. There is a copy of a deed attached with a court date. January 24, 2026, 1:00 pm, room 17. Mr. Riley goes on to say the property, located on Barber Road in Shaumet, Montana, is mine once I show up for my court date. I look at the deed which states there is a three bedroom house, out buildings and 1015 acres of property. I ask if there is a pond on the property. Mr. Riley looks at me as if I am crazy but says there is a creek that runs through a portion of the land. I shake his hand just as the bus pulls up and Marvin Riley boards the bus without asking if I will be in court. I go back into Jake's apartment, Muncer is at the window watching us. I tell him the story Mr. Riley delivered to me, show him the paperwork, and inform Muncer that I had put in my notice Thanksgiving weekend.

Muncer says he was going to ask if I had thought about joining the force with Metevior retiring. That I have done good work in assisting and helping to capture some fugitives. "There are many more out there, but I would go to Montana if I were you, too. Will you be asking Raven to go?" I am unsure of answering that question with him and Rubio being friends. I want to ask Raven before anyone else tells her the news. Muncer asks if there was any money in the backpack, I reply with, "Yes, just over $17,000.00." He rubs his forehead and says, "That money is Allard's." I know that at that moment I could have denied its existence, but Allard may need that money to be buried. It will be held in the court registry until an investigation has been held. I don't expect Raven to see that money returned to her.

I ask Muncer for a ride back to my Jeep, holding tightly onto my paperwork, my new life. Once I am in my Jeep, I call Raven not abiding to our agreement of time. She answers, knowing something has changed. I ask if I can come over, she says, "Only if it is good news." I tell her the bad news now about the money. She says she had thought about donating it to Charlene's Place or Ethan's Edge anyway so the only bad news is they may not receive it. "Please come over and tell me the other news."

I take I-5 to Graham Street and wind my way over to Lake Washington in anticipation of asking Raven to leave with me or will her decision be to stay here on the lake. Will she be shocked at my request to take her and Enzo with me since she had felt she had overstepped a short time ago speaking of us. Tonight, we will communicate, lay out our options and find direction.

I pull in, realizing it is too late for Raven to be up and get to work tomorrow on time. I regret bringing this news to her now instead of waiting for a better time, but here I sit with Raven, watching me in anticipation, knowing this is something big. I get out holding the file containing the possibility of our lives together and go in out of the wind that is whipping off the lake.

We sit silently at the kitchen table where we recently ate turkey sandwiches. I don't know what to say with the possibility of all this happening. My words don't wish to come out. I hand Raven the file, open it for her to read. The first thing she says is "1015 acres, I think this is a quarter acre." We sit comparing the vast difference and she asks, "What will you do?" I ask her if she wants to go to Montana. She nods yes and says, "Not tonight. I only have two things to do before I can leave. See Mel, I would never forgive myself if I didn't thank him and give proper notice to August."

We plan to leave around the first of the year that gives a few weeks to wrap up loose ends, like listing this house. Raven needs to tell Rubio and has asked for me to be there. I need to tell Mr. Owens about my departure, paying an extra month's rent due to the late notice and figure out a way to transport Gus.

I am so tired tonight with the highs and lows of this evening. We move to the sofa, Raven asks if I think we should still get a tree. I tell her of the lady on the bus saying that is her favorite part and say, "We should get one." That was my last thought of the night as I glance at the paperwork on the table making sure this is real.

The week rolls by both Raven and I are in thought most of the time and tired. Possibly from everything that has transpired the past few months and the journey we will be taking. We only texted once during the week making plans to purchase a Christmas tree on Saturday and Raven says she wants to get a 2025 ornament to remember our year. She will go on Sunday to visit Mel; he will be going back home soon. Her visit isn't scheduled, she will just show up.

Saturday morning, we head north enjoying the view of the lake to get a tree at Hop in Christmas Trees. The enormity of what will come after our tree is purchased is weighing heavy on our minds. We look at each other at the same moment and ask, "Are you sure you want to do this?" I respond with, "I am at least going to check it out and would like you to come if you want." "I haven't given my notice yet and would like to go to Montana before doing that even for a weekend but not next one." "Ok I will book the flight we could leave the night of the 20th and be back on the 21st." I think we have a plan. After picking out a tall, crooked tree that Enzo wanted, we return to Raven's, neither of us in the Christmas spirit with so much on our minds. At dinner, a delivered cheese pizza, we decide to buy each other a winter coat, scarf, hat and gloves as presents for our trip. We book our flights for the night of the 20th costing double due to the holiday season, rent a truck for two days and return flight for the 21st.

Sunday Raven visits with Mel at the hospital. She says the first thing he asked was if I had gotten the money from him. That was all his mom had left him besides the house. She assured him she has it but would need proof of where it came from. He wants to go to the bank for statements since his mom had gone paperless. She informs him she wants to return it and of our move. He doesn't want the money back; she tells him of Donny's truck being stolen and no longer there. He says he will find it and file for lost title. Raven agrees to take him to the bank on the day he discharges then help figure out the truck. She tells Mel of Ethan's Edge and Charlene's Place and that was where she would donate the money if he wanted her to have it. She urges him to keep it.

She returns home with the story. I call Muncer and tell him the money was Mel's, and he will have proof, I also inform him on Mel's plans with the truck. Something has changed in our friendship that has only lasted a few months. I guess when life and death are held at each encounter it brings more depth. I am sad to leave here too.

48

Detective Muncer

DECEMBER 2025

It only made sense yesterday for me to take Naomi to retrieve a car from the rental place I had used for our date on New Years Eve. So long ago, nearly four years, simply thinking about 2021 and everything that has transpired since then is hard to fathom. I gather my ratty old suitcase, the one that was purchased for my trip to Mexico that didn't happen and think of the rest of my family and Jill just as Naomi pulls up next to my cruiser, double parked since there is no other parking nearby.

She is dressed up more formal than I have ever seen her. Usually, she is in her classic black scrubs but today she has a dress made of light blue lace with a soft layer underneath, shoes I have no idea how she can walk in, or drive for that matter. It only made sense for her to pick me up since we are making our second trip to the Virginia V. I tell her we had never discussed this before, but do you have a driver's license? She laughs not answering my question and pulls from the curb. Truthfully, I am nervous to leave our lives behind but can count on Jill to water my only real responsibility "Margo," the plant I saved years back.

Naomi pops the trunk, an old pro at this fancy car already. I wonder where she may have gone last night since she already knows the operations of the car so well. There wasn't talk of us spending any time together yesterday. Packing was the only task on my mind. Neither of us have taken two weeks off work before. I have never had an entire week off in my two decades with the department. Last night my mind kept wandering, what about my cases, what happens if a lead comes through, and I am not here? All that thought is behind me now and I have left my SPD issued cell phone on top of the refrigerator.

I place my suitcase in the trunk alongside Naomi's, suddenly wishing I had bought a new one and wondering where she has been with hers. Are there other dates for her besides our haphazard ones put together randomly. Most of our time is spent in the cafeteria just resting in the middle of the night. Looking back, I wish I had tried harder but have never pushed assuming we have both been content.

I get in, having never seen Naomi behind the wheel as she doesn't own a car, this feels out of place. We make our way to Westlake, riding along in silence as we pass the beautiful views of Lake Union as the sun will be ready to set in a couple of hours. I ask if she would like some music, the silence thick with our unknown thoughts. We have never gone away together before, certainly not for ten days. We will drop the car at Sea Tac and board a plane to Honolulu. We sat and made choices of our hotel, reserved airfare and rental car, found entertainment months ago but today this is a reality. Tonight, we will be sleeping far from Seattle. In the trunk there are not any items made of polyester. My required SPD clothing remains at home, I have packed my swimming trunks, flip flops and tank tops.

Making one important stop before the airport, we pull into the boat slip parking lot just as we did a few months ago. I jump out and open the door for Naomi, thanking her for her safe driving. She takes my arm, we proceed up the ramp, take the stairs to the top deck on this cold day. Being glad I brought my suit jacket and thankful for the sun. Naomi doesn't seem chilled; she has excitement in her eyes. We are seated on wooden chairs with spotless white cushions. The place bathed in splotches of pale yellow and pink toning down life as we know it.

I think this is a time to relax and enjoy, there are other people besides us who can carry the load for a bit. I look up and see Metro and Raven, Jill bounces in sitting next to me. I have not seen Jill, Metro or Raven in clothing other than their normal street attire. Fancy is the first word that comes to mind tonight.

Just as I think of all the time I have lost with Jill the quiet music starts, and in walks Hector with a lady on his arm I do not recognize. I glance at Jill, who is beaming but stays seated by my side as she holds my arm, I take joy in knowing she is so happy. Then another set of people, a lady in her fifties or so comes in with a man about the same age and are seated up front. The ship is filling with people and excitement. The captain enters from a door I had not seen before his appearance. August comes in from the same direction we entered. I am thinking back to the last time I saw him in person and cannot remember but today it appears a load has been lifted; he is comfortable and, in a tuxedo, and we are not here fighting crime. He waves at everyone as he makes his way to the front and joins Hector next to the captain, turning to face us. Moments later the music starts, the photographer glides from seat to seat for the best angles and in walks Willow. Her gown sweeping the highly polished deck of the ship. She is here but only has her eyes on one person, August. She whispers, "I do" as she walks up the aisle looking at August.

The ceremony goes on, dancing, the best cake, the DJ plays some popular wedding music. Naomi and I slip out after saying our congratulations and meeting August's mom and her date, an owner of a lawn care company. They had met last year when she was overhauling her yard.

In the car we both sigh at once, I break the silence by saying, "That was sweet." Naomi laughs, "Our life doesn't roll like that, and we would need other music." We know we are on the same wavelength and hope this time in Hawaii is good for us. We kiss, then pull out and head towards Sea Tac to catch our flight.

49

Vernon

DECEMBER 2025

THE DAY IS FINALLY here, we have dropped off Enzo for the wedding and will pick him up after on our way to the airport. I don't think Raven has told Rubio that we are leaving town this evening or of the plans to possibly move to Montana. It is a big decision for all of us. I think back on the small town living I have done over the past few years and that is where I get stuck. Once I am there, I crave the life and energy of the city. I know for sure we will go today, and I will be there on January 24th to claim my land.

Before the wedding we pack three bags. Enzo makes sure we have books, his blanket and favorite stuffed duck. The bags are placed in the back of Raven's car, we drive to Rubio's then make our way to the Virginia V for the wedding. I don't think I have ever attended one before. I picture Raven and I in the places that August and Willow are and wonder what their story is, how long they have known each other and hope they communicate. We are seated behind Muncer, Naomi and Jill who runs around the end of the chair to hug Raven. I picture our bags in the car and our life here almost at an end. The ceremony starts. I recognize Hector but hardly anyone else, Raven knows a few people from work. The reception is a soft and easy part of our day, the meal, cake and music are calming. We get up to leave checking the time and head for the car to retrieve Enzo. We say our goodbyes to Muncer, Jill, August and Willow. Once we are at the car dressed in our best clothing we sigh, drive south, get Enzo and park at the airport. Enzo says he told papa his duck was in the car. We pass through security easily without baggage to check, take the subway through the airport and get to our gate, watching the planes through the window by our gate. I hear, "Metro" as we pass the bar. It is Muncer and Naomi on their way to Honolulu.

Our flight was uneventful, Enzo loved to fly and had brought his cape. I think of Muncer flying to the heat and us to below zero. The trip went well, the property was vacant, and everything is still in the house. We stayed there the night of the 20th, being too late to seek out a motel if there even is one way out here. I found pictures of Birdie all the way through school, she apparently left at eighteen. There is one photo of her and a boy about her age that looks like me. I turn it over and it says Bridget and Vernon. I never knew Birdie's real name was Bridget and I think that is my father with her. Another box contains a letter to me.

Dear Vernon,
We know you exist somewhere out there. Wherever Bridget took you. We will always be here for you.
Love Grandma Evelyn and Grandpa Jovis Edwards.

We walk the property the best we can making our assessments at twenty below. Return to the airport and Seattle. I know Muncer is in Hawaii, but I expect to see him when we return. Enzo is asleep by the time we reach Raven's house. I return home after the long trip and need time to process the trip and research Vernon. I am sure Raven needs to get ready for tomorrow. I also need to wrap up one last loose end, figuring out when will my twelve-week commitment will be up for Ethan's Edge and Kernal.

I got home after reassuring Raven we both need to get ready for tomorrow, no matter what the future holds. I calculate my weeks and the last commitment for this twelve-week program ends the first week of January. Kernal would be another person I would have to say goodbye to. I have kind of grown attached to him and Darius.

I get off my phone and move to my laptop. Vernon Cannon is all over, he is a musician with Facebook, Instagram, TikTok. Videos everywhere. I will continue to watch them but today I am not ready to make contact with him or anyone else. I just found out about my grandparents then realize I may have another set, the Cannons.

I get a call from Raven at 7:00 am, Enzo is chattering in the background. She has made a decision concerning Montana and hopes it is the same as mine. She wants to stay here but be together, not just see each other on the weekend. She doesn't know what my thoughts are about Montana. I one hundred percent agree. Montana is nice and I could sell the acreage and invest anywhere but right now Gus, and I will be moving to Lake Washington.